Advance Praise for *An Indiana Christmas*

"*An Indiana Christmas* is a real treat, a guest list for the ideal Hoosier literary Yuletide dinner party . . . old friends sharing the table with charming new company. Any home in the state would do itself proud to have this delightful book placed above the hearth, at the ready for aloud sampling throughout the holiday season."

—Nathan Montoya, Proprietor, Village Lights Bookstore

"A grand and thrilling selection of Hoosier writing presented through the fraught lens of Christmas. Both the new voices and the Pulitzer Prize winners here remind us of the dangers of nostalgia while also giving license to the deepest pleasures of memory. This is a fascinating and utterly enjoyable read, and I'm sure I'll pick it up again over many Christmases to come."

—Michael Dahlie, author of *A Gentleman's Guide to Graceful Living*

"The stories, poems, and essays in *An Indiana Christmas* will stay with you long after reading, no matter the season. The anthology brings to life all manner of Hoosiers: bearing casseroles, pierogi, and trifles; snowblowing neighbors' driveways just because; losing and finding religion; and posing as Santa or his grinchy counterpart. You'll see yourself in this book made by, for, and about people searching for identity in a place as complex as any."

—Sarah Layden, author of *Trip Through Your Wires*

"In this anthology, Furuness has successfully captured both the uniqueness and the universality of an Indiana Christmas. Some experiences—like a child's wish for a Red Ryder BB gun—transcend time, age, and circumstance; others—like Susan Neville's depiction of a country Christmas party—remind longtime Hoosiers of holiday gatherings as reprieves from dark, cold nights in a 'landlocked state.' The collection brings Indiana's great writers— past and present—into conversation with each other, exploring the way in which this special time of year connects us with community and, ultimately, brings us home."

—Megan Telligman, Program Manager, Indiana Humanities

An
INDIANA
Christmas

An
INDIANA
Christmas

Edited by

BRYAN FURUNESS

INDIANA UNIVERSITY PRESS

This book is a publication of

INDIANA UNIVERSITY PRESS
Office of Scholarly Publishing
Herman B Wells Library 350
1320 East 10th Street
Bloomington, Indiana 47405 USA
iupress.indiana.edu

Manufactured in the United States of America

Library of Congress Cataloging-in-Publication Data

Names: Furuness, Bryan, editor.
Title: An Indiana Christmas / Bryan Furuness.
Description: Bloomington, Indiana : Indiana University Press, 2020.
Identifiers: LCCN 2019050616 (print) | LCCN 2019050617 (ebook) |
ISBN 9780253050281 (hardback) | ISBN 9780253050298 (ebook)
Subjects: LCSH: Christmas—Literary collections.
Classification: LCC PS509.C56 I53 2020 (print) |
LCC PS509.C56 (ebook) | DDC 813/.01080334—dc23
LC record available at https://lccn.loc.gov/2019050616
LC ebook record available at https://lccn.loc.gov/2019050617

1 2 3 4 5   25 24 23 22 21 20

Reprinted by Permission

Excerpt from *Mr. Bingle* by George Barr McCutcheon, published by Dodd, Mead and Company. Copyright © 1915. Reprinted from public domain.

"The *Schneebrunzer*" from *Looking for God's Country* by Norbert Krapf. Reprinted in *Bloodroot: Indiana Poems* by Indiana University Press. Copyright © 2005. Reprinted by permission of the author.

"The Myth of the Perfect Christmas Photo Family" by Kelsey Timmerman, originally published on www.whereamiwearing.com. Copyright © 2015. Reprinted by permission of the author.

"Treasure!" by Eliza Tudor, originally published in *Flock*. Copyright © 2019. Reprinted by permission of the author.

Excerpt from "December" in *Abe Martin's Almanack* by Kin Hubbard, published by The Bobbs-Merrill Company. Copyright © 1908. Reprinted from public domain.

Excerpt from *Beasley's Christmas Party* by Booth Tarkington, published by Harper and Brothers. Copyright © 1909. Reprinted from public domain.

Excerpt from *In God We Trust: All Others Pay Cash* by Jean Shepherd. Copyright © 1966 by Jean Shepherd. Used by permission of Doubleday, an imprint of the Knopf Doubleday Publishing Group, a division of Penguin Random House, LLC. All rights reserved.

"While Mortals Sleep" from *While Mortals Sleep: Unpublished Short Fiction* by Kurt Vonnegut. Copyright © 2011 by The Kurt Vonnegut, Jr., Trust. Used by permission of Delacorte Press, an imprint of Random House, a division of Penguin Random House LLC. All rights reserved.

This book is dedicated to all the readers and writers in our fair state. Here's to a new golden age of Indiana literature.

Contents

PREFACE

THE OTHER DAY I WAS HAVING COFFEE with Megan from Indiana Humanities. Her organization has a lending library that sends books to reading groups all over the state at no charge. When I told her about this anthology, she said that a book club had just checked out a set of Christmas books.

"*Really*," I said.

It was August.

Maybe I shouldn't have been puzzled. After all, I had passed a happy summer reading Christmas stories and poems and essays for this anthology. I may have been sitting on my deck in a tank top and sunglasses, but in my mind I was tromping through the snow on a Christmas tree farm with Kelsey Timmerman, or riding a horse-drawn sleigh to Jessamyn West's clapboard house, or standing in a stubbly field with the December barns of a George Kalamaras poem.

Of course, my excuse was an August deadline. Why would a book club choose to read about Christmas in the summer?

Christmas can't be the sole source of the appeal. If it was, you'd hear Christmas music in July—and to my knowledge, that doesn't happen.

The appeal must come from the intersection of Christmas and reading. When you cross those wires, you get a strange and powerful synergy.

Picture a deep chair, a soft blanket, a crackling fire, thin branches tapping against a dark windowpane, a Manhattan on the end table, glowing in the fire-light like a ruby (I didn't even mention a book, but you imagined one in your lap, didn't you?). Forget coziness; this scene evokes a deep contentment. A nested feeling. *Hygge*, as the Danes call it.

Or picture yourself as a child, on your belly on the floor, paging through a book while music plays low on the stereo and the grown-ups murmur on the couch, someone chuckling, someone stringing popcorn. Now we're in the territory of nostalgia—for your childhood, or maybe for the childhood you wish you'd had.

Obvious answers, perhaps. But I wonder if the appeal of Christmas stories goes deeper than *hygge* and nostalgia. Further back than childhood.

You know how sometimes, when you're drifting off, you suddenly feel like you're falling? Someone told me this is a vestigial remnant of our old monkey-selves, from the nights we slept in trees and the worst thing that could happen was to fall down to the forest floor where the predators prowled.

This explanation is probably BS. Even so, it's the kind of BS I like: wrapped in a story, harming no one. It's like an old myth, the kind the ancients would make up to explain the world around us, to explain ourselves to ourselves. Like the kind of story you tell around a fire with the cold and the dark pressing in all around, which makes you feel like you're in a diving bell of light and heat. Stories are best when nights are long.

Let's stay with that image of a fire and all the listeners gathered around. It's not unlike the nativity scene, is it? A little group, looking inward, huddled together in a vast universe. Christmas is a story of togetherness, a story set and told on a long, dark night.

Picture one more thing for me, and then I'll let you go to the next fire, the next gathering in this book.

Close your eyes. Imagine yourself falling, back into your past, or into a better dream of your past. When you land, don't open your eyes. Not yet. Not until you feel warm hands on your cheeks, cradling your face. Not until you hear that voice, the one you thought you would never hear again, say, "Welcome home."

You're right where you belong. That's how you know it's Christmas.

ACKNOWLEDGMENTS

THANK YOU TO THE FOLLOWING: INDIANA UNIVERSITY Press for trusting me with this anthology and for bringing this book into the world. Butler Libraries, for their help with research and tech tools, especially Amanda Starkel, Jennifer Raye, and the dean, Julie Miller. George Hanlin of Indiana Humanities, for pointing me in the right direction on that Nicholson story and for a hundred dazzling bits of Indiana history. Kasey Kirchner, my literary assistant, for handling fun stuff like retyping ancient stories and creating citations for the frontmatter. Pip, my dachshund, for helping me stay on task by settling into my lap and groaning loudly every time I tried to get up.

An

INDIANA

Christmas

EARTHBOUND

Barbara Shoup

WE WERE SPINNING ON THE GREEN CHAIRS. They were ugly modern chairs my father had bought when my mother said we needed new chairs for our new house. He'd been so pleased to surprise her with them that she hadn't had the heart to tell him to take them back and get two sensible, earthbound chairs.

My brother and I spun to outer space on those chairs. We time-traveled to the places I read about in books. Blindfolded, we spun each other silly. We loved to time how long it took us to get our bearings and stop walking into walls. It drove our mother crazy. During the daytime, she'd yell at us and make us stop; but at night, when our father was home, she'd let us spin to our hearts' content. Eventually he'd snap, and she'd give him her how-could-you-be-so-dumb expression. Anyone could have told you that if you buy chairs that spin, kids will spin them.

Tonight she was letting us spin even though our father wasn't there. It was Christmas Eve. As long as we were spinning, we weren't asking her when he was coming home. We weren't fussing to be allowed to open just one present early. We'd had our dinner and our baths. Our good clothes were laid out on our beds. Waiting for our father so we could go to the party at Aunt Rachel's house, we spread-eagled ourselves on the green chairs as if held there by gravity, pretending we were on the Tilt-a-Whirl we rode each summer at the Catholic Carnival.

I stopped when the phone rang, but my brother kept spinning. Each time the chair went around it wobbled and brushed the wall, leaving a mark. "Mom's going to kill you," I said.

He jumped up and went to the window.

I eavesdropped. My mother had a telephone voice that was completely different from her regular voice—breathless, girlish. "Mmmm," she said, and giggled. "Oh, good grief. So, he's at the Reynolds's now?"

Who? If I asked, she'd realize I'd been listening.

So I joined my brother, rubbed a circle into the fogged window, and looked out. But I saw nothing but the empty front yard, the Christmas lights in the windows of the houses across the street. Ice glittered on the spindly trees.

Thump. I heard a loud sound on the roof. *Thump. Thump.* Then bells.

"Santa! Mom, it's Santa!" my brother cried. He was five and believed absolutely.

I was eight. A girl in my class had sworn to me that last Christmas she saw her parents get her presents from the coat closet. All parents did that, she said. I didn't believe her, but I meant to stay awake all night and make sure.

The bells grew louder. My brother ran around in circles, wild with joy. Now the stomping was on our porch. Someone pounded on the door. I rubbed the window where my breath had already refogged it, and I saw him.

"Ho!" Santa pulled up his red muffler, rubbed his gloved hands in the cold. "Ho, ho! It's John and Mary Frances Corrigan I'm looking for. Is this their new house? I want to make sure I leave their presents in the right place!"

My brother flung open the door. "I'm John," he shouted. "I've been good! I'm leaving your reindeer some carrots!" When our mother joined him, he remembered his manners and added, "Won't you come in?"

"Nope," Santa said. "Can't dally. But I've heard about you two. Heard you're pretty decent kiddos. Thought I'd just come see for myself. You still have that sister?"

I came out from behind the curtain and, speechless, presented myself.

Santa pulled a black book from his pocket and consulted it. "Mary Frances Corrigan," he said. "Not bad. Not bad at all. She spins on those green chairs in the living room though she's been told a thousand times to sit still. Could be nicer to her mother. But all in all, very good. Smart, too, her teacher says. I've got a note on that."

He flipped the pages. "John Corrigan. Hmmm. JohnJohnJohnJohnJohn."

"What?" my brother cried. "I've been good. Honest!"

"Ah, here you are," Santa said. "Yes. You've been very good this year. And you'll be good the rest of this evening, won't you? I bet you'll go right to bed when your dad tells you to."

"I will! I will! I promise!"

"Ho," Santa said. "I sure hope so, because I'll be back later, and I'll fly right over if I don't find the two of you asleep!" He jangled the bells on the strap of his black bag, laughed a deep belly laugh. "Merry Christmas," he bellowed, and before we could say "Merry Christmas" back, he was gone.

The three of us stood in the suddenly empty doorway. Its light cast a silver rectangle across the narrow porch, across the sidewalk, barely touching the frozen yard. That was when I heard the voices.

They were faint at first, children's voices calling, "Santa, Santa." I thought I had imagined them. But when my mother opened the screen door and poked her head out, the voices grew louder. I knew they were real.

"Those damn Dougherty kids," she said. It was something she said a lot, and so did all the other mothers in the neighborhood. Duane and Petey Dougherty ran wild at all hours of the day and night while their mom did who-knows-what down at the Elks Club. We kids were half-afraid of the Dougherty boys, half-enamored of them. They burned snakes in trashcans and invented weird gadgets in their backyard with wood and wire and old flashlight batteries. Now there they were under the streetlight, howling for Santa.

Soon, a few of the other big boys joined them. They wrestled, slipping and sliding in their slick-soled shoes. Petey saw us watching. "Hey, Mrs. Corrigan!" he yelled. "You guys seen Santa? We heard he was at your house a coupla minutes ago. We wanna ask him to bring us some toys."

My mother closed the door. "I don't like this," she said. "Those darn boys—"

We heard them laughing as they pounded through the narrow passageway between our house and our next door neighbor's into what, those days, still seemed like one huge communal backyard.

My mother dialed the telephone and stood tapping her foot, waiting. "Lois," she said, "has Santa been to your house yet? No? Oh, yes," she said. "The kids were thrilled. But those damn Daugherty kids are on the loose again. I think they're after Santa." She laughed. "You're so right. Coal would be too good for them. But listen—" She spoke in an odd voice, at the same time playful and strained. "We don't want to get Santa mad at our nice new neighborhood, do we? Maybe it would be a good idea to send Joe out to check around. Just to be safe."

I didn't hear a word she said after that. Why had we moved to this stupid neighborhood anyway? I missed our comfortable creaky old house, the railroad yard behind it, and the workers, who had thrown me some of the fat pieces of chalk they used to mark the boxcars. I missed the dark, cluttered corner store with its big jar of penny pretzels. When we lived in our old house, I could walk right across the tracks to my grandmother's. Or to the dime store. I could ride my bike to the library and fill my basket with books.

Our new neighborhood was miles away from anything, and all the ugly little houses looked the same. It was a wonder Santa had found us at all. Now the

Daugherty kids were chasing him. If he managed to get away from them, who could blame him if he never came back?

The phone rang a half-dozen times. My mother and the other mothers in the neighborhood tracked Santa from one house to another, trying to figure out where he had been seen last. But why didn't she worry about where our father was or about missing the party at Aunt Rachel's house?

The presents for our cousins waited on the dining room table along with the fruitcake my mother had been asked to bring. Only the few presents we'd bought for each other were under our tree now, sprinkled with fallen pine needles that were dry and sharp to the touch. Our empty stockings lay there, too. In our new house, there was no mantel to hang them on. I felt like a poor child, without hope.

"You go get dressed, Mary Frances," my mother said in between calls. "Then help your brother."

"But where's Dad?"

She drew her lips straight and gave a sharp nod in the direction of my bedroom.

We'd just finished dressing and returned to the living room when the front door opened, and my father stepped in, wet and disheveled, laughing. I didn't dare throw my arms around him with my good clothes on. His coat was soaked through and bits of dead grass stuck to it. Our neighbor, Mr. Sankowski, had followed him in and held an old felt hat, ringing it round and round with his fingers, water dripping from it onto the carpet.

"Those goddamn Daughertys," my father said, wheezing, and burst into fresh peals of laughter. "By Christ, they chased—"

"Herb," said my mother.

He saw me then and pulled me to him. The dampness in his coat soaked into my taffeta party dress, making it go limp.

"Herb," my mother said again.

He held me at arm's length. "So, kiddo," he said, "I hear you had a visitor."

I burst into tears. "Santa," I cried, "and the Daugherty kids are chasing him right now and even if he gets away from them, he'll never come back. I hate those kids. Dad, I hate it here. Why do we have to live here, anyway? Why can't we go back to our other house?"

The room grew suddenly silent. My father knelt before me, swaying slightly. There was a sweet, medicine-y smell to his breath, which, I know now, was whiskey. "Oh, honey," he said, "Santa Claus is fine. Just fine. Isn't he, Chick? Didn't we just see him?"

"Hell, we saved him," said Mr. Sankowski.

"That's right." My father collapsed on the floor Indian style and pulled me down to join him. "You listen," he said, his face right next to mine. "Chick and me got a late start from work. Missed the damn bus. So there we were hurrying up the street toward home, and what do we see? Santa running to beat the band and those damn Daugherty kids and their buddies running after him. Whoa, were we mad! We took off after the whole pack of them."

He grabbed his soggy coat, brushed at his ruined pants, and looked at my mother earnestly. "How do you think we got to be such a mess? By God, we chased those little sons of bitches through every yard in this subdivision! Finally, Chick headed them off, and I took a shortcut through Benson's yard and caught up with the old guy. Boy, he was beat. Was he ever glad to see us."

"Herb," my mother said. "Please. We're already a half-hour late for your sister's."

But my father was into the story now. "Santa says to me, 'I hope your kids aren't anything like those Daughertys.' 'No, sir,' I said. 'They certainly are not. They're not even allowed to play with those punks. Juvenile delinquents,' I told him."

"I got them good," Mr. Sankowski said. "I got them. Cracked their two dumb heads together, Petey and Duane. Huh. Marched them right up to the front door and told their old lady, 'Lock these two up or they're dead boys.' Those other kids took off real fast after that."

"I hid with Santa in Benson's shed," my father said. "Until Chick came back and told me the coast was clear."

Mr. Sankowski guffawed, then he caught himself. "I'll tell you, I made sure," he said. "I wasn't about to take any chances. Not with Santa Claus, no sir. Me and your dad, we saved him, Mary Frances. He'll be back later tonight, no doubt at all."

I looked at my father, who nodded solemnly.

We were late to Aunt Rachel's, of course. I was sure that once everyone understood what had happened, there would be no bad feeling. But when I tried to tell my aunt about how my father had saved Santa Claus, she said distractedly, "Yes, dear. *Yes*, dear." She hovered over the silver platters of cookies, stirred the spiced cider. She wouldn't look at me.

My cousin, Christine, said, "Honestly, Mary Frances, you're such a baby. You believe that?"

"Yes, I believe it." Tears sprung to my eyes. "It's true. Isn't it, Dad?"

"Mary Frances," my mother said, "I want you to calm down. Now."

But I was agitated. I couldn't help my bad behavior. I would not stand in line to say "Merry Christmas" on the telephone to my Aunt Laurie and Uncle Lou in Cincinnati. I argued with my cousins. I whipped Aunt Rachel's dog into a frenzy throwing the tennis ball and nearly broke one of her porcelain birds. I was not duly grateful for the embroidered handkerchiefs, the bubble bath, the crisp new dollar bill I was given.

I had to stay up all night and wait for Santa, I told myself. So I could say sorry.

My mother tucked me into bed and kissed me on the forehead, just as if I'd been a perfectly wonderful child all evening. The sheets were cool. My eyes still stung from crying, and I longed to close them. But I sat up in my bed, pressed my back against the knobby headboard, and played games with myself to stay awake. I went through the alphabet and made myself think of five hard words for each letter. I thought up stories.

I got up and cracked my door open, so I could see my parents in the living room. When would they go to bed? I imagined Santa Claus circling and circling above us, waiting till the lights went off so he could land and bring us our presents. The radio in the living room droned on; the Christmas carols drifting back to my room were as faint as the voices of my brother's kindergarten class had been singing their song in the school pageant. My parents' voices rose and fell. Though I couldn't understand what they said, I knew my mother was mad. Her voice rose, questioning. My father's voice was persuasive, rushed.

"Shhh," they said to each other now and then. "Shhh."

Then they began to laugh. Softly, first, then harder and harder. I wanted to be with them, cozy between them—the way the three of us had been a long, long time ago, before my brother. It always charmed me when they laughed like that, but tonight, left out, it made me sad. I grew even sadder when I tried to remember the last time I had heard them laughing and could not.

My father worked hard. Most nights he came home dirty and bone-tired from his long shift at the steel mill. I knew even then how my mother had to scrimp and save to make ends meet. But that night they were happy. They were still young enough to believe a house of their own was the first step toward a better life. So young that when my father took the half-pint bottle from his jacket pocket, my mother smiled and raised a glass for him to fill.

I saw him pour the golden liquid into it then lift the bottle to his lips and drink right from it. He poured and drank again. Again. Their voices grew louder.

"Honest to God, Betty," my father said, "I thought those kids were going to kill me. I haven't run since the army! And if that weren't bad enough, there were those goddamn pillows. Every step I took, they slid farther and farther down my pants. Plus, Chick lost his kid's basketball when they took off after us—you know, the reindeer. He'll be in hot water about that.

"Jesus, Mary, and Joseph! The two of us ended up in Ed Benson's shed. Freezing our butts! But we had to stay there until I could get the damn Santa suit off. It was so wet, and my fingers were like ice. It's still over there. The beard's wrecked."

My mother giggled and yawned.

"The kids loved it, though," my father said. "John and Mary Frances. They loved it, didn't they? That Mary Frances. Hook, line, and sinker. I thought for sure we'd lose her this year. After all, she's eight. She's no dummy." He moved to the green chair I'd spun on earlier and gave it a twirl. In the deep ho-ho voice I had believed was Santa's, he said, "She spins on the green chair in the living room, though she's been told a thousand times to sit still."

"Honestly, Herb," my mother said. But she was laughing.

"You believe that?" my cousin Christine had said. "You're such a baby, Mary Frances."

I was a baby. A big fat stupid baby. A fool. At that moment, I hated my parents more than I would ever hate anyone again. They could have told me there was no Santa Claus. I was half-ready to hear it. I would have taken the news just fine. But to find out this way, to be tricked by my own parents, made a fool of! I would never, never forgive them.

I watched them bring out the presents. They set John's fire truck and my bride doll under the tree, unwrapped. There were other, smaller, presents, too, but I couldn't see what those were. My mother must have wrapped them while John was napping, while I was at school.

Finished, they stood in front of the Christmas tree and surveyed what they had done.

They kissed. Arm in arm, they walked to their bedroom. I heard the door close behind them, heard the creak of the bedsprings as they settled into their bed.

When I had heard nothing but the whisper of the furnace for a long time, I went into the living room. There was my bulging stocking. My grandmother had knitted it for me before I was born. Bending to touch it, I could feel the round shape of an orange. There was always an orange. And candy canes and gum. And little gifts: coloring books, funny wind-up toys, number puzzles for car trips. I could feel all these things with my fingers.

I saw the books then, and I knelt to examine them. *Heidi*, *The Three Musketeers*, *Hans Brinker and the Silver Skates*. There were twelve in the set. I could tell they were expensive, probably more than my parents could afford.

"Smart, too." Remembering my father's Santa voice, I pulled my hand from the books as if it had been burned. I sat down on the green chair and stared at them. They were beautiful books, bound in bright colors, the pages edged in gold. I longed to claim them.

But, as young as I was, I understood that only by not claiming them could I hurt my parents as much as they had hurt me. I sat a long time that night, staring at the books they had bought for me. I sat on the green chair, absolutely still.

WINTER SCENE, PAST MIDNIGHT

Matthew Brennan

Past midnight, long after lovemaking,
The light patter of snow,
Like the voice of a dead child or parent,
Taps at the panes and abruptly wakes you.
You go to the window that opens
To the park of oaks and, beyond,
To the art museum's portico—
Through frost you see no moon, just clouds
Arched low like a blown-glass bowl.

You lift the window, lean into the cold,
And try to remember what you were dreaming
When, moments ago, you shuddered and woke,
Drawn for some reason into this scene.
But it's like trying to recall the instant
Your life was conceived. All you can see
Is snow falling on the still, white park,
Falling on the sculpted bronze flesh
Of some forgotten city father
Until even this solitary shape
Is nothing but white.

THE FABLE OF THE CUT-UP WHO CAME VERY NEAR LOSING HIS TICKET, BUT WHO TURNED DEFEAT INTO VICTORY

George Ade

IN A PRAIRIE HAMLET, FAR FROM THE maddening Department Store, where arrogant Wealth did not flaunt itself before the Humble, and where the People were so Primitive that they did not know how to get Money except by Working for it, they were making large Preparations to tear Things wide open at Christmas.

All through the abbreviated Community, the Women Folks were feverishly popping Corn and cracking Hickory Nuts on a Flatiron and making homemade Candy. The Unmarried Kind were secretively working on Yarn Mittens.

There was to be a Tree at the Church and preceding the Distribution of Presents there was to be a Show, alias a Methodist Vaudeville, which consists of Pieces, Responsive Readings, and the best that the Choir can do. The Druggist in this Village had laid in what he called an Elegant Assortment of Holiday Goods. He had all of Will Carleton's Poems and a Counter covered with fragile Toys that smelled of the Paint, also an attractive Line of Perfumeries and some Toilet Sets. One of these Toilet Sets was the Prize Exhibit. The Comb and Brushes were of Celluloid, the Amber and White being scrambled in a very effective Manner. The Druggist was willing to give a Guarantee that the Bristles were Real. This Toilet Set reposed in a puckered Nest of Yellow Satin. The Box was of Blue Plush with a neat Clasp, and on the Lid was the Following, in Silver Letters: "Merry X-Mas."

Every Girl in Town came into the Drugstore and leaned on the Showcase and gazed longingly at the Work of Art. It was evident that the local Beau who loosened up for $6.50 would win in a Canter. But there was general Doubt as to whether anyone would be so Reckless as to fork over $6.50, just for Foolishness. All who went into the Drugstore and Stood in Solemn Silence, admiring the Blue Plush, the Yellow Satin, and the gleaming Celluloid, conceded that the Outfit was Purty, but they allowed it was too Fine for Actual Use. It was supposed that the Box alone would come to $3. Some said the Letters on the Lid were genuine Silver. Others contended that they were merely Plated.

In every Household the Toilet Set was a fruitful Topic. The general Verdict appeared to be that, in all probability, the Druggist would either have to knock off something on the Price or else be Stuck. There had been one or two Offers of $5 for the *Pièce de Résistance*, but the Druggist claimed that he had paid more than that for it, Wholesale.

Three Days before Christmas there appeared on the Yellow Satin a Card marked "Sold." The News spread like Wildfire that someone had blown himself to the Limit. There was but one Question agitating the whole Village for the next two Days. "Who will get the Toilet Set for Christmas?" Speculation ran rife, and every Girl who kept Company was hoping against Hope, even though her cold Judgment told her that, in all likelihood, her Fellow had not seen $6.50 in six long Months.

The Druggist had been pledged to Secrecy, and it became evident that the Populace would have to wait until Christmas to have its Curiosity appeased. So it waited with a lot of Impatience.

The Village Wag, whose name was Amos, had been one of Several who looked at the Toilet Set and counted their Money and passed out. He loved a Girl named Luella, but he had a Frugal Mind. It seemed to him that it would be more Sensible to save his Money and make a First Payment on a Home. Besides, the Poultry Business had been a little Slack, and he couldn't see himself giving up $6.50 for a dosh-burned Gimcrack that was no Account except to look at. So he gave up Sixty Cents for an Autograph Album and let it go at that. He would have gone ahead and bought something for a Dollar, only Amos thought he had a Cinch. His only Rival for the Hand of Luella was Tallmadge N. Crockett, proprietor of the Livery and Feed Stable. Amos was so much more Comic and Conversational than Tallmadge and had such a Taking Way that he wasn't for a Minute afraid of being Cut Out by Tallmadge.

Being the recognized Village Wag, Amos was called upon to impersonate Santa Claus at the Christmas Tree Entertainment. Amos was a born Romp, and the Congregation was sure of many a Hearty Laugh when he came in as Santy and began to cut Didoes.

Amos borrowed a Buffalo Robe, a Strand of Bells, and a Fur Cap. He rigged up a Set of Cotton Whiskers and prepared to be even Funnier than usual.

On Christmas Eve the Church put them in the Aisles, so great was the Interest in the Tree. The Superintendent of the Sunday School, looking unusually pale and scrubbed-up and smelling of Bay Rum, stood up in front of the Tree and made an Address that was Facetious, from his Point of View. The Choir sang one of its hardest Anthems, and after two or three other Inflictions, Amos, the Merry Andrew, came in as Santa Claus and did some of his best Comedy Acting. He galloped up and down the Aisles and scared several Children in Arms into Convulsions. Then he went up to the Tree to assist the droll Superintendent in distributing Presents. As a Team they were expected to spring a great many timely Quips, right on the Spur of the Moment.

While standing by the Tree, waiting for the Infant Class to conclude a Carol, Amos saw on a Table the magnificent Toilet Set, with the $6.50 Mark still on it. He drew nearer to read the attached Card and almost fainted with Horror when he saw the Name of Luella in the well-known Handwriting of Tallmadge N. Crockett. The Shock was so great that everything Swam before his Gaze, the same as in a Natatorium. He could not see anything except his own Finish. When Luella came to compare the superb Toilet Set and the Sixty-Cent Autograph Album, he knew that he would not be One-Two-Seven. He was inspired to a Desperate Action. He happened to remember that Celluloid contains Gun Cotton and Camphor and other high Explosives. The Infant Class stood between him and the Congregation. Stealthily he plucked a lighted Candle from the Tree and dropped it on the Toilet Set. Then he leaped over the Rail. There was a terrific Report, a flash of Fire, an odor of Camphor, and the Air was full of Infant Class. A Panic ensued. Throwing off his Disguise of White Cotton Whiskers, Amos gathered Luella in his Arms and carried her to a Place of Safety. She called him "Preserver" and refused to let go of him. When Quiet was restored, there was nothing left of the Toilet Set except the Clasp and the letters spelling "Merry X-Mas."

MORAL: True Love will prevail against the Vulgar Bank Roll, even at Christmastime.

MAKING PIEROGI ON CHRISTMAS EVE

Karen Kovacik

The dough is not turning out. It refuses
to stretch, sticks to the sides of the pink bowl.
You work in another half scoop of flour,
click your tongue, stamp your slippered foot.
And the flutter in my stomach quickens:
instinctive response to your anger, thrum
of guilt, my fault. In this room, once
dove gray, attic gold, brushed peach,
you presided in alligator flats,
though you could have been on stilts,
so tall you towered over us. You wanted
the gold-flecked linoleum to gleam,
the turquoise wool coat of your design
to disguise my sloping back, every plate
to be safe in its nesting place.
                                    You are smaller now,
more comic, a banner of unbleached flour
on your belly pressed against the table edge
as you thump the rolling pin over the dough's
thin skin. My own body feels bigger,
too big for the braided mat of this chair,
flushed with the insight that you have become
my serious gray-haired girl. How stubbornly
you hold your shoulders, your pastry wheel

flaying the flat expanse of dough into strips.
Flour on my fingers, I crimp your tiny pillows
of plum and cheese, watch them bob
and float in the salty water, and rescue them
again and again.

KEEPING CHRISTMAS OUR WAY

Gene Stratton-Porter

<u>CHARACTERS</u>

LADDIE, Who Loved and Asked No Questions.

THE PRINCESS, From the House of Mystery.

LEON, Our Angel Child.

LITTLE SISTER, Who Tells What Happened.

MR. and MRS. STANTON, Who Faced Life Shoulder to Shoulder.

ELIZABETH, SHELLEY, MAY, and Other Stanton Children.

CANDACE, the Cook.

Interested Relatives, Friends, and Neighbors.

"I remember, I remember
How my childhood fleeted by,
The mirth of its December,
And the warmth of its July."

WHEN DUSK CLOSED IN IT WOULD BE Christmas Eve. All day I had three points—a chair beside the kitchen table, a lookout melted through the frost on the front window, and the big sitting-room fireplace.

All the perfumes of Araby floated from our kitchen that day. There was that delicious smell of baking flour from big snowy loaves of bread, light biscuit, golden coffee cake, and cinnamon rolls dripping a waxy mixture of sugar, butter, and spice, much better than the finest butterscotch ever brought from the city. There was the tempting odor of boiling ham and baking pies. The air was filled with the smell of more herbs and spices than I knew the names of, that went into mincemeat, fruitcake, plum pudding, and pies. There was a teasing fragrance in the spiced vinegar heating for pickles, a reminder of winesap and rambo in the boiling cider, while the newly opened bottles of grape juice filled the house with the tang of Concord and muscadine. It seemed to me I never got nicely fixed where I could take a sly dip in the cake dough or snipe a fat raisin from the mincemeat but Candace would say: "Don't you suppose the backlog is halfway down the lane?"

Then I hurried to the front window, where I could see through my melted outlook on the frosted pane, across the west eighty to the woods, where father and Laddie were getting out the Christmas backlog. It was too bitterly cold to keep me there while they worked, but Laddie said that if I would watch, and come to meet them, he would take me up, and I might ride home among the Christmas greens on the log.

So I flattened my nose against the pane and danced and fidgeted until those odors teased me back to the kitchen; and no more did I get nicely located beside a jar of pudding sauce than Candace would object to the place I had hung her stocking. It was my task, my delightful all-day task, to hang the stockings. Father had made me a peg for each one, and I had ten feet of mantel front along which to arrange them. But it was no small job to do this to everyone's satisfaction. No matter what happened to anyone else, Candace had to be pleased, for did not she so manage that most fowls served on Mother's table went gizzardless to the carving? She knew and acknowledged the great importance of trying cookies, pies, and cake while they were hot. She was forever overworked and tired, yet she always found time to make gingerbread women with currant buttons on their frocks, and pudgy doughnut men with clove eyes and cigars of cinnamon. If my own stocking lay on the hearth, Candace's had to go in a place that satisfied her—that was one sure thing. Besides, I had to make up to her for what Leon did, because she was crying into the corner of her apron about that.

He slipped in and stole her stocking, hung it over the broomstick, and marched around the breakfast table singing to the tune of

"Ha, ha, ha, who wouldn't go—
Up on the housetop click, click, click?
Down through the chimney,
With good Saint Nick—"

words he made up himself. He walked just fast enough that she couldn't catch him, and sang as he went:

"Ha, ha, ha, good Saint Nick,
Come and look at this stocking, quick!
If you undertake its length to fill,
You'll have to bust a ten-dollar bill.
Who does it belong to? Candace Swartz.
Bring extra candy,—seven quarts—"

She got so angry she just roared, so father made Leon stop it, but I couldn't help laughing myself. Then we had to pet her all day, so she'd cheer up, and not salt the Christmas dinner with her tears. I never saw such a monkey as Leon! I trotted out to comfort her, and snipped bites, until I wore a triangle on the carpet between the kitchen and the mantel, the mantel and the window, and the window and the kitchen, while every hour things grew more exciting.

There never had been such a flurry at our house since I could remember; for tomorrow would be Christmas and bring home all the children, and a house full of guests. My big brother, Jerry, who was a lawyer in the city, was coming with his family, and so were Frank, Elizabeth, and Lucy with theirs, and of course Sally and Peter—I wondered if she would still be fixing his tie—and Shelley came yesterday, blushing like a rose, and she laughed if you pointed your finger at her.

Something had happened to her in Chicago. I wasn't so sure as I had been about a city being such a dreadful place of noise, bad air, and wicked people. Nothing had hurt Shelley. She had grown so much that you could see she was larger. Her hair and face—all of Shelley just shone. Her eyes danced, she talked and laughed all the time, and she hugged everyone who passed her. She never loved us so before. Leon said she must have been homesick and coming back had given her a spell. I did hope it would be a bad one, and last forever. I would have liked for all our family to have had a spell if it would have made them act and look like Shelley. The Princess was not a speck lovelier, and she didn't act any nicer.

If I could have painted, I'd have made a picture of Shelley with a circle of light above her head like the one of the boy Jesus where he talked with the wise men in the temple. I asked Father if he noticed how much prettier and nicer she was, and he said he did. Then I asked him if he thought now, that a city was such a bad place to live in, and he said where she was had nothing to do with it, the same thing would happen here, or anywhere, when life's greatest experience came to a girl. That was all he would say, but figuring it out was easy. The greatest experience that happened to our girls was when they married, like Sally, so it meant that Shelley had gone and fallen in love with that lawyer man, and she liked sitting on the sofa with him, and no doubt she fixed his ties. But if anyone thought I would tell anything I saw when he came they were badly mistaken.

All of us rushed around like we were crazy. If Father and Mother hadn't held steady and kept us down, we might have raised the roof. We were all so glad about getting Leon and the money back; mother hadn't been sick since the fish cured her; the new blue goose was so like the one that had burst, even Father never noticed any difference; all the children were either home or coming, and after we had our gifts and the biggest dinner we ever had, Christmas night all of us would go to the schoolhouse to see our school try to spell down three others to whom they had sent saucy invitations to come and be beaten.

Mother sat in the dining room beside the kitchen door, so that she could watch the baking, brewing, pickling, and spicing. It took four men to handle the backlog, which I noticed Father pronounced every year "just a little the finest we ever had," and Laddie strung the house with bittersweet, evergreens, and the most beautiful sprays of myrtle that he raked from under the snow. Father drove to town in the sleigh, and the list of things to be purchased Mother gave him as a reminder was almost a yard long.

The minute they finished the outdoor work Laddie and Leon began bringing in baskets of apples, golden bellflowers, green pippins, white winter pearmains, Rhode Island greenings, and striped rambos all covered with hoarfrost, yet not frozen, and so full of juice you had to bite into them carefully or they dripped and offended Mother. These they washed and carried to the cellar ready for use.

Then they cracked big dishes of nuts; and popped corn that popped with the most resounding pops in all my experience—popped a tubful, and Laddie melted maple sugar and poured over it and made big balls of fluff and sweetness. He took a pan and filled it with grains, selected one at a time, the very largest and whitest, and made an especial ball, in the middle of which he put a lovely pink candy heart on which was printed in red letters: "How can this heart be mine, yet yours, unless our hearts are one?" He wouldn't let any of them see it except me, and he only let me because he knew I'd be delighted.

It was almost dusk when Father came through the kitchen loaded with bundles and found Candace and the girls still cooking.

We were so excited we could scarcely be gathered around the supper table, and Mother said we chattered until she couldn't hear herself think. After a while Laddie laid down his fork and looked at our father.

"Have you any objection to my using the sleigh tomorrow night?" he asked.

Father looked at Mother.

"Had you planned to use it, Mother?"

Mother said: "No. If I go, I'll ride in the big sled with all of us. It is such a little way, and the roads are like glass."

So Father said politely, as he always spoke to us: "Then it will give me great pleasure for you to take it, my son."

That made Leon bang his fork loudly as he dared and squirm in his chair, for well he knew that if he had asked, the answer would have been different. If Laddie took the sleigh he would harness carefully, drive fast, but reasonably, blanket his horse, come home at the right time, and put everything exactly where he found it. But Leon would pitch the harness on some way, race every step, never think of his steaming horse, come home when there was no one so wild as he left to play pranks with, and scatter the harness everywhere. He knew our father would love to trust him the same as he did Laddie. He wouldn't always prove himself trustworthy, but he envied Laddie.

"You think you'll take the Princess to the spelling bee, don't you?" he sneered.

"I mean to ask her," replied Laddie.

"Maybe you think she'll ride in our old homemade, hickory cheesebox, when she can sail all over the country like a bird in a velvet-lined cutter with a real buffalo robe."

There was a quick catch in Mother's breath and I felt her hand on my chair tremble. Father's lips tightened and a frown settled on his face, while Laddie fairly jumped. He went white to the lips, and one hand dropped on the table, palm up, the fingers closing and unclosing, while his eyes turned first to Mother, and then to Father, in dumb appeal. We all knew that he was suffering. No one spoke, and Leon having shot his arrow straight home, saw as people so often do in this world that the damage of unkind words could not easily be repaired; so he grew red in the face and squirmed uncomfortably.

At last Laddie drew a deep, quivering breath. "I never thought of that," he said. "She has seemed happy to go with me several times when I asked her, but of course she might not care to ride in ours, when she has such a fine sleigh of her own."

Father's voice fairly boomed down the length of the table.

"Your mother always has found our sleigh suitable," he said.

The fact was, Father was rarely proud of it. He had selected the hickory in our woods, cut and hauled it to the mill, cured the lumber, and used all his spare time for two winters making it. With the exception of having the runners turned at a factory and iron-bound at a smithy, he had completed it alone with great care, even to staining it a beautiful cherry color, and fitting white sheepskins into the bed. We had all watched him and been so proud of it, and now Leon was sneering at it. He might just as well have undertaken to laugh at Father's wedding suit or to make fun of "Clark's Commentaries."

Laddie appealed to Mother: "Do you think I'd better not ask her?"

He spoke with an effort.

"Laddie, that is the first time I ever heard you propose to do any one an injustice," she said.

"I don't see how," said Laddie.

"It isn't giving the Princess any chance at all," replied Mother. "You've just said that she has seemed pleased to accompany you before, now you are proposing to cut her out of what promises to be the most delightful evening of the winter, without even giving her the chance to say whether she'd go with you or not. Has she ever made you feel that anything you offered her or wanted to do for her was not good enough?"

"Never!" exclaimed Laddie fervently.

"Until she does, then, do you think it would be quite manly and honorable to make decisions for her? You say you never thought of anything except a pleasant time with her; possibly she feels the same. Unless she changes, I would scarcely let a boy's foolish tongue disturb her pleasure. Moreover, as to the matter of wealth, your father may be as rich as hers; but they have one, we have many. If what we spend on all our brood could be confined to one child, we could easily duplicate all her luxuries, and I think she has the good sense to realize the fact as quickly as anyone. I've no doubt she would gladly exchange half she has for the companionship of a sister or a brother in her lonely life."

Laddie turned to Father, and Father's smile was happy again. Mother was little but she was mighty. With only a few words she had made Leon feel how unkind and foolish he had been, quieted Laddie's alarm, and soothed the hurt Father's pride had felt in that he had not been able to furnish her with so fine a turnout as Pryors had.

Next morning when the excitement of gifts and greetings was over, and Laddie's morning work was all finished, he took a beautiful volume of poems and his popcorn ball and started across the fields due west; all of us knew that he was going to call on and offer them to the Princess, and ask to take her to the spelling bee. I suppose Laddie thought he was taking that trip alone, but really he was surrounded. I watched him from the window, and my heart went with him. Presently Father went and sat beside Mother's chair, and stroking her hand, whispered softly: "Please don't worry, little mother. It will be all right. Your boy will come home happy."

"I hope so," she answered, "but I can't help feeling dreadfully nervous. If things go wrong with Laddie, it will spoil the day."

"I have much faith in the Princess's good common sense," replied Father, "and considering what it means to Laddie, it would hurt me sore to lose it."

Mother sat still, but her lips moved so that I knew she was making soft little whispered prayers for her best loved son. But Laddie, plowing through the drift, never dreamed that all of us were with him. He was always better looking than any other man I ever had seen, but when, two hours later, he stamped into the kitchen he was so much handsomer than usual, that I knew from the flush on his cheek and the light in his eye, that the Princess had been kind, and by the package in his hand, that she had made him a present. He really had two, a beautiful book and a necktie. I wondered to my soul if she gave him that, so she could fix it! I didn't believe she had begun on his ties at that time; but of course when he loved her as he did, he wished she would.

It was the very jolliest Christmas we ever had, but the day seemed long. When night came we were in a precious bustle. The wagon bed on bobs, filled with hay and covers, drawn by Ned and Jo, was brought up for the family, and the sleigh made spick-and-span and drawn by Laddie's thoroughbred, stood beside it. Laddie had filled the kitchen oven with bricks and hung up a comfort at four o'clock to keep the Princess warm.

Because he had to drive out of the way to bring her, Laddie wanted to start early; and when he came down dressed in his college clothes, and looking the manliest of men, some of the folks thought it funny to see him carefully rake his hot bricks from the oven, and pin them in an old red breakfast shawl. I thought it was fine, and I whispered to Mother: "Do you suppose that if Laddie ever marries the Princess he will be good to her as he is to you?"

Mother nodded with tear-dimmed eyes, but Shelley said: "I'll wager a strong young girl like the Princess will laugh at you for babying over her."

"Why?" inquired Laddie. "It is a long drive and a bitter night, and if you fancy the Princess will laugh at anything I do, when I am doing the best I know for her comfort, you are mistaken. At least, that is the impression she gave me this morning."

I saw the swift glance Mother shot at Father, and Father laid down his paper and said, while he pretended his glasses needed polishing: "Now there is the right sort of a girl for you. No foolishness about her, when she has every chance. Hurrah for the Princess!"

It was easy to see that she wasn't going to have nearly so hard a time changing Father's opinion as she would Mother's. It was not nearly a year yet, and here he was changed already. Laddie said good-bye to Mother—he never forgot—gathered up his comfort and bricks, and started for Pryors' downright happy. We went to the schoolhouse a little later, all of us scoured, curled, starched, and wearing our very best clothes. My! but it was fine. There were many lights in the room and it was hung with greens. There was a crowd even though it was early. On

Miss Amelia's table was a volume of history that was the prize, and everyone was looking and acting the very best he knew how, although there were cases where they didn't know so very much.

Our Shelley was the handsomest girl there, until the Princess came, and then they both were. Shelley wore one of her city frocks and a quilted red silk hood that was one of her Christmas gifts, and she looked just like a handsome doll. She made every male creature in that room feel that she was pining for him alone. May had a gay plaid frock and curls nearly a yard long, and so had I, but both our frocks and curls were homemade; Mother would have them once in a while; Father and I couldn't stop her.

But there was not a soul there who didn't have some sort of gift to rejoice over, and laughter and shouts of "Merry Christmas!" filled the room. It was growing late and there was some talk of choosers, when the door opened and in a rush of frosty air the Princess and Laddie entered. Every one stopped short and stared. There was good reason. The Princess looked as if she had accidentally stepped from a frame. She was always lovely and beautifully dressed, but tonight she was prettier and finer than ever before. You could fairly hear their teeth click as some of the most envious of those girls caught sight of her, for she was wearing a new hat!—a black velvet store hat, fitting closely over her crown, with a rim of twisted velvet, a scarlet bird's wing, and a big silver buckle. Her dress was of scarlet cloth cut in forms, and it fitted as if she had been melted and poured into it. It was edged around the throat, wrists, and skirt with narrow bands of fur, and she wore a loose, long, silk-lined coat of the same material, and worst of all, furs—furs such as we had heard wealthy and stylish city ladies were wearing. A golden brown cape that reached to her elbows, with ends falling to the knees, finished in the tails of some animal, and for her hands a muff as big as a nail keg.

Now, there was not a girl in that room, except the Princess, and she had those clothes, who wouldn't have flirted like a peacock, almost bursting with pride; but because the Princess had them, and they didn't, they sat stolid and sullen, and cast glances at each other as if they were saying: "The stuck-up thing!" "Thinks she's smart, don't she?"

Many of them should have gone to meet her and made her welcome, for she was not of our district and really their guest. Shelley did go, but I noticed she didn't hurry.

The choosers began at once, and Laddie was the first person called for our side, and the Princess for the visitors'. Everyone in the room was chosen on one side or the other; even my name was called, but I only sat still and shook my head, for I very well knew that no one except Father would remember to pronounce easy ones for me, and besides I was so bitterly disappointed I could scarcely have stood up. They had put me in a seat near the fire; the spellers lined either wall, and a goodly number that refused to spell occupied the middle seats. I couldn't get a glimpse of Laddie or the home folks, or worst of all, of my idolized Princess.

I never could bear to find a fault with Laddie, but I sadly reflected that he might as well have left me at home, if I were to be buried where I could neither hear nor see a thing. I was just wishing it was summer so I could steal out to the cemetery, and have a good visit with the butterflies that always swarmed around Georgiana Jane Titcomb's grave at the corner of the church. I never knew Georgiana Jane, but her people must have been very fond of her, for her grave was scarlet with geraniums, and pink with roses from earliest spring until frost, and the bright colors attracted swarms of butterflies. I had learned that if I stuck a few blossoms in my hair, rubbed some sweet-smelling ones over my hands, and knelt and kept so quiet that I fitted into the landscape, the butterflies would think me a flower too, and alight on my hair, dress, and my hands, even. God never made anything more beautiful than those butterflies, with their wings of brightly painted velvet down, their bright eyes, their curious antennae, and their queer, tickly feet. Laddie had promised me a book telling all about every kind there was, the first time he went to a city, so I was wishing I had it, and was among my pet beauties with it, when I discovered him bending over me.

He took my arm, and marching back to his place, helped me to the deep window seat beside him, where with my head on a level, and within a foot of his, I could see everything in the whole room. I don't know why I ever spent any time pining for the beauties of Georgiana Jane Titcomb's grave, even with its handsome headstone on which was carved a lamb standing on three feet and holding a banner over its shoulder with the fourth, and the geraniums, roses, and the weeping willow that grew over it, thrown in. I might have trusted Laddie. He never had forgotten me; until he did, I should have kept unwavering faith.

Now, I had the best place of anyone in the room, and I smoothed my new plaid frock and shook my handmade curls just as near like Shelley as ever I could. But it seems that most of the ointment in this world has a fly in it, like in the Bible, for fine as my location was, I soon knew that I should ask Laddie to put me down, because the window behind me didn't fit its frame, and the night was bitter. Before half an hour I was stiff with cold; but I doubt if I would have given up that location if I had known I would freeze, because this was the most fun I had ever seen.

Miss Amelia began with McGuffey's spelling book, and whenever some poor unfortunate made a bad break the crowd roared with laughter. Peter Justice stood up to spell and before three rounds he was nodding on his feet, so she pronounced *sleepy* to him. Someone nudged Pete and he waked up and spelled it, s-l-e, sle, p-e, pe, and because he really was so sleepy it made everyone laugh. James Whittaker spelled *compromise* with a k, and Isaac Thomas spelled *soap*, s-o-a-p-e, and it was all the funnier that he couldn't spell it, for from his looks you could tell that he had no acquaintance with it in any shape. Then Miss Amelia gave out *marriage* to the spooniest young man in the district, and *stepfather* to a man who was courting a widow with nine children; and *coquette* to our Shelley, who had been making sheep's eyes at Johnny Myers, so it took her by surprise and she joined the majority, which by that time occupied seats.

There was much laughing and clapping of hands for a time, but when Miss Amelia had let them have their fun and thinned the lines to half a dozen on each side who could really spell, she began business, and pronounced the hardest words she could find in the book, and the spellers caught them up and rattled them off like machines.

"Incompatibility," she gave out, and before the sound of her voice died away the Princess was spelling: "I-n, in, c-o-m, com, incom, p-a-t, pat, incompat, i, incompati, b-i-l, bil, incompatibil, i, incompatibili, t-y, ty, incompatibility."

Then Laddie spelled *incomprehensibility* and they finished up the *-bilities* and the *-alities* with a rush and changed McGuffey's for Webster, with five on Laddie's side and three on the Princess's, and when they quit with it, the Princess was alone, and Laddie and our little May facing her.

From that on you could call it real spelling. They spelled from the grammars, *hyperbole, synecdoche,* and *epizeuxis.* They spelled from the physiology, *chlorophyll, coccyx, arytenoid,* and the names of the bones and nerves, and all the hard words inside you. They tried the diseases and spelled *jaundice, neurasthenia,* and *tongue-tied.* They tried all the occupations and professions, and went through the stores and spelled all sorts of hardware, china and dry goods. Each side kept cheering its own and urging them to do their best, and every few minutes some man in the back of the house said something that was too funny. When Miss Amelia pronounced *bombazine* to Laddie our side cried, "Careful, Laddie, careful! You're out of your element!"

And when she gave *swivel-tree* to the Princess, her side whispered, "Go easy! Do you know what it is? Make her define it."

They branched over the country. May met her Jonah on the mountains. *Katahdin* was too much for her, and Laddie and the Princess were left to fight it out alone. I didn't think Laddie liked it. I'm sure he never expected it to turn out that way. He must have been certain he could beat her, for after he finished English there were two or three other languages he knew, and everyone in the district felt that he could win, and expected him to do it. It was an awful place to put him in, I could see that. He stood a little more erect than usual, with his eyes toward the Princess, and when his side kept crying, "Keep the prize, Laddie! Hold up the glory of the district!" he ground out the words as if he had a spite at them for not being so hard that he would have an excuse for going down.

The Princess was poised lightly on her feet, her thick curls, just touching her shoulders, shining in the light; her eyes like stars, her perfect, dark oval face flushed a rich red, and her deep bosom rising and falling with excitement. Many times in later years I have tried to remember when the Princess was loveliest of all, and that night always stands first.

I was thinking fast. Laddie was a big man. Men were strong on purpose so they could bear things. He loved the Princess so, and he didn't know whether she loved him or not; and every marriageable man in three counties was just aching for the chance to court her, and I didn't feel that he dared risk hurting her feelings.

Laddie said, to be the man who conquered the Princess and to whom she lifted her lips for a first kiss was worth life itself. I made up my mind that night that he knew just exactly what he was talking about. I thought so too. And I seemed to understand why Laddie—Laddie in his youth, strength, and manly beauty, Laddie, who boasted that there was not a nerve in his body—trembled before the Princess.

It looked as if she had set herself against him and was working for the honors, and if she wanted them, I didn't feel that he should chance beating her, and then, too, it was beginning to be plain that it was none too sure he could. Laddie didn't seem to be the only one who had been well drilled in spelling.

I held my jaws set a minute, so that I could speak without Laddie knowing how I was shivering, and then I whispered: "Except her eyes are softer, she looks just like a cardinal."

Laddie nodded emphatically and moving a step nearer laid his elbow across my knees. Heavens, how they spelled! They finished all the words I ever heard and spelled like lightning through a lot of others the meaning of which I couldn't imagine. Father never gave them out at home. They spelled *epiphany*, *gaberdine*, *ichthyology*, *gewgaw*, *kaleidoscope*, and *troubadour*. Then Laddie spelled one word two different ways; and the Princess went him one better, for she spelled another three.

They spelled from the Bible, *Nebuchadnezzar*, *Potiphar*, *Peleg*, *Belshazzar*, *Abimelech*, and a host of others I never heard the minister preach about. Then they did the most dreadful thing of all. *Broom*, pronounced the teacher, and I began mentally, b-r-o-o-m, but Laddie spelled "b-r-o-u-g-h-a-m," and I stared at him in a daze. A second later Miss Amelia gave out *Beecham* to the Princess, and again I tried it, b-e-e-c-h, but the Princess was spelling "B-e-a-u-c-h-a-m-p," and I almost fell from the window.

They kept that up until I was nearly crazy with nervousness; I forgot I was half frozen. I pulled Laddie's sleeve and whispered in his ear: "Do you think she'll cry if you beat her?"

I was half crying myself, the strain had been awful. I was torn between these dearest loves of mine.

"Seen me have any chance to beat her?" retorted Laddie.

Miss Amelia seemed to have used most of her books, and at last picked up an old geography and began giving out points around the coast, while Laddie and the Princess took turns snatching the words from her mouth and spelling them. Father often did that, so Laddie was safe there. They were just going at it when Miss Amelia pronounced, "Terra del Fuego," to the Princess. "T-e-r-r-a, Terra, d-e-l, del, F-i-e-u-g-o," spelled the Princess, and sat down suddenly in the midst of a mighty groan from her side, swelled by a wail from one little home district deserter.

"Next!" called Miss Amelia.

"T-e-r-r-a, Terra, d-e-l, del, F-e-u-g-o," spelled Laddie.

"Wrong!" wailed Miss Amelia, and our side breathed one big groan in concert, and I lifted up my voice in that also. Then everyone laughed and pretended they didn't care, and the Princess came over and shook hands with Laddie, and Laddie said to Miss Amelia: "Just let me take that book a minute until I see how the thing really does go." It was well done and satisfied the crowd, which clapped and cheered; but as I had heard him spell it many, many times for Father, he didn't fool me.

Laddie and the Princess drew slips for the book and it fell to her. He was so pleased he kissed me as he lifted me down and never noticed I was so stiff I could scarcely stand—and I did fall twice going to the sleigh. My bed was warm and my room was warm, but I chilled the night through and until the next afternoon, when I grew so faint and sleepy I crept to Miss Amelia's desk, half dead with fright—it was my first trip to ask an excuse—and begged: "Oh teacher, I'm so sick. Please let me go home."

I think one glance must have satisfied her that it was true, for she said very kindly that I might, and she would send Leon along to take care of me. But my troubles were only half over when I had her consent. It was very probable I would be called a baby and sent back when I reached home, so I refused company and started alone. It seemed a mile past the cemetery. I was so tired I stopped, and leaning against the fence, peeped through at the white stones and the whiter mounds they covered, and wondered how my mother would feel if she were compelled to lay me beside the two little whooping cough and fever sisters already sleeping there. I decided that it would be so very dreadful, that the tears began to roll down my cheeks and freeze before they fell.

Down the Big Hill slowly I went. How bare it looked then! Only leafless trees and dried seedpods rattling on the bushes, the sand frozen, and not a rush to be seen for the thick blanket of snow. A few rods above the bridge was a footpath, smooth and well worn, that led down to the creek, beaten by the feet of children who raced it every day and took a running slide across the ice. I struck into the path as always; but I was too stiff to run, for I tried. I walked on the ice, and being almost worn out, sat on the bridge and fell to watching the water bubbling under the glassy crust. I was so dull a horse's feet struck the bridge before I heard the bells—for I had bells in my ears that day—and when I looked up it was the Princess—the Princess in her red dress and furs, with a silk hood instead of her hat, her sleigh like a picture, with a buffalo robe, that it was whispered about the country, cost over a hundred dollars, and her thoroughbred mare Maud dancing and prancing. "Bless me! Is it you, Little Sister?" she asked. "Shall I give you a ride home?"

Before I could scarcely realize she was there, I was beside her and she was tucking the fine warm robe over me. I lifted a pair of dull eyes to her face.

"Oh Princess, I am so glad you came," I said. "I don't think I could have gone another step if I had frozen on the bridge."

The Princess bent to look in my face. "Why, you poor child!" she exclaimed, 'you're white as death! Where are you ill?"

I leaned on her shoulder, though ordinarily I would not have offered to touch her first, and murmured: "I am not ill, outdoors, only dull, sleepy, and freezing with the cold."

"It was that window!" she exclaimed. "I thought of it, but I trusted Laddie."

That roused me a little.

"Oh Princess," I cried, "you mustn't blame Laddie! I knew it was too cold, but I wouldn't tell him, because if he put me down I couldn't see you, and we thought, but for your eyes being softer, you looked just like a cardinal."

The Princess hugged me close and laughed merrily. "You darling!" she cried.

Then she shook me up sharply: "Don't you dare go to sleep!" she said. "I must take you home first."

Once there she quieted my mother's alarm, put me to bed, drove three miles for Dr. Fenner, and had me started nicely on the road to a month of lung fever, before she left. In my delirium I spelled volumes; and the miracle of it was I never missed a word until I came to "Terra del Fuego," and there I covered my lips and stoutly insisted that it was the Princess's secret.

To keep me from that danger sleep on the road, she shook me up and asked about the spelling bee. I thought it was the grandest thing I had ever seen in my life, and I told her so. She gathered me close and whispered: "Tell me something, Little Sister, please."

The minx! She knew I thought that a far finer title than hers.

"Would Laddie care?" I questioned.

"Not in the least!"

"Well then, I will."

"Can Laddie spell 'Terra del Fuego?'" she whispered.

I nodded.

"Are you sure?"

"I have heard him do it over and over for Father."

The Princess forgot I was so sick, forgot her horse, forgot everything. She threw her head back and her hands up, until her horse stopped in answer to the loosened line, and she laughed and laughed. She laughed until peal on peal re-echoed from our Big Woods clear across the west eighty. She laughed until her ringing notes set my slow pulses on fire, and started my numbed brain in one last effort. I stood up and took her lovely face between my palms, turning it until I could see whether the thought that had come to me showed in her eyes, and it did.

"Oh you darling, splendid Princess!" I cried. "You missed it on purpose to let Laddie beat! You can spell it too!"

DIGGING AND GROUSING

Ernie Pyle

ON THE NORTH AFRICAN DESERT, MARCH 23, 1943—When our Sahara salvage expedition finally found the wrecked airplanes far out on the endless desert, the mechanics went to work taking off usable parts, and four others of us appointed ourselves the official ditchdiggers of the day.

We were all afraid of being strafed if the Germans came over and saw men working around the planes, and we wanted a nice ditch handy for diving into. The way to have a nice ditch is to dig one. We wasted no time.

Would that all slit trenches could be dug in soil like that. The sand was soft and moist; just the kind children like to play in. The four of us dug a winding ditch forty feet long and three feet deep in about an hour and a half.

The day got hot, and we took off our shirts. One sweating soldier said: "Five years ago you couldn't a got me to dig a ditch for five dollars an hour. Now look at me.

"You can't stop me digging ditches. I don't even want pay for it; I just dig for love. And I sure do hope this digging today is all wasted effort; I never wanted to do useless work so bad in my life.

"Any time I get fifty feet from my home ditch you'll find me digging a new ditch, and brother I ain't joking. I love to dig ditches."

Digging out here in the soft desert sand was paradise compared with the claylike digging back at our base. The ditch went forward like a prairie fire. We measured it with our eyes to see if it would hold everybody.

"Throw up some more right here," one of the boys said, indicating a low spot in the bank on either side. "Do you think we've got it deep enough?"

"It don't have to be so deep," another one said. "A bullet won't go through more than three inches of sand. Sand is the best thing there is for stopping bullets."

A growth of sagebrush hung over the ditch on one side. "Let's leave it right there," one of the boys said. "It's good for the imagination. Makes you think you're covered up even when you ain't."

That's the new outlook, the new type of conversation, among thousands of American boys today. It's hard for you to realize, but there are certain moments when a plain old ditch can be dearer to you than any possession on earth. For all bombs, no matter where they may land eventually, do all their falling right straight at your head. Only those of you who know about that can ever know all about ditches.

While we were digging, one of the boys brought up for the thousandth time the question of that letter in *Time* magazine. What letter, you ask? Why, it's a letter you probably don't remember, but it has become famous around these parts.

It was in the November 23[, 1942] issue, which eventually found its way over here. Somebody read it, spoke to a few friends, and pretty soon thousands of men were commenting on this letter in terms which the fire department won't permit me to set to paper.

To get to the point, it was written by a soldier, and it said: "The greatest Christmas present that can be given to us this year is not smoking jackets, ties, pipes, or games. If people will only take the money and buy war bonds . . . they will be helping themselves and helping us to be home next Christmas. Being home next Christmas is something which would be appreciated by all of us boys in service!"

The letter was all right with the soldiers over here until they got down to the address of the writer and discovered he was still in camp in the States. For a soldier back home to open his trap about anything concerning the war is like waving a red flag at the troops over here. They say they can do whatever talking is necessary.

"Them poor dogfaces back home," said one of the ditchdiggers with fine soldier sarcasm, "they've really got it rugged. Nothing to eat but them old greasy pork chops and them three-inch steaks all the time. I wouldn't be surprised if they don't have to eat eggs several times a week."

"And they're so lonely," said another. "No entertainment except to rassle them old dames around the dance floor. The USO closes at ten o'clock and the night-clubs at three. It's mighty tough on them. No wonder they want to get home."

"And they probably don't get no sleep," said another, "sleeping on them old cots with springs and everything, and scalding themselves in hot baths all the time."

"And nothing to drink but that nasty old ten-cent beer and that awful Canadian Club whiskey," chimed in another philosopher with a shovel.

"And when they put a nickel in the box nothing comes out but Glenn Miller and Artie Shaw and such trash as that. My heart just bleeds for them poor guys."

"And did you see where he was?" asked another. "At the Albuquerque Air Base. And he wants to be home by next Christmas. Hell, if I could just see the Albuquerque Air Base again I'd think I was in heaven."

That's the way it goes. The boys feel a soldier isn't qualified to comment unless he's on the wrong side of the ocean. They're gay and full of their own wit when they get started that way, but just the same they mean it. It's a new form of the age-old soldier pastime of grousing. It helps take your mind off things.

THE FARM WIFE FINDS GRACE IN HER EMPTY BARN

Shari Wagner

Inside the house, dust is dust,
but here it looks holy, suspended

in slanted light that slips between
boards. Jacob's ladder could be

rungs to a loft where barn swallows
brush the dark with the curve

of their wings. Every joint is pegged
tight as Noah's ark, but there's room

for everyone—nesting sparrows
and mice that scatter from burlap sacks.

When I slide the big door back,
sunlight rushes in to fill the empty bin

where Jesus could be reaching up
to touch black and white faces

gazing down. I like to picture him
swaddled by the breath of cows.

THE FARM WIFE MAKES HER CHRISTMAS LIST

Shari Wagner

Give me sisters and brothers with crockpots full
and running over. A bed piled high with coats

and diaper bags. Leaves to extend the kitchen table.
Thick catalogs to booster seat the kids.

A percolator perking thirty cups as we pass
plates of monster cookies and whoopee pies.

Albums with ancestors solid as their barns.
Battered Rook cards we use to shoot the moon

and dominoes branching in every direction.
Paper snowflakes till strings of hearts

replace them. The old piano we can't afford
to tune, that gives us our pitch when we sing

"Praise God from Whom All Blessings Flow,"
the version with echoing alleluias and amens.

Silence washing over us as we wave to the last
car pulling out, side by side like newlyweds.

INDIANA WINTER

Susan Neville

IT'S THE DEAD OF WINTER. A LANDLOCKED state. Seven cars maneuver between frozen bean fields under gray skies. Seven men drive. Six women hold warm casseroles wrapped in towels.

Each car pushes its own small horn of light, scraping the road and frozen waves of soil until it blends with the others in the dim floodlights of one driveway.

The men and women leave their cars and go to the front door of a farmhouse. The women hug the casseroles. The men stand behind them. Their breath plumes as they wait.

Inside there is movement! Noise! Bright light! A party, hot spiced tea on the stove. Divinity! Take the casseroles in the kitchen, the hostess says, pile the coats on the bed.

The guests move into the large kitchen, into the brick-walled family room, around the wood stove, past the rack of shining guns. Some of the women stay in the kitchen and arrange dishes. The one old man stays with them. He stands at the kitchen counter with a toothed knife and homemade bread. His spotted hands make precise cuts. The rest of the men and some of the women move close to the basketball game on television.

The women talk about their children. Some of the men talk about money. A million dollars at retirement, a banker says, guaranteed. Honey, a woman yells to her husband, listen to this. Her husband has gone in the kitchen with the host to inspect a leaking pipe. The wealth we could have when we retire, she thinks. Honey, imagine, the security. There's a roar around the flickering television. Damnit, Uwe, the host booms, coming back from the kitchen, you were wide open. If I had been that tall, he says, I'd own the damn state and throw in Kentucky.

We're ready, the hostess calls. Come. Eat.

Glass casseroles, clouds of steam. Yams sweet in orange sauce. Almond cookies. Home-canned beans, red tomatoes, ham. Yeast breads, risen. Sugar pies. Cranberry ice in pink glasses. Paper plates stamped with holly. There is no wine. Taste. Shh. The host. Please, give us grace. The clatter of silver on glass. The flash of fire from knives, candle flames cradled in spoons. Your bread, Reverend, is delicious. Outside the house, the frost line is two feet deep. A rabbit run over by a car, its fur frozen. Inside the house, the air is as thick and warm and yellow as clotted cream. If only we lived here, the guests believe, we would never be unhappy.

She bought the skirt to wear tonight, but the waist button is already tight. She had no idea it would happen so fast. Under the table, her husband's knee presses hers. Still their secret, the child curled like a spoon under the paper napkin. Conceived in the dead of winter, lucky child, the mother hopes. Less danger of miscarriage than those children begun in the season of dogwood and iris, red discing, herbicide and dust. Half the women here seem cloudy with never-born children. There was that spring when three of the women miscarried in April. At the end of nine months, one had said, she felt the child's presence like a phantom limb.

Last spring it had happened to her too. The three months of growth, then the blood, then the waiting, then this new baby who would always feel like two. Later that spring there had been the fragile green of early corn, the good, kind faces of farmers in town, and no real connection between anything.

The candles carve out the slight hollows underneath her husband's cheekbones, the cold glow of early silver in his hair. Husband, do you know how much I love you? Sometimes this world seems so temporary. The whole table laughs at something the host said. Her husband looks ecstatic. Life is wonderful, she knows he is thinking, marvelous. Husband, I'm frightened. Do you know how much I love you?

The Reverend's hand is dry on the pink water glass. His lips are unsteady. He sees the exhilaration on the face of the young man beside him. The young man turns to him, out of politeness says, And for Christmas, Reverend, where will you be? The Reverend says he's not sure yet and the young man looks for a second guiltily at his wife until the Reverend says he has several offers and the husband relaxes and touches his wife's hand.

I hope, she says, this holiday won't be difficult for you, and the Reverend says, Oh no, I'm going to try to keep busy. I read a lot, you know.

He starts to tell them about an Eskimo book he's been reading, forgetting the vows he had made as a young man when old retired uncles would talk endlessly at family dinners about birds or former presidents, the vows that he could never bore young people like that. But the pleasure of conversation! Of hearing himself tell someone about the things he's filled his mind with—ice houses and frozen seals and lamps of fat and hot tea. Though it seems to come out odd. For a moment he feels dizzy, like that kayak sickness when the sky and water are such a blinding blue and white that you can't tell up from down.

The host's face and neck are as red as sunburn. He shouts across two women. The game should have started. A father with a son on the team looks up nervously from his plate, a cookie in his hand. You think so? He's been aware of every minute. Yes, it's time. The host reaches for a radio on the table behind him. His wife looks at him, and he doesn't turn it on.

The basketball player's father thinks of the drive back through the country to town. Hundreds of gravestones along the highway leading to the fieldhouse. On Saturday nights, when the traffic gets heavy, the gravestones snap with sharp, reflected light, like rows of cameras aimed right for his son.

The fieldhouse is a sea of green sweatshirts by now. Teenagers cruise the perimeter in two concentric circles, their eyes headlights. Scoreboards flashing, steamed eyeglasses, candy wrappers, old men and babies. Everyone in town is there, and his son! The father looks up to see if anyone's looking at him. He takes another cookie. My God, his son. Legs like a racehorse, just as fast. Only a sophomore, but already some people know. The old Reverend knows, the way he clasps the boy's hand on the Sundays they bring him out of retirement to preach, the way he leans forward in his thin tie and white shirt, his hands on his knees, focusing always on his son as intently as he, the father, focuses. Everyone in town is unemployed or just holding on, waiting for something. And it's his son. Never misses a free throw. Hits from halfway down the court. But still inconsistent, young. Not everyone knows what he'll be: best point guard in the state, in the country. Records that will stand. He has a gift. Everyone is waiting for something, and it's his son they're waiting for.

He holds his own small hand a few inches above the table, looks at the top, then the palm. Where did he come from, his son? A game tonight, and he let his wife talk him into missing it for this party. Already he's regretting that he's come. This party, she said, I look forward all year. A game tonight.

The host jumps up, says, To the best cooks in the county. A toast with this piece of fudge. He picks up the radio and heads for the family room. One by one the men follow, scraping chairs, joking. The old Reverend and the young husband stay behind, helping the women clear dishes. The cold presses against the bay window by the table, comes down the chimney in the living room by the tree.

Start another fire, the hostess says.

There is the sound of basketball from the family room, the odor of wood burning in the stove and the fireplace, of smoke from the snuffed-out candles. The women's faces are glowing from the warmth, stomachs round as bubbles.

When the old man runs out of things he can see to do and stands with his hands at his sides, the women send him into the family room and begin comparing childbirth stories. They all know each other's stories but pretend, for the pleasure of telling them again. Labor started in the car, in the bathroom, in bed, at work, in the grocery. Tipped uterus, dilated cervix, placenta praevia, I was so scared. Four children, says one woman, they were all a breeze; I could do it every day. Twenty hours of labor, says another, I almost died. Forty-eight hours for me, says another.

The young husband helping with the dishes goes into the living room to stand by the fire.

I knew right away when I was pregnant, one woman says, my breasts so sore I couldn't sleep on them. With Todd, another says, I was on the pill for two months and didn't know; when I found out, I worried the whole time.

They outdo one another with horror stories, secondhand, and casually told. A child born without ears, stillborn children wrapped in magazines at the foot of a teenager's bed. A two-pound baby born too early who fits in the palm of her mother's hand.

Slowly they bring up their own worries. A child who doesn't crawl. A boy who cries at night. A baby who hasn't yet turned over—Mine didn't turn until he was ever so old, the hostess says, and now he's gifted. One woman's daughter with leukemia, in remission, her lips so dry in the hospital the mother rubbed them with the strawberry lip gloss she sells door to door, a beautiful child. They'll be well, the women reassure one another, they all will be well. Remember the way a baby's soft hair feels on your cheek, the way you hate to give up nursing.

The woman in the wool skirt wants to tell but is afraid to bring bad luck. Some days, she thinks, it feels like a festival, and some days I'm so frightened. The hostess takes powdered cream from a shelf and pours it into a small pitcher with a silver spoon. She turns to the woman in the wool skirt who has nothing to add to the conversation. Now which grade is it you teach again? The woman in the wool skirt answers, smiles, goes into the living room to find her husband.

The husband and wife stand in the living room by the tree. How do you feel? he asks her. She smiles and looks into the tree: planets and stars brought inside against the winter. She lets her eyes lose focus and leans into her husband, galaxies of light multiplied and spinning, filling the room, her husband's body the only stable, unchanging thing in a universe too large, the tiny child the size of her thumb. A log cracks and falls through the fireplace grate, an explosion of orange sparks. He puts his arm around her waist. I never realized it, she says, for so long, how people have had the courage to have children.

The temperature drops below zero. The wind blows dark branches of evergreens outside the windows. The women see the branches and move into the family room. The husband and wife hear the wind and move into the family room. The men are laughing at something they can't explain.

The old Reverend sits uncomfortably in the best overstuffed chair. When he sees the couple come in from the living room, he offers it to the woman and moves to a stiff, wooden one.

Please, he thinks. Listen to me. For months my house has been darker than I remember it ever being, the outside gray seeping in and nothing I do will keep it out. The northern winters that last six months, a warm light from seal fat shining through ice and one family living by itself until the air gets close and then running miles through the black cold to another place just like it, all ice and dark, and a new house in hours, the universe shrunk to a bright warm dot. If my house could feel as warm as that, as warm as this place, please listen.

The host opens the wood-burning stove. The room seems smaller. Maybe it will snow, someone says. Not a chance, says the basketball player's father. It only snows in March during basketball play-offs. Right now it's the middle of the gray season, not a chance for snow.

The hostess passes pecans in the shell. The host picks up a book from the coffee table. He shows it to the woman in the wool skirt. The inscription reads "to my friend." It was signed by the author. The cover is bright yellow with orange. We were in Vietnam together, the host says. He shot himself after the book was published. The host says this with bravado, his knees spread wide.

Pecan shells cracking dust in the air. Black windows sweating. We got lost coming here, the woman says to him, ended up by the grain elevators.

They are the host's elevators, round white silos. In the fall farmers bring him their crops. In the spring he sells them poisons.

The woman remembers high school, another party. She didn't know anyone there. She'd gone with a boy she wasn't supposed to even talk to. Most of the boys she knew were college-bound and not worried. This was one of the expendable ones. There was nothing he wanted to do with his life, no job worth waiting for, probably no job at all.

She can't remember how she got there, whose car they went in. It was a frame working-class house close to other houses just like it. They all had porches. There were no adults, or rather, no authority. Someone's older brother was there.

There were a lot of people in the living room. She remembers orange-flowered upholstery, a windowsill covered with chips of putty and paint, the shells of bugs. She doesn't remember faces. The older brother had short hair. He was home on some sort of leave. He laughed hard, his arm crooked around the neck of a short, long-haired girl. It was like he was choking her.

He got out a white screen and set it up against a wall. He had a case of slides. The projector was old and the slides kept sticking. It bothered him when one of the slides was in backward, though no one else could tell. She thinks she remembers him laughing as he showed them but doesn't trust that memory. She turned away from the screen.

And what does that have to do with this room, earthy nut taste, lingering cinnamon and cranberry, hot coffee, her child. The host and that boy pulled out of the county, her future husband sitting safe in an accounting class. Just from watching the news, she says now to the host, even to me, there's something terrifying about helicopters.

We're living in dark times, the host says, and she nods.

Dark times, the host says, and the men agree. Smoke from pipes and one or two cigarettes. The largest all-brick factory in the world, now a quiet old fossil in the center of town. Windows are broken out and covered with paper. Acres of empty parking lots full of trash. There are For Sale signs in every neighborhood, many of them foreclosures. Last fall a stomping death out by the county high school. Of course the banks are holding on, one or two of the furniture stores. Churches are still open, the children at school dreaming about the future. The hostess passes ribbon candy.

She goes to an exercise class twice a week in the basement under the B&G Gym. The class is downtown, near the courthouse, and most of the stores around it are empty, the windows blank. The basement is unfinished: block walls, bare bulb lights, a slanting, cracked concrete floor with rusted drains, years of dust and cobwebs, exposed pipes and supporting beams holding up the gym floor. The children paly to the side, by the furnace, on a tumbling mat. It's a dreary place to be but the new, light-filled gym behind the Baptist church, where prayer concerns precede each session and a head of Christ fills one whole wall in a paint-by-numbers style, has no provision for children and meets at an inconvenient time.

The instructor brings a small tape player with tapes of rock music and routines she drives to Indianapolis every other month to learn and they all jump and dance and breathe while overhead men drop hundred-pound weights on an old plank floor and the women imitate their clumsy instructor and watch their children play and pray for grace.

In town, the fieldhouse is packed. The crowd roars as the boys run through the tunnel and onto the floor. The radio announcers interview the mascot, a Roman soldier. An Indian from the visiting school runs around the outside of the court with a tomahawk and the home crowd boos. The soldier walks across the floor on his hands.

The Reverend stares at the radio, trying to picture that tall, confident boy. Sitting on the bench probably while the others start to practice, his head between his hands, praying most likely. Some coaches would mind, but this is a town where the prayer at last year's graduation turned into a revival, with the seniors who thought they were saved raising their hands and shouting.

The Reverend has known that boy since he was born. They were neighbors. He and his wife would sit out on the porch and watch him play. He can remember the boy during that cute toddler stage, when he'd come over to their porch tangling his fingers together and holding his fists up to him as a gift; this is a flower, he'd say, and then untangle them and twist them back together as a star or a bird that only he could see. This is a church, the Reverend would say, showing the boy his own hands and conventional patterns, and this the steeple.

He was like their child. Sometimes he envied the boy's parents but would never say that to his wife. They had both accepted their inability to have children and had not looked back. But it amazed him now when he thinks about it how much of their time they spent watching this boy, how much of their time they spent talking about him. His wife worried when she heard that metallic ringing of the basketball on the concrete driveway in all kinds of weather, the boy unable to let himself come in until he made a hundred shots in a row, starting over if he missed one, even in cold rain.

Last year during the closest thing Methodists ever had to a revival, on the fifth night of services when the minister had asked for the fifth time for people to come forward in rededication and everyone but two or three old women who had sat still all their lives and were tired of it stayed, as usual, politely in their seats, the boy had come forward and taken the pulpit, quietly, *quietly*, and with dignity, chastising the congregating for their lack of fervor.

And first his parents had come forward, his mother crying and his father large and uncomfortable kneeling at the altar, and then the teenagers and then the others around the parents' age, the ones here tonight, and then most of the rest, only a small ring of the ever-polite left sitting on the oak benches at the perimeter.

Dark times, the host says, and the men and one or two women talk about nuclear war. Within the next decade, the host says, and some of the men agree. There's no way it won't happen. These are end times, a teacher says, and he begins enumerating the seven horsemen, forgetting four. The host, excited, remembers one—famine. It's like the seven dwarves, the teacher says, any group can only usually remember part of them, and I'm sure there are more. But I think there may only be four, a woman says. How many, Reverend? she asks. There are four horsemen of the apocalypse, he says; but I can't believe it has much to do with this.

At any rate, the host says, you have to believe it's true, within the decade. A banker agrees. The economy is falling apart, he says, you know this year the bank didn't hold its Christmas party. And it's happening everywhere. That always comes before war. We can't live with this tension anymore, sooner or later one of us, maybe even it will be us, will decide to hell with it and start the whole thing going.

It could happen by accident, one of the women says.

And probably will, says the host.

Maybe we'll be safe out here, the hostess says.

An accountant who had just read an article in a magazine shakes his head. One of the newer missiles hits Indianapolis, Chicago, or Dayton, and we've all had it.

Why would anyone aim at those cities, a woman asks; they're not New York or Washington.

The Russians will want to save the Rockettes, the banker says—and anyway, who had ever heard of Nagasaki?

Summer, gray-green jets from Wright Patterson practice maneuvers over the farmhouse while the hostess hangs out laundry. They fly so fast she would miss them if it weren't for the sound. Her youngest boy hides under a red maple. When the planes fly back into the morning sun they turn white and fragile as tiny, brittle bones.

She excuses herself and goes into the kitchen for more coffee. When she comes back to the party she sits on the other side of the room where a few of the women are huddled around a table.

According to this article, the accountant says, you can make a quick shelter against the foundation of your house, kind of like a deep window well—that is, if you have an hour or so warning, and if you're far enough away that all you have to worry about is fallout. Sounds like a grave, says a banker. You can survive fallout, the husband of the woman in the wool skirt says. At least for a day or two, says the host.

He's already got twenty-eight points, the father says to the room, and the game's only half over.

I've got my wife drying vegetables, the host says, and we've got ammunition for all those guns. You'd let all of us in, wouldn't you, says the banker with a cane. If we had enough, the host says, looking uncomfortable. We have a lot of friends.

The school record is forty-eight, and he's only a sophomore, says the father.

The host shifts position in his chair and looks at the banker. Of course we'd let you in, he says.

The other banker says he put an electric fence around his place last summer. He cracks a pecan into his handkerchief. The shock waves from one missile in a strategic place, says the accountant, will knock out all the electricity, all the computers, all the cars, everything.

The world's going up in flames, says the host, there aren't any leaders anymore that aren't idiots. Look at our last mayoral election, the teacher says—well-meaning alcoholics and bag ladies and a couple of addicts, the biggest qualification for the job that they're unemployed and have plenty of time to devote to it. Anyone with something to do, a business or family, wouldn't want the job, the banker with the fence says. Not much hope in it.

It's funny, the husband says, looking away from the radio. The day of the big train wreck in Dunreith the plaster cracked in every room in our house, the sky was red from the fire. I woke up and for a minute I was terrified, sure that the Russians had finally dropped the bomb on us. I never stopped to ask why they would choose a town of ten or twelve families and three antique stores as a target. I was sure, the fear so deep in me. At any time, depending on your mood, the most likely two targets seem to be exactly where you are or exactly where you aren't.

If I'm really quiet, his wife thinks, maybe I can feel him move. She stretches her legs out, listens to the logs in the fire and the pleasant crackling of the radio, glad the Reverend gave her the chair in the middle of the men where she can just listen to the drone of their voices, not feeling like she needs to join in the conversation the way she would if she were with the women. She can sit there feeling secret and warm, as though she's the only one this has ever happened to. It will be a boy. She's sure of that already. She and her husband and the boy will come together so tightly they will never need anyone else, never be afraid of anything, never lonely. They will live forever.

One of the women brings a plate of Christmas cookies into the family room and puts it on the coffee table. The host notices the gold lights above the mantel aren't plugged in, and he turns them on. The accountant eats a green-sugared bell, a banker a silver wreath with cinnamon hearts. Dark times, the men agree.

They're silent and then turn uncomfortably to the women. The teacher clears his throat, says, Well anyway, tell us about the new retirement accounts, and the bankers produce calculators and sheets of the paper to prove how if you start now you really could be a millionaire when you retire.

The accountant and the host go into the basement to inspect some new wiring. The ball player's father eats a piece of vanilla fudge. The skin above his sweater is purple. A quiet repairman talks about the deck he's building on the back of his house, the banker with a fence asks him about a leak in his hot water heater.

The room is cold, the light dimming. They all notice the Reverend, poor thing, sitting with his eyes milky, missing his wife.

The basketball player's mother leans forward in her chair, catching the eye of her husband. My God! he shouts and jumps up from his chair. Forty-four points. What's the record? a woman asks. I think it's forty-eight, says the repairman. A nervous excitement bubbles up like tree lights. The accountant and the host come back up from the basement. The banker stops talking about his hot water heater. The women get up from the table and squeeze onto sofas next to their husbands. Three of four men and women sit on the floor. They all face the radio, their backs to the windows.

Who set the record?

Scott Lewis in '68. Maybe Troy Schweikart in '57.

It was Scott, says the Reverend, in '67.

How could I let her talk me out of being there? thinks the father. He stands up and paces.

Thousands of people are crowded into the fieldhouse, others around radios, late on one of the darkest nights of the year. And his son, her son, takes the ball down the floor and from twenty feet outside right through the net without hitting the rim, their son, so quiet when I carried him, where did he come from? The arc of the basketball beginning at a point deep in all of their chests, this boy they know, who is part of them, the arc ending, how could it be otherwise, in the sweet center of the basket, a record set years ago by a boy two years older and, with a foul shot, on this night quietly broken.

The host takes a deep breath of pine from the roping on the mantel. The heat from the crowded room. Dark times, he repeats without thinking, everyone excited, including the host, congratulating the father, who is hugging his wife and hugging the other wives and his friends, a great party. The host slaps one of the bankers on the back. End times.

The woman in the wool skirt touches her husband's hand. Life is wonderful, he thinks, marvelous. Are you ready? she asks. Yes, it's late.

A crowding in the kitchen. Was that your casserole? It was delicious. Don't forget the spoon. Smooth satin lining on coats, voices like bells. The old man with his hands in his pockets hesitates at the door.

Four older model cars and three new ones head into the black night. For a while the house lights blaze. Then the host and hostess turn off the outside lights and turn and lock the door. And the fields, the trees, the faces in the cars, fade into the winter night.

HOME FOR THE HOLIDAYS

Liz Whiteacre

This ornate golden dragon's head,
the glass flask hidden inside its wooden shaft,
isn't the cane Grandpa used most often
after his knees' parts were re-engineered
with metal and plastic, but the one given to him
as a gift—half joke—willed to Dad.

I'm just graduated from crutches, home on holiday,
and I fit the dragon in my palm.
Cold, short like the fireplace poker, it bites:
I know why Grandpa rejected it
—his great hands could smother my own.

My brown cane, bought at a medical supply store
in a southern Illinois strip mall, has a candy-cane arc
nearly at my hip, a sturdy third leg, utilitarian,
not flashy, a necessity when balance is fragile.
I reject the ill-fitting, cold head, lean it against the hearth,
picture it nestled with other novelty canes at Grandpa's home
—gifts from people who've not yet needed a prop.

Try as I might, I cannot conjure his daily cane
—was it aluminum or wood—the third appendage
that lent him swagger to my school plays, ballet recitals,
midnight church services in Decatur, the dinner table
my Grandma set—it remains translucent in my mind
when I picture him, like the exact hue of denim
he liked to wear, the twangy song playing
on the bathroom radio, the L'Amour or McMurtry title
that sat near his recliner.

The details fade like snowflakes on the panes tonight,
but when I feel my cane's heft, its smooth curve pressed
into my palm, I remember his grace, the affectionate poke
he gave Grandma's bottom when she served dinner,
the grip of his hand when we played later
while dishes were cleared: he'd grab my fist
and I'd pull and pull to let go
and he'd laugh until his fingers sprang open,
catching me, always catching me, before I fell.

A REVERSIBLE SANTA CLAUS

Meredith Nicholson

I

Mr. William B. Aikins, *alias* "Softy" Hubbard, *alias* Billy The Hopper, paused for breath behind a hedge that bordered a quiet lane and peered out into the highway at a roadster whose taillight advertised its presence to his felonious gaze. It was Christmas Eve, and after a day of unseasonable warmth a slow, drizzling rain was whimsically changing to snow.

The Hopper was blowing from two hours' hard travel over rough country. He had stumbled through woodlands, flattened himself in fence corners to avoid the eyes of curious motorists speeding homeward or flying about distributing Christmas gifts, and he was now bent upon committing himself to an interurban trolley line that would afford comfortable transportation for the remainder of his journey. Twenty miles, he estimated, still lay between him and his domicile.

The rain had penetrated his clothing and vigorous exercise had not greatly diminished the chill in his blood. His heart knocked violently against his ribs and he was dismayed by his shortness of wind. The Hopper was not so young as in the days when his agility and genius for effecting a quick "get-away" had earned for him his sobriquet. The last time his Bertillon measurements were checked (he was subjected to this humiliating experience in Omaha during the Ak-Sar-Ben carnival three years earlier) official note was taken of the fact that The Hopper's hair, long carried in the records as black, was rapidly whitening.

At forty-eight a crook—even so resourceful and versatile a member of the fraternity as The Hopper—begins to mistrust himself. For the greater part of his life, when not in durance vile, The Hopper had been in hiding, and the state or condition of being a fugitive, hunted by keen-eyed agents of justice, is not, from all accounts, an enviable one. His latest experience of involuntary servitude had been under the auspices of the state of Oregon, for a trifling indiscretion in the way of safe-blowing. Having served his sentence, he skillfully effaced himself by a year's siesta on a pineapple plantation in Hawaii. The island climate was not wholly pleasing to The Hopper, and when pineapples palled he took passage from Honolulu as a stoker, reached San Francisco (not greatly chastened in spirit), and by a series of characteristic hops, skips, and jumps across the continent landed in Maine by way of the Canadian provinces. The Hopper needed money. He was not without a certain crude philosophy, and it had been his dream to acquire by some brilliant coup a sufficient fortune upon which to retire and live as a decent, law-abiding citizen for the remainder of his days. This ambition, or at least the means to its fulfillment, can hardly be defended as praiseworthy, but The Hopper was a singular character and we must take him as we find him. Many prison chaplains and jail visitors bearing tracts had striven with little success to implant moral ideals in the mind and soul of The Hopper, but he was still to be cataloged among the impenitent; and as he moved southward through the commonwealth of Maine he was so oppressed by his poverty, as contrasted with the world's abundance, that he lifted forty thousand dollars in a neat bundle from an express car which Providence had sidetracked, apparently for his personal enrichment, on the upper waters of the Penobscot. Whereupon he began perforce playing his old game of artful dodging, exercising his best powers as a hopper and skipper. Forty thousand dollars is no inconsiderable sum of money, and the success of this master stroke of his career was not to be jeopardized by careless moves. By craftily hiding in the big woods and making himself agreeable to isolated lumberjacks who rarely saw newspapers, he arrived in due course on Manhattan Island, where with shrewd judgment he avoided the haunts of his kind while planning a future commensurate with his new dignity as a capitalist.

He spent a year as a diligent and faithful employee of a garage which served a fashionable quarter of the metropolis; then, animated by a worthy desire to continue to lead an honest life, he purchased a chicken farm fifteen miles as the crow flies from Center Church, New Haven, and boldly opened a bank account in that academic center in his newly adopted name of Charles S. Stevens, of Happy Hill Farm. Feeling the need of companionship, he married a lady somewhat his junior, a shoplifter of the second class, whom he had known before the vigilance of the metropolitan police necessitated his removal to the Far West. Mrs. Stevens's inferior talents as a petty larcenist had led her into many difficulties, and she gratefully availed herself of The Hopper's offer of his heart and hand.

They had added to their establishment a retired yegg who had lost an eye by the premature popping of the "soup" (i.e., nitroglycerin) poured into the crevices of a country post office in Missouri. In offering shelter to Mr. James Whitesides, *alias* "Humpy" Thompson, The Hopper's motives had not been wholly unselfish, as Humpy had been entrusted with the herding of poultry in several penitentiaries and was familiar with the most advanced scientific thought on chicken culture.

The roadster was headed toward his home and The Hopper contemplated it in the deepening dusk with greedy eyes. His labors in the New York garage had familiarized him with automobiles, and while he was not ignorant of the pains and penalties inflicted upon lawless persons who appropriate motors illegally, he was the victim of an irresistible temptation to jump into the machine thus left in the highway, drive as near home as he dared, and then abandon it. The owner of the roadster was presumably eating his evening meal in peace in the snug little cottage behind the shrubbery, and The Hopper was aware of no sound reason why he should not seize the vehicle and further widen the distance between himself and a suspicious-looking gentleman he had observed on the New Haven local.

The Hopper's conscience was not altogether at ease, as he had, that afternoon, possessed himself of a bill-book that was protruding from the breast pocket of a dignified citizen whose strap he had shared in a crowded subway train. Having foresworn crime as a means of livelihood, The Hopper was chagrined that he had suffered himself to be beguiled into stealing by the mere propinquity of a piece of red leather. He was angry at the world as well as himself. People should not go about with bill-books sticking out of their pockets; it was unfair and unjust to those weak members of the human race who yield readily to temptation.

He had agreed with Mary when she married him and the chicken farm that they would respect the Ten Commandments and all statutory laws, state and federal, and he was painfully conscious that when he confessed his sin she would deal severely with him. Even Humpy, now enjoying a peace that he had rarely known outside the walls of prison, even Humpy would be bitter. The thought that he was again among the hunted would depress Mary and Humpy, and he knew that their harshness would be intensified because of his violation of the unwritten law of the underworld in resorting to purse-lifting, an infringement upon a branch of felony despicable and greatly inferior in dignity to safe-blowing.

These reflections spurred The Hopper to action, for the sooner he reached home the more quickly he could explain his protracted stay in New York (to which metropolis he had repaired in the hope of making a better price for eggs with the commission merchants who handled his products), submit himself to Mary's chastisement, and promise to sin no more. By returning on Christmas Eve, of all times, again a fugitive, he knew that he would merit the unsparing condemnation that Mary and Humpy would visit upon him. It was possible, it was even quite likely, that the short, stocky gentleman he had seen on the New Haven local was not a "bull"—not really a detective who had observed the little transaction in the subway—but the very uncertainty annoyed The Hopper. In his happy and profitable year at Happy Hill Farm he had learned to prize his personal comfort, and he was humiliated to find that he had been frightened into leaving the train at Bansford to continue his journey afoot, and merely because a man had looked at him a little queerly.

Any Christmas spirit that had taken root in The Hopper's soul had been disturbed, not to say seriously threatened with extinction, by the untoward occurrences of the afternoon.

II

The Hopper waited for a limousine to pass and then crawled out of his hiding place, jumped into the roadster, and was at once in motion. He glanced back, fearing that the owner might have heard his departure, and then, satisfied of his immediate security, negotiated a difficult turn in the road and settled himself with a feeling of relief to careful but expeditious flight. It was at this moment, when he had urged the car to its highest speed, that a noise startled him—an amazing little chirrupy sound which corresponded to none of the familiar forewarnings of engine trouble. With his eyes to the front he listened for a repetition of the sound. It rose again—it was like a perplexing cheep and chirrup, changing to a chortle of glee.

"Goo-goo! Goo-goo-goo!"

The car was skimming a dark stretch of road and a superstitious awe fell upon The Hopper. Murder, he gratefully remembered, had never been among his crimes, though he had once winged a too-inquisitive policeman in Kansas City. He glanced over his shoulder, but saw no pursuing ghost in the snowy highway; then, looking down apprehensively, he detected on the seat beside him what appeared to be an animate bundle, and, prompted by a louder "goo-goo," he put out his hand. His fingers touched something warm and soft and were promptly seized and held by Something.

The Hopper snatched his hand free of the tentacles of the unknown and shook it violently. The nature of the Something troubled him. He renewed his experiments, steering with his left hand and exposing the right to what now seemed to be the grasp of two very small mittened hands.

"Goo-goo! Goody; teep wunnin'!"

"A kid!" The Hopper gasped.

That he had eloped with a child was the blackest of the day's calamities. He experienced a strange sinking feeling in the stomach. In moments of apprehension a crook's thoughts run naturally into periods of penal servitude, and the punishment for kidnapping, The Hopper recalled, was severe. He stopped the car and inspected his unwelcome fellow passenger by the light of matches. Two big blue eyes stared at him from a hood and two mittens were poked into his face. Two small feet, wrapped tightly in a blanket, kicked at him energetically.

"Detup! Mate um skedaddle!"

Obedient to this command The Hopper made the car skedaddle, but superstitious dread settled upon him more heavily. He was satisfied now that from the moment he transferred the strap-hanger's bill-book to his own pocket he had been hoodooed. Only a jinx of the most malevolent type could have prompted his hurried exit from a train to dodge an imaginary "bull." Only the blackest of evil spirits could be responsible for this involuntary kidnapping!

"Mate um wun! Mate um 'ippity stip!"

The mittened hands reached for the wheel at this juncture and an unlooked-for "jippity skip" precipitated the young passenger into The Hopper's lap.

This mishap was attended with the jolliest baby laughter. Gently but with much firmness The Hopper restored the youngster to an upright position and supported him until sure he was able to sustain himself.

"Ye better set still, little feller," he admonished.

The little feller seemed in no wise astonished to find himself abroad with a perfect stranger and his courage and good cheer were not lost upon The Hopper. He wanted to be severe, to vent his rage for the day's calamities upon the only human being within range, but in spite of himself he felt no animosity toward the friendly little bundle of humanity beside him. Still, he had stolen a baby and it was incumbent upon him to free himself at once of the appalling burden; but a baby is not so easily disposed of. He could not, without seriously imperiling his liberty, return to the cottage. It was the rule of housebreakers, he recalled, to avoid babies. He had heard it said by burglars of wide experience and unquestioned wisdom that babies were the most dangerous of all burglar alarms. All things considered, kidnapping and automobile theft were not a happy combination with which to appear before a criminal court. The Hopper was vexed because the child did not cry; if he had shown a bad disposition The Hopper might have abandoned him; but the youngster was the cheeriest and most agreeable of traveling companions. Indeed, The Hopper's spirits rose under his continued "goo-gooing" and chirruping.

"Nice little Shaver!" he said, patting the child's knees.

Little Shaver was so pleased by this friendly demonstration that he threw up his arms in an effort to embrace The Hopper.

"Bil-lee," he gurgled delightedly.

The Hopper was so astonished at being addressed in his own lawful name by a strange baby that he barely averted a collision with a passing motor truck. It was unbelievable that the baby really knew his name, but perhaps it was a good omen that he had hit upon it. The Hopper's resentment against the dark fate that seemed to pursue him vanished. Even though he had stolen a baby, it was a merry, brave little baby who didn't mind at all being run away with! He dismissed the thought of planting the little shaver at a door, ringing the bell and running away; this was no way to treat a friendly child that had done him no injury, and The Hopper highly resolved to do the square thing by the youngster even at personal inconvenience and risk.

The snow was now falling in generous Christmasy flakes, and the high speed the car had again attained was evidently deeply gratifying to the young person, whose reckless tumbling about made it necessary for The Hopper to keep a hand on him.

"Steady, little un; steady!" The Hopper kept mumbling.

His wits were busy trying to devise some means of getting rid of the youngster without exposing himself to the danger of arrest. By this time someone was undoubtedly busily engaged in searching for both baby and car; the police far and near would be notified, and would be on the lookout for a smart roadster containing a stolen child.

"Merry Christmas!" a boy shouted from a farm gate.

"M'y Kwismus!" piped Shaver.

The Hopper decided to run the machine home and there ponder the disposition of his blithe companion with the care the unusual circumstances demanded.

"'Urry up; me's goin' 'ome to me's gwanpa's kwismus t'ee!"

"Right ye be, little un; right ye be!" affirmed The Hopper.

The youngster was evidently blessed with a sanguine and confiding nature. His reference to his grandfather's Christmas tree impinged sharply upon The Hopper's conscience. Christmas had never figured very prominently in his scheme of life. About the only Christmases that he recalled with any pleasure were those that he had spent in prison, and those were marked only by Christmas dinners varying with the generosity of a series of wardens.

But Shaver was entitled to all the joys of Christmas, and The Hopper had no desire to deprive him of them.

"Keep a-larfin', Shaver, keep a-larfin'," said the Hopper. "Ole Hop ain't a-goin' to hurt ye!"

The Hopper, feeling his way cautiously round the fringes of New Haven, arrived presently at Happy Hill Farm, where he ran the car in among the chicken sheds behind the cottage and carefully extinguished the lights.

"Now, Shaver, out ye come!"

Whereupon Shaver obediently jumped into his arms.

III

The Hopper knocked twice at the back door, waited an instant, and knocked again. As he completed the signal the door was opened guardedly. A man and woman surveyed him in hostile silence as he pushed past them, kicked the door shut, and deposited the blinking child on the kitchen table. Humpy, the one-eyed, jumped to the windows and jammed the green shades close into the frames. The woman scowlingly waited for the head of the house to explain himself, and this, with the perversity of one who knows the dramatic value of suspense, he was in no haste to do.

"Well," Mary questioned sharply. "What ye got there, Bill?"

The Hopper was regarding Shaver with a grin of benevolent satisfaction. The youngster had seized a bottle of catsup and was making heroic efforts to raise it to his mouth, and the Hopper was intensely tickled by Shaver's efforts to swallow the bottle. Mrs. Stevens, *alias* Weeping Mary, was not amused, and her husband's enjoyment of the child's antics irritated her.

"Come out with ut, Bill!" she commanded, seizing the bottle. "What ye been doin'?"

Shaver's big blue eyes expressed surprise and displeasure at being deprived of his plaything, but he recovered quickly and reached for a plate with which he began thumping the table.

"Out with ut, Hop!" snapped Humpy nervously. "Nothin' wuz said about kidnappin', an' I don't stand for ut!"

"When I heard the machine comin' in the yard I knowed somethin' was wrong an' I guess it couldn't be no worse," added Mary, beginning to cry. "You hadn't no right to do ut, Bill. Hookin' a buzz-buzz an' a kid an' when we wuz playin' the white card! You ought t' 'a' told me, Bill, what ye went to town fer, an' it bein' Christmas, an' all."

That he should have chosen for his fall the Christmas season of all times was reprehensible, a fact which Mary and Humpy impressed upon him in the strongest terms. The Hopper was fully aware of the inopportuneness of his transgressions, but not to the point of encouraging his wife to abuse him.

As he clumsily tried to unfasten Shaver's hood, Mary pushed him aside and with shaking fingers removed the child's wraps. Shaver's cheeks were rosy from his drive through the cold; he was a plump, healthy little shaver and The Hopper viewed him with intense pride. Mary held the hood and coat to the light and inspected them with a sophisticated eye. They were of excellent quality and workmanship, and she shook her head and sighed deeply as she placed them carefully on a chair.

"It ain't on the square, Hop," protested Humpy, whose lone eye expressed the most poignant sorrow at The Hopper's derelictions. Humpy was tall and lean, with a thin, many-lined face. He was an ill-favored person at best, and his habit of turning his head constantly as though to compel his single eye to perform double service gave one an impression of restless watchfulness.

"Cute little Shaver, ain't 'e? Give Shaver somethin' to eat, Mary. I guess milk'll be the right ticket considerin' th' size of 'im. How ole you make 'im? Not more'n three, I reckon?"

"Two. He ain't more'n two, that kid."

"A nice little feller; you're a cute un, ain't ye, Shaver?"

Shaver nodded his head solemnly. Having wearied of playing with the plate he gravely inspected the trio; found something amusing in Humpy's bizarre countenance and laughed merrily. Finding no response to his friendly overtures he appealed to Mary.

"Me wants me's paw-widge," he announced.

"Porridge," interpreted Humpy with the air of one whose superior breeding makes him the proper arbiter of the speech of children of high social station. Whereupon Shaver appreciatively poked his forefinger into Humpy's surviving optic.

"I'll see what I got," muttered Mary. "What ye used t' eatin' for supper, honey?"

The "honey" was a concession, and The Hopper, who was giving Shaver his watch to play with, bent a commendatory glance upon his spouse.

"Go on an' tell us what ye done," said Mary, doggedly busying herself about the stove.

The Hopper drew a chair to the table to be within reach of Shaver and related succinctly his day's adventures.

"A dip!" moaned Mary as he described the seizure of the purse in the subway.

"You hadn't no right to do ut, Hop!" bleated Humpy, who had tipped his chair against the wall and was sucking a cold pipe. And then, professional curiosity overmastering his shocked conscience, he added: "What'd she measure, Hop?"

The Hopper grinned.

"Flubbed! Nothin' but papers," he confessed ruefully.

Mary and Humpy expressed their indignation and contempt in unequivocal terms, which they repeated after he told of the suspected "bull" whose presence on the local had so alarmed him. A frank description of his flight and of his seizure of the roadster only added to their bitterness.

Humpy rose and paced the floor with the quick, short stride of men habituated to narrow spaces. The Hopper watched the telltale step so disagreeably reminiscent of evil times and shrugged his shoulders impatiently.

"Set down, Hump; ye make me nervous. I got thinkin' to do."

"Ye'd better be quick about doin' ut!" Humpy snorted with an oath.

"Cut the cussin'!" The Hopper admonished sharply. Since his retirement to private life he had sought diligently to free his speech of profanity and thieves' slang, as not only unbecoming in a respectable chicken farmer, but likely to arouse suspicions as to his origin and previous condition of servitude. "Can't ye see Shaver ain't use to ut? Shaver's a little gent; he's a reg'ler little juke; that's wot Shaver is."

"The more 'way up he is the worse fer us," whimpered Humpy. "It's kidnappin', that's wot ut is!"

"That's wot it *ain't*," declared The Hopper, averting a calamity to his watch, which Shaver was swinging by its chain. "He was took by accident I tell ye! I'm goin' to take Shaver back to his ma—ain't I, Shaver?"

"Take 'im back!" echoed Mary.

Humpy crumpled up in his chair at this new evidence of The Hopper's insanity.

"I'm goin' to make a Chris'mas present o' Shaver to his ma," reaffirmed The Hopper, pinching the nearer ruddy cheek of the merry, contented guest.

Shaver kicked The Hopper in the stomach and emitted a chortle expressive of unshakable confidence in The Hopper's ability to restore him to his lawful owners. This confidence was not, however, manifested toward Mary, who had prepared with care the only cereal her pantry afforded, and now approached Shaver, bowl and spoon in hand. Shaver, taken by surprise, inspected his supper with disdain and spurned it with a vigor that sent the spoon rattling across the floor.

"Me wants me's paw-widge bowl! Me wants me's *own* paw-widge bowl!" he screamed.

Mary expostulated; Humpy offered advice as to the best manner of dealing with the refractory Shaver, who gave further expression to his resentment by throwing The Hopper's watch with violence against the wall. That the table-service of The Hopper's establishment was not to Shaver's liking was manifested in repeated rejections of the plain white bowl in which Mary offered the porridge. He demanded his very own porridge bowl with the increasing vehemence of one who is willing to starve rather than accept so palpable a substitute. He threw himself back on the table and lay there kicking and crying. Other needs now occurred to Shaver: he wanted his papa; he wanted his mamma; he wanted to go to his gwan'pa's. He clamored for Santa Claus and numerous Christmas trees which, it seemed, had been promised him at the houses of his kinsfolk. It was amazing and bewildering that the heart of one so young could desire so many things that were not immediately attainable. He had begun to suspect that he was among strangers who were not of his way of life, and this was fraught with the gravest danger.

"They'll hear 'im hollerin' in China," wailed the pessimistic Humpy, running about the room and examining the fastenings of doors and windows. "Folks goin' along the road'll hear 'im, an' it's terms fer the whole bunch!"

The Hopper began pacing the floor with Shaver, while Humpy and Mary denounced the child for unreasonableness and lack of discipline, not overlooking the stupidity and criminal carelessness of The Hopper in projecting so lawless a youngster into their domestic circle.

"Twenty years, that's wot ut is!" mourned Humpy.

"Ye kin get the chair fer kidnappin'," Mary added dolefully. "Ye gotta get 'im out o' here, Bill."

Pleasant predictions of a long prison term with capital punishment as the happy alternative failed to disturb The Hopper. To their surprise and somewhat to their shame he won the Shaver to a tractable humor. There was nothing in The Hopper's known past to justify any expectation that he could quiet a crying baby, and yet Shaver with a child's unerring instinct realized that The Hopper meant to be kind. He patted The Hopper's face with one fat little paw, chokingly declaring that he was hungry.

"'Course Shaver's hungry; an' Shaver's goin' to eat nice porridge Aunt Mary made fer 'im. Shaver's goin' to have 'is own porridge bowl to-morry—yes, sir-ee, oo is, little Shaver!"

Restored to the table, Shaver opened his mouth in obedience to The Hopper's patient pleading and swallowed a spoonful of the mush, Humpy holding the bowl out of sight in tactful deference to the child's delicate aesthetic sensibilities. A tumbler of milk was sipped with grateful gasps.

The Hopper grinned, proud of his success, while Mary and Humpy viewed his efforts with somewhat grudging admiration, and waited patiently until The Hopper took the wholly surfeited Shaver in his arms and began pacing the floor, humming softly. In normal circumstances The Hopper was not musical, and Humpy and Mary exchanged looks which, when interpreted, pointed to nothing less than a belief that the owner of Happy Hill Farm was bereft of his senses. There was some question as to whether Shaver should be undressed. Mary discouraged the idea and Humpy took a like view.

"Ye gotta chuck 'im quick; that's what ye gotta do," said Mary hoarsely. "We don't want 'im sleepin' here."

Whereupon The Hopper demonstrated his entire independence by carrying the Shaver to Humpy's bed and partially undressing him. While this was in progress, Shaver suddenly opened his eyes wide and raising one foot until it approximated the perpendicular, reached for it with his chubby hands.

"Sant' Claus comin'; m'y Kwismus!"

"Jes' listen to Shaver!" chuckled The Hopper. "'Course Santy is comin',' an' we're goin' to hang up Shaver's stockin', ain't we, Shaver?"

He pinned both stockings to the footboard of Humpy's bed. By the time this was accomplished under the hostile eyes of Mary and Humpy, Shaver slept the sleep of the innocent.

IV

They watched the child in silence for a few minutes and then Mary detached a gold locket from his neck and bore it to the kitchen for examination.

"Ye gotta move quick, Hop," Humpy urged. "The white card's what we wuz all goin' to play. We wuz fixed nice here, an' things goin' easy; an' the yard full o' br'ilers. I don't want to do no more time. I'm an ole man, Hop."

"Cut ut!" ordered The Hopper, taking the locket from Mary and weighing it critically in his hand. They bent over him as he scrutinized the face on which was inscribed:—

Roger Livingston Talbot
June 13, 1913

"Lemme see; he's two an' a harf. Ye purty nigh guessed 'im right, Mary."

The sight of the gold trinket, the probability that the Shaver belonged to a family of wealth, proved disturbing to Humpy's late protestations of virtue.

"They'd be a heap o' kale in ut, Hop. His folks is rich, I reckon. Ef we wuzn't playin' the white card—"

Ignoring this shocking evidence of Humpy's moral instability, The Hopper became lost in reverie, meditatively drawing at his pipe.

"We ain't never goin' to quit playin' ut square," he announced, to Mary's manifest relief. "I hadn't ought t' 'a' done th' dippin'. It were a mistake. My ole head wuzn't workin' right er I wouldn't 'a' slipped. But ye needn't jump on me no more."

"Wot ye goin' to do with that kid? Ye tell me that!" demanded Mary, unwilling too readily to accept The Hopper's repentance at face value.

"I'm goin' to take 'im to 'is folks, that's wot I'm goin' to do with 'im," announced The Hopper.

"Yer crazy—yer plum crazy!" cried Humpy, slapping his knees excitedly. "Ye kin take 'im to an orphant asylum an' tell um ye found 'im in that machine ye lifted. And mebbe ye'll git by with ut an' mebbe ye won't, but ye gotta keep me out of ut!"

"I found the machine in th' road, right here by th' house; an' th' kid was in ut all by hisself. An' bein' humin an' respectible I brought 'im in to keep 'im from freezin' t' death," said The Hopper, as though repeating lines he was committing to memory. "They ain't nobody can say as I didn't. Ef I git pinched, that's my spiel to th' cops. It ain't kidnappin'; it's life-savin', that's wot ut is! I'm a-goin' back an' have a look at that place where I got 'im. Kind o' queer they left the kid out there in the buzz-wagon; *mighty* queer, now's I think of ut. Little house back from the road; lots o' trees an' bushes in front. Didn't seem to be no lights. He keeps talkin' about Chris'mas at his grandpa's. Folks must 'a' been goin' to take th' kid somewheres fer Chris'mas. I guess it'll throw a skeer into 'em to find him up an' gone."

"They's rich, an' all the big bulls'll be lookin' fer 'im; ye'd better 'phone the New Haven cops ye've picked 'im up. Then they'll come out, an' yer spiel about findin' 'im'll sound easy an' sensible like."

The Hopper, puffing his pipe philosophically, paid no heed to Humpy's suggestion even when supported warmly by Mary.

"I gotta find some way o' puttin' th' kid back without seein' no cops. I'll jes' take a sneak back an' have a look at th' place," said The Hopper. "I ain't goin' to turn Shaver over to no cops. Ye can't take no chances with 'em. They don't know nothin' about us bein' here, but they ain't fools, an' I ain't goin' to give none o' 'em a squint at me!"

He defended his plan against a joint attack by Mary and Humpy, who saw in it only further proof of his tottering reason. He was obliged to tell them in harsh terms to be quiet, and he added to their rage by the deliberation with which he made his preparations to leave.

He opened the door of a clock and drew out a revolver, which he examined carefully and thrust into his pocket. Mary groaned; Humpy beat the air in impotent despair. The Hopper possessed himself also of a jimmy and an electric lamp. The latter he flashed upon the face of the sleeping Shaver, who turned restlessly for a moment and then lay still again. He smoothed the coverlet over the tiny form, while Mary and Humpy huddled in the doorway. Mary wept; Humpy was awed into silence by his old friend's perversity. For years he had admired The

Hopper's cleverness, his genius for extricating himself from difficulties; he was deeply shaken to think that one who had stood so high in one of the most exacting of professions should have fallen so low. As The Hopper imperturbably buttoned his coat and walked toward the door, Humpy set his back against it in a last attempt to save his friend from his own foolhardiness.

"Ef anybody turns up here an' asks for th' kid, ye kin tell 'em wot I said. We finds 'im in th' road right here by the farm when we're doin' th' night chores an' takes 'im in t' keep 'im from freezin'. Ye'll have th' machine an' kid here to show 'em. An' as fer me, I'm off lookin' fer his folks."

Mary buried her face in her apron and wept despairingly. The Hopper, noting for the first time that Humpy was guarding the door, roughly pushed him aside and stood for a moment with his hand on the knob.

"They's things wot is," he remarked with a last attempt to justify his course, "an' things wot ain't. I reckon I'll take a peek at that place an' see wot's th' best way t' shake th' kid. Ye can't jes' run up to a house in a machine with his folks all settin' round cryin' an' cops askin' questions. Ye got to do some plannin' an' thinkin'. I'm goin' t' clean ut all up before daylight, an' ye needn't worry none about ut. Hop ain't worryin'; jes' leave ut t' Hop!"

There was no alternative but to leave it to Hop, and they stood mute as he went out and softly closed the door.

V

The snow had ceased and the stars shone brightly on a white world as The Hopper made his way by various trolley lines to the house from which he had snatched Shaver. On a New Haven car he debated the prospects of more snow with a policeman who seemed oblivious to the fact that a child had been stolen—shamelessly carried off by a man with a long police record. Merry Christmas passed from lip to lip as if all creation were attuned to the note of love and peace, and crime were an undreamed of thing.

For two years The Hopper had led an exemplary life and he was keenly alive now to the joy of adventure. His lapses of the day were unfortunate; he thought of them with regret and misgivings, but he was zestful for whatever the unknown held in store for him. Abroad again with a pistol in his pocket, he was a lawless being, but with the difference that he was intent now upon making restitution, though in such manner as would give him something akin to the old thrill that he experienced when he enjoyed the reputation of being one of the most skillful yeggs in the country. The successful thief is of necessity an imaginative person; he must be able to visualize the unseen and to deal with a thousand hidden contingencies. At best the chances are against him; with all his ingenuity the broad, heavy hand of the law is likely at any moment to close upon him from some unexpected quarter. The Hopper knew this, and knew, too, that in yielding to the exhilaration of the hour he was likely to come to grief. Justice has a long memory, and if he again made himself the object of police scrutiny that little forty-thousand-dollar affair in Maine might still be fixed upon him.

When he reached the house from whose gate he had removed the roadster with Shaver attached, he studied it with the eye of an experienced strategist. No gleam anywhere published the presence of frantic parents bewailing the loss of a baby. The cottage lay snugly behind its barrier of elms and shrubbery as though its young heir had not vanished into the void. The Hopper was a deliberating being and he gave careful weight to these circumstances as he crept round the walk, in which the snow lay undisturbed, and investigated the rear of the premises. The lattice door of the summer kitchen opened readily, and, after satisfying himself that no one was stirring in the lower part of the house, he pried up the sash of a window and stepped in. The larder was well stocked, as though in preparation for a Christmas feast, and he passed on to the dining room, whose appointments spoke for good taste and a degree of prosperity in the householder.

Cautious flashes of his lamp disclosed on the table a hamper, in which were packed a silver cup, plate, and bowl which at once awoke the Hopper's interest. Here indubitably was proof that this was the home of Shaver, now sleeping sweetly in Humpy's bed, and this was the porridge bowl for which Shaver's soul had yearned. If Shaver did not belong to the house, he had at least been a visitor there, and it struck The Hopper as a reasonable assumption that Shaver had been deposited in the roadster while his lawful guardians returned to the cottage for the hamper preparatory to an excursion of some sort. But The Hopper groped in the dark for an explanation of the calmness with which the householders accepted the loss of the child. It was not in human nature for the parents of a youngster so handsome and in every way so delightful as Shaver to permit him to be stolen from under their very noses without making an outcry. The Hopper examined the silver pieces and found them engraved with the name borne by the locket. He crept through a living room and came to a Christmas tree—the smallest of Christmas trees. Beside it lay a number of packages designed clearly for none other than young Roger Livingston Talbot.

Housebreaking is a very different business from the forcible entry of country post offices, and The Hopper was nervous. This particular house seemed utterly deserted. He stole upstairs and found doors open and a disorder indicative of the occupants' hasty departure. His attention was arrested by a small room finished in white, with a white enameled bed, and other furniture to match. A generous litter of toys was the last proof needed to establish the house as Shaver's true domicile. Indeed, there was every indication that Shaver was the central figure of this home of whose charm and atmosphere The Hopper was vaguely sensible. A frieze of dancing children and watercolor sketches of Shaver's head, dabbed here and there in the most unlooked-for places, hinted at an artistic household. This impression was strengthened when The Hopper, bewildered and baffled, returned to the lower floor and found a studio opening off the living room. The Hopper had never visited a studio before, and satisfied now that he was the sole occupant of the house, he passed about shooting his light upon unfinished canvases, pausing finally before an easel supporting a portrait of Shaver—newly finished, he discovered, by poking his finger into the wet paint. Something fell to the floor and he picked up a large sheet of drawing paper on which this message was written in charcoal:—

Six-thirty.

Dear Sweetheart:—

This is a fine trick you have played on me, you dear girl! I've been expecting you back all afternoon. At six I decided that you were going to spend the night with your infuriated parent and thought I'd try my luck with mine! I put Billie into the roadster and, leaving him there, ran over to the Flemings's to say Merry Christmas and tell 'em we were off for the night. They kept me just a minute to look at those new Jap prints Jim's so crazy about, and while I was gone you came along and skipped with Billie and the car! I suppose this means that you've been making headway with your dad and want to try the effect of Billie's blandishments. Good luck! But you might have stopped long enough to tell me about it! How fine it would be if everything could be straightened out for Christmas! Do you remember the first time I kissed you—it was on Christmas Eve four years ago at the Billings's dance! I'm just trolleying out to Father's to see what an evening session will do. I'll be back early in the morning.

Love always,
ROGER.

Billie was undoubtedly Shaver's nickname. This delighted The Hopper. That they should possess the same name appeared to create a strong bond of comradeship. The writer of the note was presumably the child's father and the "Dear

Sweetheart" the youngster's mother. The Hopper was not reassured by these disclosures. The return of Shaver to his parents was far from being the pleasant little Christmas Eve adventure he had imagined. He had only the lowest opinion of a father who would, on a winter evening, carelessly leave his baby in a motor-car while he looked at pictures, and who, finding both motor and baby gone, would take it for granted that the baby's mother had run off with them. But these people were artists, and artists, The Hopper had heard, were a queer breed, sadly lacking in common sense. He tore the note into strips which he stuffed into his pocket.

Depressed by the impenetrable wall of mystery along which he was groping, he returned to the living room, raised one of the windows and unbolted the front door to make sure of an exit in case these strange, foolish Talbots should unexpectedly return. The shades were up and he shielded his light carefully with his cap as he passed rapidly about the room. It began to look very much as though Shaver would spend Christmas at Happy Hill Farm—a possibility that had not figured in The Hopper's calculations.

Flashing his lamp for a last survey a letter propped against a lamp on the table arrested his eye. He dropped to the floor and crawled into a corner where he turned his light upon the note and read, not without difficulty, the following:—

Seven o'clock.

Dear Roger:—

I've just got back from Father's where I spent the last three hours talking over our troubles. I didn't tell you I was going, knowing you would think it foolish, but it seemed best, dear, and I hope you'll forgive me. And now I find that you've gone off with Billie, and I'm guessing that you've gone to *your* father's to see what you can do. I'm taking the trolley into New Haven to ask Mamie Palmer about that cook she thought we might get, and if possible I'll bring the girl home with me. Don't trouble about me, as I'll be perfectly safe, and, as you know, I rather enjoy prowling around at night. You'll certainly get back before I do, but if I'm not here don't be alarmed.

We are so happy in each other, dear, and if only we could get our foolish fathers to stop hating each other, how beautiful everything would be! And we could all have such a merry, merry Christmas!

MURIEL.

The Hopper's acquaintance with the epistolary art was the slightest, but even to a mind unfamiliar with this branch of literature it was plain that Shaver's parents were involved in some difficulty that was attributable, not to any lessening of affection between them, but to a row of some sort between their respective fathers. Muriel, running into the house to write her note, had failed to see Roger's letter in the studio, and this was very fortunate for The Hopper; but Muriel might return at any moment, and it would add nothing to the plausibility of the story he meant to tell if he were found in the house.

VI

Anxious and dejected at the increasing difficulties that confronted him, he was moving toward the door when a light, buoyant step sounded on the veranda. In a moment the living-room lights were switched on from the entry and a woman called out sharply:—

"Stop right where you are or I'll shoot!"

The authoritative voice of the speaker, the quickness with which she had grasped the situation and leveled her revolver, brought The Hopper to an abrupt halt in the middle of the room, where he fell with a discordant crash across the keyboard of a grand piano. He turned, cowering, to confront a tall, young woman in a long ulster who advanced toward him slowly, but with every mark of determination upon her face. The Hopper stared beyond the gun, held in a very steady hand, into a pair of fearless dark eyes. In all his experiences he had never been cornered by a woman, and he stood gaping at his captor in astonishment. She was a very pretty young woman, with cheeks that still had the curve of youth, but with a chin that spoke for much firmness of character. A fur toque perched a little to one side gave her a boyish air.

This undoubtedly was Shaver's mother who had caught him prowling in her house, and all The Hopper's plans for explaining her son's disappearance and returning him in a manner to win praise and gratitude went glimmering. There was nothing in the appearance of this Muriel to encourage a hope that she was either embarrassed or alarmed by his presence. He had been captured many times, but the trick had never been turned by anyone so cool as this young woman. She seemed to be pondering with the greatest calmness what disposition she should make of him. In the intentness of her thought the revolver wavered for an instant, and The Hopper, without taking his eyes from her, made a cat-like spring that brought him to the window he had raised against just such an emergency.

"None of that!" she cried, walking slowly toward him without lowering the pistol. "If you attempt to jump from that window I'll shoot! But it's cold in here and you may lower it."

The Hopper, weighing the chances, decided that the odds were heavily against escape, and lowered the window.

"Now," said Muriel, "step into that corner and keep your hands up where I can watch them."

The Hopper obeyed her instructions strictly. There was a telephone on the table near her and he expected her to summon help; but to his surprise she calmly seated herself, resting her right elbow on the arm of the chair, her head slightly tilted to one side, as she inspected him with greater attention along the blue-black barrel of her automatic. Unless he made a dash for liberty this extraordinary woman would, at her leisure, turn him over to the police as a housebreaker and his peaceful life as a chicken farmer would be at an end. Her prolonged silence troubled The Hopper. He had not been more nervous when waiting for the report of the juries which at times had passed upon his conduct, or for judges to fix his term of imprisonment.

"Yes'm," he muttered, with a view to ending a silence that had become intolerable.

Her eyes danced to the accompaniment of her thoughts, but in no way did she betray the slightest perturbation.

"I ain't done nothin'; hones' to God, I ain't!" he protested brokenly.

"I saw you through the window when you entered this room and I was watching while you read that note," said his captor. "I thought it funny that you should do that instead of packing up the silver. Do you mind telling me just why you read that note?"

"Well, miss, I jes' thought it kind o' funny there wuzn't nobody round an' the letter was layin' there all open, an' I didn't see no harm in lookin'."

"It was awfully clever of you to crawl into the corner so nobody could see your light from the windows," she said with a tinge of admiration. "I suppose you thought you might find out how long the people of the house were likely to be gone and how much time you could spend here. Was that it?"

"I reckon ut wuz somethin' like that," he agreed.

This was received with the noncommittal "Um" of a person whose thoughts are elsewhere. Then, as though she were eliciting from an artist or man of letters a frank opinion as to his own ideas of his attainments and professional standing, she asked, with a meditative air that puzzled him as much as her question:—

"Just how good a burglar are you? Can you do a job neatly and safely?"

The Hopper, staggered by her inquiry and overcome by modesty, shrugged his shoulders and twisted about uncomfortably.

"I reckon as how you've pinched me I ain't much good," he replied, and was rewarded with a smile followed by a light little laugh. He was beginning to feel pleased that she manifested no fear of him. In fact, he had decided that Shaver's mother was the most remarkable woman he had ever encountered, and by all odds the handsomest. He began to take heart. Perhaps after all he might hit upon some way of restoring Shaver to his proper place in the house of Talbot without making himself liable to a long term for kidnapping.

"If you're really a successful burglar—one who doesn't just poke around in empty houses as you were doing here, but clever and brave enough to break into houses where people are living and steal things without making a mess of it; and if you can play fair about it—then I think—I think—maybe—we can come to terms!"

"Yes'm!" faltered The Hopper, beginning to wonder if Mary and Humpy had been right in saying that he had lost his mind. He was so astonished that his arms wavered, but she was instantly on her feet and the little automatic was again on a level with his eyes.

"Excuse me, miss, I didn't mean to drop 'em. I weren't goin' to do nothin'. Hones' I wuzn't!" he pleaded with real contrition. "It jes' seemed kind o' funny what ye said."

He grinned sheepishly. If she knew that her Billie, *alias* Shaver, was not with her husband at his father's house, she would not be dallying in this fashion. And if the young father, who painted pictures, and left notes in his studio in a blind faith that his wife would find them,—if that trusting soul knew that Billie was asleep in a house all of whose inmates had done penance behind prison bars, he would very quickly become a man of action. The Hopper had never heard of such careless parenthood! These people were children! His heart warmed to them in pity and admiration, as it had to little Billie.

"I forgot to ask you whether you are armed," she remarked, with just as much composure as though she were asking him whether he took two lumps of sugar in his tea; and then she added, "I suppose I ought to have asked you that in the first place."

"I gotta gun in my coat—right side," he confessed. "An' that's all I got," he added, batting his eyes under the spell of her bewildering smile.

With her left hand she cautiously extracted his revolver and backed away with it to the table.

"If you'd lied to me I should have killed you; do you understand?"

"Yes'm," murmured The Hopper meekly.

She had spoken as though homicide were a common incident of her life, but a gleam of humor in the eyes she was watching vigilantly abated her severity.

"You may sit down—there, please!"

She pointed to a much bepillowed davenport and The Hopper sank down on it, still with his hands up. To his deepening mystification she backed to the windows and lowered the shades, and this done she sat down with the table between them, remarking,—

"You may put your hands down now, Mr.——?"

He hesitated, decided that it was unwise to give any of his names; and respecting his scruples she said with great magnanimity:—

"Of course you wouldn't want to tell me your name, so don't trouble about that."

She sat, wholly tranquil, her arms upon the table, both hands caressing the small automatic, while his own revolver, of different pattern and larger caliber, lay close by. His status was now established as that of a gentleman making a social call upon a lady who, in the pleasantest manner imaginable and yet with undeniable resoluteness, kept a deadly weapon pointed in the general direction of his person.

A clock on the mantel struck eleven with a low, silvery note. Muriel waited for the last stroke and then spoke crisply and directly.

"We were speaking of that letter I left lying here on the table. You didn't understand it, of course; you couldn't—not really. So I will explain it to you. My husband and I married against our fathers' wishes; both of them were opposed to it."

She waited for this to sink into his perturbed consciousness. The Hopper frowned and leaned forward to express his sympathetic interest in this confidential disclosure.

"My father," she resumed, "is just as stupid as my father-in-law and they have both continued to make us just as uncomfortable as possible. The cause of the trouble is ridiculous. There's nothing against my husband or me, you understand; it's simply a bitter jealousy between the two men due to the fact that they are rival collectors."

The Hopper stared blankly. The only collectors with whom he had enjoyed any acquaintance were persons who presented bills for payment.

"They are collectors," Muriel hastened to explain, "of ceramics—precious porcelains and that sort of thing."

"Yes'm," assented The Hopper, who hadn't the faintest notion of what she meant.

"For years, whenever there have been important sales of these things, which men fight for and are willing to die for—whenever there has been something specially fine in the market, my father-in-law—he's Mr. Talbot—and Mr. Wilton—he's my father—have bid for them. There are auctions, you know, and people come from all over the world looking for a chance to buy the rarest pieces. They've explored China and Japan hunting for prizes, and they are experts—men of rare taste and judgment—what you call connoisseurs."

The Hopper nodded gravely at the unfamiliar word, convinced that not only were Muriel and her husband quite insane, but that they had inherited the infirmity.

"The trouble has been," Muriel continued, "that Mr. Talbot and my father both like the same kind of thing; and when one has got something the other wanted, of course it has added to the ill-feeling. This has been going on for years and recently they have grown more bitter. When Roger and I ran off and got married, that didn't help matters any; but just within a few days something has happened to make things much worse than ever."

The Hopper's complete absorption in this novel recital was so manifest that she put down the revolver with which she had been idling and folded her hands.

"Thank ye, miss," mumbled The Hopper.

"Only last week," Muriel continued, "my father-in-law bought one of those pottery treasures—a plum-blossom vase made in China hundreds of years ago and very, very valuable. It belonged to a Philadelphia collector who died not long ago and Mr. Talbot bought it from the executor of the estate, who happened to be an old friend of his. Father was very angry, for he had been led to believe that this vase was going to be offered at auction and he'd have a chance to bid on it. And just before that Father had got hold of a jar—a perfectly wonderful piece of red Lang-Yao—that collectors everywhere have coveted for years. This made Mr. Talbot furious at Father. My husband is at his father's now trying to make him see the folly of all this, and I visited *my* father today to try to persuade him to stop being so foolish. You see I wanted us all to be happy for Christmas! Of course, Christmas ought to be a time of gladness for everybody. Even people in your—er—profession must feel that Christmas is one day in the year when all hard feelings should be forgotten and everybody should try to make others happy."

"I guess yer right, miss. Ut sure seems foolish fer folks t' git mad about jugs like you says. Wuz they empty, miss?"

"Empty!" repeated Muriel wonderingly, not understanding at once that her visitor was unaware that the "jugs" men fought over were valued as art treasures and not for their possible contents. Then she laughed merrily, as only the mother of Shaver could laugh.

"Oh! Of course they're *empty*! That does seem to make it sillier, doesn't it? But they're like famous pictures, you know, or any beautiful work of art that only happens occasionally. Perhaps it seems odd to you that men can be so crazy about such things, but I suppose sometimes you have wanted things very, very much, and—oh!"

She paused, plainly confused by her tactlessness in suggesting to a member of his profession the extremities to which one may be led by covetousness.

"Yes, miss," he remarked hastily; and he rubbed his nose with the back of his hand, and grinned indulgently as he realized the cause of her embarrassment. It crossed his mind that she might be playing a trick of some kind; that her story, which seemed to him wholly fantastic and not at all like a chronicle of the acts of veritable human beings, was merely a device for detaining him until help arrived. But he dismissed this immediately as unworthy of one so pleasing, so beautiful, so perfectly qualified to be the mother of Shaver!

"Well, just before luncheon, without telling my husband where I was going, I ran away to Papa's, hoping to persuade him to end this silly feud. I spent the afternoon there and he was very unreasonable. He feels that Mr. Talbot wasn't fair about that Philadelphia purchase, and I gave it up and came home. I got here a little after dark and found my husband had taken Billie—that's our little boy— and gone. I knew, of course, that he had gone to *his* father's hoping to bring him round, for both our fathers are simply crazy about Billie. But you see I never go to Mr. Talbot's and my husband never goes—Dear me!" she broke off suddenly. "I suppose I ought to telephone and see if Billie is all right."

The Hopper, greatly alarmed, thrust his head forward as she pondered this. If she telephoned to her father-in-law's to ask about Billie, the jig would be up! He drew his hand across his face and fell back with relief as she went on, a little absently:—

"Mr. Talbot hates telephoning, and it might be that my husband is just getting him to the point of making concessions, and I shouldn't want to interrupt. It's so late now that of course Roger and Billie will spend the night there. And Billie and Christmas ought to be a combination that would soften the hardest heart! You ought to see—you just ought to see Billie! He's the cunningest, dearest baby in the world!"

The Hopper sat pigeon-toed, beset by countless conflicting emotions. His ingenuity was taxed to its utmost by the demands of this complex situation. But for his returning suspicion that Muriel was leading up to something; that she was detaining him for some purpose not yet apparent, he would have told her of her husband's note and confessed that the adored Billie was at that moment enjoying the reluctant hospitality of Happy Hill Farm. He resolved to continue his policy of silence as to the young heir's whereabouts until Muriel had shown her hand. She had not wholly abandoned the thought of telephoning to her father-in-law's, he found, from her next remark.

"You think it's all right, don't you? It's strange Roger didn't leave me a note of some kind. Our cook left a week ago and there was no one here when he left."

"I reckon as how yer kid's all right, miss," he answered consolingly.

Her voluble confidences had enthralled him, and her reference of this matter to his judgment was enormously flattering. On the rough edges of society where he had spent most of his life, fellow craftsmen had frequently solicited his advice, chiefly as to the disposition of their ill-gotten gains or regarding safe harbors of refuge, but to be taken into counsel by the only gentlewoman he had ever met roused his self-respect, touched a chivalry that never before had been wakened in The Hopper's soul. She was so like a child in her guilelessness, and so brave amid her perplexities!

"Oh, I know Roger will take beautiful care of Billie. And now," she smiled radiantly, "you're probably wondering what I've been driving at all this time. Maybe"—she added softly—"maybe it's providential, your turning up here in this way!"

She uttered this happily, with a little note of triumph and another of her smiles that seemed to illuminate the universe. The Hopper had been called many names in his varied career, but never before had he been invested with the attributes of an agent of Providence.

"They's things wot is an' they's things wot ain't, miss; I reckon I ain't as bad as some. I mean to be on the square, miss."

"I believe that," she said. "I've always heard there's honor among thieves, and"—she lowered her voice to a whisper—"it's possible I might become one myself!"

The Hopper's eyes opened wide and he crossed and uncrossed his legs nervously in his agitation.

"If—if"—she began slowly, bending forward with a grave, earnest look in her eyes and clasping her fingers tightly—"if we could only get hold of Father's Lang-Yao jar and that plum-blossom vase Mr. Talbot has—if we could only do that!"

The Hopper swallowed hard. This fearless, pretty young woman was calmly suggesting that he commit two felonies, little knowing that his score for the day already aggregated three—purse snatching, the theft of an automobile from her own door, and what might very readily be construed as the kidnapping of her own child!

"I don't know, miss," he said feebly, calculating that the sum total of even minimum penalties for the five crimes would outrun his natural life and consume an eternity of reincarnations.

"Of course it wouldn't be stealing in the ordinary sense," she explained. "What I want you to do is to play the part of what we will call a reversible Santa Claus, who takes things away from stupid people who don't enjoy them anyhow. And maybe if they lost these things they'd behave themselves. I could explain afterward that it was all my fault, and of course I wouldn't let any harm come to *you*. I'd be responsible, and of course I'd see you safely out of it; you would have to rely on me for that. I'm trusting *you* and you'd have to trust *me*!"

"Oh, I'd trust ye, miss! An' ef I was to get pinched I wouldn't never squeal on ye. We don't never blab on a pal, miss!"

He was afraid she might resent being called a "pal," but his use of the term apparently pleased her.

"We understand each other, then. It really won't be very difficult, for Papa's place is over on the Sound and Mr. Talbot's is right next to it, so you wouldn't have far to go."

Her utter failure to comprehend the enormity of the thing she was proposing affected him queerly. Even among hardened criminals in the underworld such undertakings are suggested cautiously; but Muriel was ordering a burglary as though it were a pound of butter or a dozen eggs!

"Father keeps his most valuable glazes in a safe in the pantry," she resumed after a moment's reflection, "but I can give you the combination. That will make it a lot easier."

The Hopper assented, with a pontifical nod, to this sanguine view of the matter.

"Mr. Talbot keeps his finest pieces in a cabinet built into the bookshelves in his library. It's on the left side as you stand in the drawing-room door, and you look for the works of Thomas Carlyle. There's a dozen or so volumes of Carlyle, only they're not books,—not really,—but just the backs of books painted on the steel of a safe. And if you press a spring in the upper right-hand corner of the shelf just over these books the whole section swings out. I suppose you've seen that sort of hiding place for valuables?"

"Well, not exactly, miss. But havin' a tip helps, an' ef there ain't no soup to pour—"

"Soup?" inquired Muriel, wrinkling her pretty brows.

"That's the juice we pour into the cracks of a safe to blow out the lid with," The Hopper elucidated. "Ut's a lot handier ef you've got the combination. Ut usually ain't jes' layin' around."

"I should hope not!" exclaimed Muriel.

She took a sheet of paper from the leathern stationery rack and fell to scribbling, while he furtively eyed the window and again put from him the thought of flight.

"There! That's the combination of Papa's safe." She turned her wrist and glanced at her watch. "It's half-past eleven and you can catch a trolley in ten minutes that will take you right past Papa's house. The butler's an old man who forgets to lock the windows half the time, and there's one in the conservatory with a broken catch. I noticed it today when I was thinking about stealing the jar myself!"

They were established on so firm a basis of mutual confidence that when he rose and walked to the table she didn't lift her eyes from the paper on which she was drawing a diagram of her father's house. He stood watching her nimble fingers, fascinated by the boldness of her plan for restoring amity between Shaver's grandfathers, and filled with admiration for her resourcefulness.

He asked a few questions as to exits and entrances and fixed in his mind a very accurate picture of the home of her father. She then proceeded to enlighten him as to the ways and means of entering the home of her father-in-law, which she sketched with equal facility.

"There's a French window—a narrow glass door—on the veranda. I think you might get in *there!*" She made a jab with the pencil. "Of course I should hate awfully to have you get caught! But you must have had a lot of experience, and with all the help I'm giving you—!"

A sudden lifting of her head gave him the full benefit of her eyes and he averted his gaze reverently.

"There's always a chance o' bein' nabbed, miss," he suggested with feeling.

Shaver's mother wielded the same hypnotic power, highly intensified, that he had felt in Shaver. He knew that he was going to attempt what she asked; that he was committed to the project of robbing two houses merely to please a pretty young woman who invited his cooperation at the point of a revolver!

"Papa's always a sound sleeper," she was saying. "When I was a little girl a burglar went all through our house and carried off his clothes and he never knew it until the next morning. But you'll have to be careful at Mr. Talbot's, for he suffers horribly from insomnia."

"They got any o' them fancy burglar alarms?" asked The Hopper as he concluded his examination of her sketches.

"Oh, I forgot to tell you about that!" she cried contritely. "There's nothing of the kind at Mr. Talbot's, but at Papa's there's a switch in the living room, right back of a bust—a white marble thing on a pedestal. You turn it off *there*. Half the time Papa forgets to switch it on before he goes to bed. And another thing—be careful about stumbling over that bearskin rug in the hall. People are always sticking their feet into its jaws."

"I'll look out for ut, miss."

Burglar alarms and the jaws of wild beasts were not inviting hazards. The program she outlined so light-heartedly was full of complexities. It was almost pathetic that anyone could so cheerfully and irresponsibly suggest the perpetration of a crime. The terms she used in describing the loot he was to filch were much stranger to him than Chinese, but it was fairly clear that at the Talbot house he was to steal a blue-and-white thing and at the Wilton's a red one. The form and size of these articles she illustrated with graceful gestures.

"If I thought you were likely to make a mistake I'd—I'd go with you!" she declared.

"Oh, no, miss; ye couldn't do that! I guess I can do ut fer ye. Ut's jes' a *leetle* ticklish. I reckon ef yer pa wuz to nab me ut'd go hard with me."

"I wouldn't let him be hard on you," she replied earnestly. "And now I haven't said anything about a—a—about what we will call a *reward* for bringing me these porcelains. I shall expect to pay you; I couldn't think of taking up your time, you know, for nothing!"

"Lor', miss, I couldn't take nothin' at all fer doin' ut! Ye see ut wuz sort of accidental our meetin', and besides, I ain't no housebreaker—not, as ye may say, reg'ler. I'll be glad to do ut fer ye, miss, an' ye can rely on me doin' my best fer ye. Ye've treated me right, miss, an' I ain't a-goin' t' fergit ut!"

The Hopper spoke with feeling. Shaver's mother had, albeit at the pistol point, confided her most intimate domestic affairs to him. He realized, without finding just these words for it, that she had in effect decorated him with the symbol of her order of knighthood and he had every honorable—or dishonorable!—intention of proving himself worthy of her confidence.

"If ye please, miss," he said, pointing toward his confiscated revolver.

"Certainly; you may take it. But of course you won't kill anybody?"

"No, miss; only I'm sort o' lonesome without ut when I'm on a job."

"And you do understand," she said, following him to the door and noting in the distance the headlight of an approaching trolley, "that I'm only doing this in the hope that good may come of it. It isn't really criminal, you know; if you succeed, it may mean the happiest Christmas of my life!"

"Yes, miss. I won't come back till mornin', but don't you worry none. We gotta play safe, miss, an' ef I land th' jugs I'll find cover till I kin deliver 'em safe."

"Thank you; oh, thank you ever so much! And good luck!"

She put out her hand; he held it gingerly for a moment in his rough fingers and ran for the car.

VII

The Hopper, in his role of the Reversible Santa Claus, dropped off the car at the crossing Muriel had carefully described, waited for the car to vanish, and warily entered the Wilton estate through a gate set in the stone wall. The clouds of the early evening had passed and the stars marched through the heavens resplendently, proclaiming peace on earth and goodwill toward men. They were almost oppressively brilliant, seen through the clear, cold atmosphere, and as The Hopper slipped from one big tree to another on his tangential course to the house, he fortified his courage by muttering, "They's things wot is an' things wot ain't!"—finding much comfort and stimulus in the phrase.

Arriving at the conservatory in due course, he found that Muriel's averments as to the vulnerability of that corner of her father's house were correct in every particular. He entered with ease, sniffed the warm, moist air, and, leaving the door slightly ajar, sought the pantry, lowered the shades, and, helping himself to a candle from a silver candelabrum, readily found the safe hidden away in one of the cupboards. He was surprised to find himself more nervous with the combination in his hand than on memorable occasions in the old days when he had broken into country post offices and assaulted safes by force. In his haste he twice failed to give the proper turns, but the third time the knob caught, and in a moment the door swung open disclosing shelves filled with vases, bottles, bowls, and plates in bewildering variety. A chest of silver appealed to him distractingly as a much more tangible asset than the pottery, and he dizzily contemplated a jewel case containing a diamond necklace with a pearl pendant. The moment was a critical one in The Hopper's eventful career. This dazzling prize was his for the taking, and he knew the operator of a fence in Chicago who would dispose of the necklace and make him a fair return. But visions of Muriel, the beautiful, the confiding, and of her little Shaver asleep on Humpy's bed, rose before him. He steeled his heart against temptation, drew his candle along the shelf, and scrutinized the glazes. There could be no mistaking the red Lang-Yao whose brilliant tints kindled in the candle-glow. He lifted it tenderly, verifying the various points of Muriel's description, set it down on the floor, and locked the safe.

He was retracing his steps toward the conservatory and had reached the main hall when the creaking of the stairsteps brought him up with a start. Someone was descending, slowly and cautiously. For a second time and with grateful appreciation of Muriel's forethought, he carefully avoided the ferocious jaws of the bear, noiselessly continued on to the conservatory, crept through the door, closed it, and then, crouching on the steps, awaited developments. The caution exercised by the person descending the stairway was not that of a householder who has been roused from slumber by a disquieting noise. The Hopper was keenly interested in this fact.

With his face against the glass he watched the actions of a tall, elderly man with a short, grayish beard, who wore a golf cap pulled low on his head—points noted by The Hopper in the flashes of an electric lamp with which the gentleman was guiding himself. His face was clearly the original of a photograph The Hopper had seen on the table at Muriel's cottage—Mr. Wilton, Muriel's father, The Hopper surmised; but just why the owner of the establishment should be prowling about in this fashion taxed his speculative powers to the utmost. Warned by steps on the cement floor of the conservatory, he left the door in haste and flattened himself against the wall of the house some distance away and again awaited developments.

Wilton's figure was a blur in the starlight as he stepped out into the walk and started furtively across the grounds. His conduct greatly displeased The Hopper, as likely to interfere with the further carrying out of Muriel's instructions. The Lang-Yao jar was much too large to go into his pocket and not big enough to fit snugly under his arm, and as the walk was slippery he was beset by the fear that he might fall and smash this absurd thing that had caused so bitter an enmity between Shaver's grandfathers. The soft snow on the lawn gave him a surer footing and he crept after Wilton, who was carefully pursuing his way toward a house whose gables were faintly limned against the sky. This, according to Muriel's diagram, was the Talbot place. The Hopper greatly mistrusted conditions he didn't understand, and he was at a loss to account for Wilton's strange actions.

He lost sight of him for several minutes, then the faint click of a latch marked the prowler's proximity to a hedge that separated the two estates. The Hopper crept forward, found a gate through which Wilton had entered his neighbor's property, and stole after him. Wilton had been swallowed up by the deep shadow of the house, but The Hopper was aware, from an occasional scraping of feet, that he was still moving forward. He crawled over the snow until he reached a large tree whose boughs, sharply limned against the stars, brushed the eaves of the house.

The Hopper was aroused, tremendously aroused, by the unaccountable actions of Muriel's father. It flashed upon him that Wilton, in his deep hatred of his rival collector, was about to set fire to Talbot's house, and incendiarism was a crime which The Hopper, with all his moral obliquity, greatly abhorred.

Several minutes passed, a period of anxious waiting, and then a sound reached him which, to his keen professional sense, seemed singularly like the forcing of a window. The Hopper knew just how much pressure is necessary to the successful snapping back of a window catch, and Wilton had done the trick neatly and with a minimum amount of noise. The window thus assaulted was not, he now determined, the French window suggested by Muriel, but one opening on a terrace which ran along the front of the house. The Hopper heard the sash moving slowly in the frame. He reached the steps, deposited the jar in a pile of snow, and was soon peering into a room where Wilton's presence was advertised by the fitful flashing of his lamp in a far corner.

"He's beat me to ut!" muttered The Hopper, realizing that Muriel's father was indeed on burglary bent, his obvious purpose being to purloin, extract, and remove from its secret hiding place the coveted plum-blossom vase. Muriel, in her longing for a Christmas of peace and happiness, had not reckoned with her father's passionate desire to possess the porcelain treasure—a desire which could hardly fail to cause scandal, if it did not land him behind prison bars.

This had not been in the program, and The Hopper weighed judicially his further duty in the matter. Often as he had been the chief actor in daring robberies, he had never before enjoyed the high privilege of watching a rival's labors with complete detachment. Wilton must have known of the concealed cupboard whose panel fraudulently represented the works of Thomas Carlyle, the intent spectator reflected, just as Muriel had known, for though he used his lamp sparingly Wilton had found his way to it without difficulty.

The Hopper had no intention of permitting this monstrous larceny to be committed in contravention of his own rights in the premises, and he was considering the best method of wresting the vase from the hands of the insolent Wilton when events began to multiply with startling rapidity. The panel swung open and the thief's lamp flashed upon shelves of pottery.

At that moment a shout rose from somewhere in the house, and the library lights were thrown on, revealing Wilton before the shelves and their precious contents. A short, stout gentleman with a gleaming bald pate, clad in pajamas, dashed across the room, and with a yell of rage flung himself upon the intruder with a violence that bore them both to the floor.

"Roger! Roger!" bawled the smaller man, as he struggled with his adversary, who wriggled from under and rolled over upon Talbot, whose arms were clasped tightly about his neck. This embrace seemed likely to continue for some time, so tenaciously had the little man gripped his neighbor. The fat legs of the infuriated householder pawed the air as he hugged Wilton, who was now trying to free his head and gain a position of greater dignity. Occasionally, as opportunity offered, the little man yelled vociferously, and from remote recesses of the house came answering cries demanding information as to the nature and whereabouts of the disturbance.

The contestants addressed themselves vigorously to a spirited rough-and-tumble fight. Talbot, who was the more easily observed by reason of his shining pate and the pink stripes of his pajamas, appeared to be revolving about the person of his neighbor. Wilton, though taller, lacked the rotund Talbot's liveliness of attack.

An authoritative voice, which The Hopper attributed to Shaver's father, anxiously demanding what was the matter, terminated The Hopper's enjoyment of the struggle. Enough was the matter to satisfy The Hopper that a prolonged stay in the neighborhood might be highly detrimental to his future liberty. The combatants had rolled a considerable distance away from the shelves and were near a door leading into a room beyond. A young man in a bath wrapper dashed upon the scene, and in his precipitate arrival upon the battlefield fell sprawling across the prone figures. The Hopper, suddenly inspired to deeds of prowess, crawled through the window, sprang past the three men, seized the blue-and-white vase which Wilton had separated from the rest of Talbot's treasures, and then with one hop gained the window. As he turned for a last look, a pistol cracked and he landed upon the terrace amid a shower of glass from a shattered pane.

A woman of unmistakable Celtic origin screamed murder from a third-story window. The thought of murder was disagreeable to The Hopper. Shaver's father had missed him by only the matter of a foot or two, and as he had no intention of offering himself again as a target he stood not upon the order of his going.

He effected a running pick-up of the Lang-Yao, and with this art treasure under one arm and the plum-blossom vase under the other, he sprinted for the highway, stumbling over shrubbery, bumping into a stone bench that all but caused disaster, and finally reached the road on which he continued his flight toward New Haven, followed by cries in many keys and a fusillade of pistol shots.

Arriving presently at a hamlet, where he paused for breath in the rear of a country store, he found a basket and a quantity of paper in which he carefully packed his loot. Over the top he spread some faded lettuce leaves and discarded carnations which communicated something of a blithe holiday air to his encumbrance. Elsewhere he found a bicycle under a shed, and while cycling over a snowy road in the dark, hampered by a basket containing pottery representative of the highest genius of the Orient, was not without its difficulties and dangers, The Hopper made rapid progress.

Halfway through New Haven he approached two policemen and slowed down to allay suspicion.

"Merry Chris'mas!" he called as he passed them and increased his weight upon the pedals.

The officers of the law, cheered as by a greeting from Santa Claus himself, responded with an equally hearty Merry Christmas.

VIII

At three o'clock The Hopper reached Happy Hill Farm, knocked as before at the kitchen door, and was admitted by Humpy.

"Wot ye got now?" snarled the reformed yeggman.

"He's gone and done ut ag'in!" wailed Mary, as she spied the basket.

"I sure done ut, all right," admitted The Hopper good-naturedly, as he set the basket on the table where a few hours earlier he had deposited Shaver. "How's the kid?"

Grudging assurances that Shaver was asleep and hostile glances directed at the mysterious basket did not disturb his equanimity.

Humpy was thwarted in an attempt to pry into the contents of the basket by a tart reprimand from The Hopper, who with maddening deliberation drew forth the two glazes, found that they had come through the night's vicissitudes unscathed, and held them at arm's length, turning them about in leisurely fashion as though lost in admiration of their loveliness. Then he lighted his pipe, seated himself in Mary's rocker, and told his story.

It was no easy matter to communicate to his irritable and contumelious auditors the sense of Muriel's charm, or the reasonableness of her request that he commit burglary merely to assist her in settling a family row. Mary could not understand it; Humpy paced the room nervously, shaking his head and muttering. It was their judgment, stated with much frankness, that if he had been a fool in the first place to steal the child, his character was now blackened beyond any hope by his later crimes. Mary wept copiously; Humpy most annoyingly kept counting upon his fingers as he reckoned the "time" that was in store for all of them.

"I guess I got into ut an' I guess I'll git out," remarked The Hopper serenely. He was disposed to treat them with high condescension, as incapable of appreciating the lofty philosophy of life by which he was sustained. Meanwhile, he gloated over the loot of the night.

"Them things is wurt' mints; they's more valible than di'mon's, them things is! Only eddicated folks knows about 'em. They's fer emp'rors and kings t' set up in their palaces, an' men goes nutty jes' hankerin' fer 'em. The Chinese made 'em thousand o' years back, an' th' secret died with 'em. They ain't never goin' to be no more jugs like them settin' right there. An' them two ole sports give up their business jes' t' chase things like them. They's some folks goes loony about chickens, an' hosses, an' fancy dogs, but this here kind o' collectin' 's only fer millionaires. They's more difficult t' pick than a lucky race-hoss. They's barrels o' that stuff in them houses, that looked jes' as good as them there, but nowheres as valible."

An informal lecture on Chinese ceramics before daylight on Christmas morning was not to the liking of the anxious and nerve-torn Mary and Humpy. They brought The Hopper down from his lofty heights to practical questions touching his plans, for the disposal of Shaver in the first instance, and the ceramics in the second. The Hopper was singularly unmoved by their forebodings.

"I guess th' lady got me to do ut!" he retorted finally. "Ef I do time fer ut I reckon's how she's in fer ut, too! An' I seen her pap breakin' into a house an' I guess I'd be a state's witness fer that! I reckon they ain't goin' t' put nothin' over on Hop! I guess they won't peep much about kidnappin' with th' kid safe an' us pickin' 'im up out o' th' road an' shelterin' 'im. Them folks is goin' to be awful nice to Hop fer all he done fer 'em." And then, finding that they were impressed by his defense, thus elaborated, he magnanimously referred to the bill-book which had started him on his downward course.

"That were a mistake; I grant ye ut were a mistake o' jedgment. I'm goin' to keep to th' white card. But ut's kind o' funny about that poke—queerest thing that ever happened."

He drew out the book and eyed the name on the flap. Humpy tried to grab it, but The Hopper, frustrating the attempt, read his colleague a sharp lesson in good manners. He restored it to his pocket and glanced at the clock.

"We gotta do somethin' about Shaver's stockin's. Ut ain't fair fer a kid to wake up an' think Santy missed 'im. Ye got some candy, Mary; we kin put candy into 'em; that's reg'ler."

Humpy brought in Shaver's stockings and they were stuffed with the candy and popcorn Mary had provided to adorn their Christmas feast. Humpy inventoried his belongings, but could think of nothing but a revolver that seemed a suitable gift for Shaver. This Mary scornfully rejected as improper for one so young. Whereupon Humpy produced a Mexican silver dollar, a treasured pocket-piece preserved through many tribulations, and dropped it reverently into one of the stockings. Two brass buttons of unknown history, a mouth-organ Mary had bought for a neighbor boy who assisted at times in the poultry yard, and a silver spectacle case of uncertain antecedents were added.

"We ought t' 'a' colored eggs fer 'im!" said The Hopper with sudden inspiration, after the stockings had been restored to Shaver's bed. "Some yaller an' pink eggs would 'a' been the right ticket."

Mary scoffed at the idea. Eggs wasn't proper fer Christmas; eggs was fer Easter. Humpy added the weight of his personal experience of Christian holidays to this statement. While a trusty in the Missouri penitentiary with the chicken yard in his keeping, he remembered distinctly that eggs were in demand for purposes of decoration by the warden's children sometime in the spring; mebbe it was Easter, mebbe it was Decoration Day; Humpy was not sure of anything except that it wasn't Christmas.

The Hopper was meek under correction. It having been settled that colored eggs would not be appropriate for Christmas he yielded to their demand that he show some enthusiasm for disposing of his ill-gotten treasures before the police arrived to take the matter out of his hands.

"I guess that Muriel'll be glad to see me," he remarked. "I guess me and her understands each other. They's things wot is an' things wot ain't; an' I guess Hop ain't goin' to spend no Chris'mas in jail. It's the white card an' poultry an' eggs fer us; an' we're goin' t' put in a couple more incubators right away. I'm thinkin' some o' rentin' that acre across th' brook back yonder an' raisin' turkeys. They's mints in turks, ef ye kin keep 'em from gettin' their feet wet an' dyin' o' pneumonia, which wipes out thousands o' them birds. I reckon ye might make some coffee, Mary."

The Christmas dawn found them at the table, where they were renewing a pledge to play "the white card" when a cry from Shaver brought them to their feet.

Shaver was highly pleased with his Christmas stockings, but his pleasure was nothing to that of The Hopper, Mary, and Humpy, as they stood about the bed and watched him. Mary and Humpy were so relieved by The Hopper's promises to lead a better life that they were now disposed to treat their guest with the most distinguished consideration. Humpy, absenting himself to perform his morning tasks in the poultry-houses, returned bringing a basket containing six newly hatched chicks. These cheeped and ran over Shaver's fat legs and performed exactly as though they knew they were a part of his Christmas entertainment. Humpy, proud of having thought of the chicks, demanded the privilege of serving Shaver's breakfast. Shaver ate his porridge without a murmur, so happy was he over his new playthings.

Mary bathed and dressed him with care. As the candy had stuck to the stockings in spots, it was decided after a family conference that Shaver would have to wear them wrong side out as there was no time to be wasted in washing them. By eight o'clock The Hopper announced that it was time for Shaver to go home. Shaver expressed alarm at the thought of leaving his chicks; whereupon Humpy conferred two of them upon him in the best imitation of baby talk that he could muster.

"Me's tate um to me's gwanpas," said Shaver; "chickee for me's two gwanpas,"—a remark which caused The Hopper to shake for a moment with mirth as he recalled his last view of Shaver's "gwanpas" in a death grip upon the floor of "Gwanpa" Talbot's house.

IX

When The Hopper rolled away from Happy Hill Farm in the stolen machine, accompanied by one stolen child and forty thousand dollars' worth of stolen pottery, Mary wept, whether because of the parting with Shaver, or because she feared that The Hopper would never return, was not clear.

Humpy, too, showed signs of tears, but concealed his weakness by performing a grotesque dance, dancing grotesquely by the side of the car, much to Shaver's joy—a joy enhanced just as the car reached the gate, where, as a farewell attention, Humpy fell down and rolled over and over in the snow.

The Hopper's wits were alert as he bore Shaver homeward. By this time it was likely that the confiding young Talbots had conferred over the telephone and knew that their offspring had disappeared. Doubtless the New Haven police had been notified, and he chose his route with discretion to avoid unpleasant encounters. Shaver, his spirits keyed to holiday pitch, babbled ceaselessly, and The Hopper, highly elated, babbled back at him.

They arrived presently at the rear of the young Talbots' premises, and The Hopper, with Shaver trotting at his side, advanced cautiously upon the house bearing the two baskets, one containing Shaver's chicks, the other the precious porcelains. In his survey of the landscape he noted with trepidation the presence of two big limousines in the highway in front of the cottage and decided that if possible he must see Muriel alone and make his report to her.

The moment he entered the kitchen he heard the clash of voices in angry dispute in the living room. Even Shaver was startled by the violence of the conversation in progress within, and clutched tightly a fold of The Hopper's trousers.

"I tell you it's John Wilton who has stolen Billie!" a man cried tempestuously. "Anybody who would enter a neighbor's house in the dead of night and try to rob him—rob him, yes, and *murder* him in the most brutal fashion—would not scruple to steal his own grandchild!"

"Me's gwanpa," whispered Shaver, gripping The Hopper's hand, "an' 'im's mad."

That Mr. Talbot was very angry indeed was established beyond cavil. However, Mr. Wilton was apparently quite capable of taking care of himself in the dispute.

"You talk about my stealing when you robbed me of my Lang-Yao—bribed my servants to plunder my safe! I want you to understand once for all, Roger Talbot, that if that jar isn't returned within one hour,—within one hour, sir,—I shall turn you over to the police!"

"Liar!" bellowed Talbot, who possessed a voice of great resonance. "You can't mitigate your foul crime by charging me with another! I never saw your jar; I never wanted it! I wouldn't have the thing on my place!"

Muriel's voice, full of tears, was lifted in expostulation.

"How can you talk of your silly vases when Billie's lost! Billie's been stolen—and you two men can think of nothing but pot-ter-ree!"

Shaver lifted a startled face to The Hopper.

"Mamma's cwyin'; gwanpa's hurted mamma!"

The strategic moment had arrived when Shaver must be thrust forward as an interruption to the exchange of disagreeable epithets by his grandfathers.

"You trot right in there t' yer ma, Shaver. Ole Hop ain't goin' t' let 'em hurt ye!"

He led the child through the dining room to the living-room door and pushed him gently on the scene of strife. Talbot, senior, was pacing the floor with angry strides, declaiming upon his wrongs—indeed, his theme might have been the misery of the whole human race from the vigor of his lamentations. His son was keeping step with him, vainly attempting to persuade him to sit down. Wilton, with a patch over his right eye, was trying to disengage himself from his daughter's arms with the obvious intention of doing violence to his neighbor.

"I'm sure Papa never meant to hurt you; it was all a dreadful mistake," she moaned.

"He had an accomplice," Talbot thundered, "and while he was trying to kill me there in my own house the plum-blossom vase was carried off; and if Roger hadn't pushed him out of the window after his hireling—I'd—I'd—"

A shriek from Muriel happily prevented the completion of a sentence that gave every promise of intensifying the prevailing hard feeling.

"Look!" Muriel cried. "It's Billie come back! Oh, Billie!"

She sprang toward the door and clasped the frightened child to her heart. The three men gathered round them, staring dully. The Hopper from behind the door waited for Muriel's joy over Billie's return to communicate itself to his father and the two grandfathers.

"Me's dot two chick-ees for Kwismus," announced Billie, wriggling in his mother's arms.

Muriel, having satisfied herself that Billie was intact—that he even bore the marks of maternal care—was in the act of transferring him to his bewildered father, when, turning a tear-stained face toward the door, she saw The Hopper awkwardly twisting the derby which he had donned as proper for a morning call of ceremony. She walked toward him with quick, eager step.

"You—you came back!" she faltered, stifling a sob.

"Yes'm," responded The Hopper, rubbing his hand across his nose. His appearance roused Billie's father to a sense of his parental responsibility.

"You brought the boy back! You are the kidnapper!"

"Roger," cried Muriel protestingly, "don't speak like that! I'm sure this gentleman can explain how he came to bring Billie."

The quickness with which she regained her composure, the ease with which she adjusted herself to the unforeseen situation, pleased The Hopper greatly. He had not misjudged Muriel; she was an admirable ally, an ideal confederate. She gave him a quick little nod, as much as to say, "Go on, sir; we understand each other perfectly"—though, of course, she did not understand, nor was she enlightened until sometime later, as to just how The Hopper became possessed of Billie.

Billie's father declared his purpose to invoke the law upon his son's kidnappers no matter where they might be found.

"I reckon as mebbe ut wuz a kidnappin' an' I reckon as mebbe ut wuzn't," The Hopper began unhurriedly. "I live over Shell Road way; poultry and eggs is my line; Happy Hill Farm. Stevens's the name—Charles S. Stevens. An' I found Shaver—'scuse me, but ut seemed sort o' nat'ral name fer 'im?—I found 'im a settin' up in th' machine over there by my place, chipper's ye please. I takes Vim into my house an' Mary'—that's th' missus—she gives 'im supper and puts 'im t' sleep. An' we thinks mebbe somebody'd come along askin' fer 'im. An' then this mornin' I calls th' New Haven police, an' they tole me about you folks, an' me and Shaver comes right over."

This was entirely plausible and his hearers, The Hopper noted with relief, accepted it at face value.

"How dear of you!" cried Muriel. "Won't you have this chair, Mr. Stevens!"

"Most remarkable!" exclaimed Wilton. "Some scoundrelly tramp picked up the car and finding there was a baby inside left it at the roadside like the brute he was!"

Billie had addressed himself promptly to the Christmas tree, to his very own Christmas tree that was laden with gifts that had been assembled by the family for his delectation. Efforts of Grandfather Wilton to extract from the child some account of the man who had run away with him were unavailing. Billie was busy, very busy, indeed. After much patient effort he stopped sorting the animals in a bright new Noah's Ark to point his finger at The Hopper and remark:—

"'Ims nice mans; 'ims let Bil-lee play wif 'ims watch!"

As Billie had broken the watch his acknowledgment of The Hopper's courtesy in letting him play with it brought a grin to The Hopper's face.

Now that Billie had been returned and his absence satisfactorily accounted for, the two connoisseurs showed signs of renewing their quarrel. Responsive to a demand from Billie, The Hopper got down on the floor to assist in the proper mating of Noah's animals. Billie's father was scrutinizing him fixedly and The Hopper wondered whether Muriel's handsome young husband had recognized him as the person who had vanished through the window of the Talbot home bearing the plum-blossom vase. The thought was disquieting; but feigning deep interest in the Ark he listened attentively to a violent tirade upon which the senior Talbot was launched.

"My God!" he cried bitterly, planting himself before Wilton in a belligerent attitude, "every infernal thing that can happen to a man happened to me yesterday. It wasn't enough that you robbed me and tried to murder me—yes, you did, sir!—but when I was in the city I was robbed in the subway by a pickpocket. A thief took my bill-book containing invaluable data I had just received from my agent in China giving me a clue to porcelains, sir, such as you never dreamed of! Some more of your work—Don't you contradict me! You don't contradict me! Roger, he doesn't contradict me!"

Wilton, choking with indignation at this new onslaught, was unable to contradict him.

Pained by the situation, The Hopper rose from the floor and coughed timidly.

"Shaver, go fetch yer chickies. Bring yer chickies in an' put 'em on th' boat."

Billie obediently trotted off toward the kitchen and The Hopper turned his back upon the Christmas tree, drew out the pocket-book and faced the company.

"I beg yer pardon, gents, but mebbe this is th' book yer fightin' about. Kind o' funny like! I picked ut up on th' local yistiddy afternoon. I wuz goin' t' turn ut int' th' agint, but I clean fergot ut. I guess them papers may be valible. I never touched none of 'em."

Talbot snatched the bill-book and hastily examined the contents. His brow relaxed and he was grumbling something about a reward when Billie reappeared, laboriously dragging two baskets.

"Bil-lee's dot chick-*ees*! Bil-lee's dot pitty dishes. Bil-lee make dishes go 'ippity!"

Before he could make the two jars go 'ippity, The Hopper leaped across the room and seized the basket. He tore off the towel with which he had carefully covered the stolen pottery and disclosed the contents for inspection.

"'Scuse me, gents; no crowdin'," he warned as the connoisseurs sprang toward him. He placed the porcelains carefully on the floor under the Christmas tree. "Now ye kin listen t' me, gents. I reckon I'm goin' t' have somethin' t' say about this here crockery. I stole 'em—I stole 'em fer th' lady there, she thinkin' ef ye didn't have 'em no more ye'd stop rowin' about 'em. Ye kin call th' bulls an' turn me over ef ye likes; but I ain't goin' t' have ye fussin' an' causin' th' lady trouble no more. I ain't goin' to stand fer ut!"

"Robber!" shouted Talbot. "You entered my house at the instance of this man; it was you—"

"I never saw the gent before," declared The Hopper hotly. "I ain't never had nothin' to do with neither o' ye."

"He's telling the truth!" protested Muriel, laughing hysterically. "I did it—I got him to take them!"

The two collectors were not interested in explanations; they were hungrily eyeing their property. Wilton attempted to pass The Hopper and reach the Christmas tree under whose protecting boughs the two vases were looking their loveliest.

"Stand back," commanded The Hopper, "an' stop callin' names! I guess ef I'm yanked fer this I ain't th' only one that's goin' t' do time fer housebreakin'."

This statement, made with considerable vigor, had a sobering effect upon Wilton, but Talbot began dancing round the tree looking for a chance to pounce upon the porcelains.

"Ef ye don't set down—the whole caboodle o' ye—I'll smash 'em—I'll smash 'em both! I'll bust 'em—sure as shootin'!" shouted The Hopper.

They cowered before him; Muriel wept softly; Billie played with his chickies, disdainful of the world's woe. The Hopper, holding the two angry men at bay, was enjoying his command of the situation.

"You gents ain't got no business to be fussin' an' causin' yer childern trouble. An' ye ain't goin' to have these pretty jugs to fuss about no more. I'm goin' t' give 'em away; I'm goin' to make a Chris'mas present of 'em to Shaver. They're goin' to be little Shaver's right here, all orderly an' peace'ble, or I'll tromp on 'em! Looky here, Shaver, wot Santy Claus brought ye!"

"Nice dood Sant' Claus!" cried Billie, diving under the davenport in quest of the wandering chicks.

Silence held the grown-ups. The Hopper stood patiently by the Christmas tree, awaiting the result of his diplomacy.

Then suddenly Wilton laughed—a loud laugh expressive of relief. He turned to Talbot and put out his hand.

"It looks as though Muriel and her friend here had cornered us! The idea of pooling our trophies and giving them as a Christmas present to Billie appeals to me strongly. And, besides we've got to prepare somebody to love these things after we're gone. We can work together and train Billie to be the greatest collector in America!"

"Please, Father," urged Roger as Talbot frowned and shook his head impatiently.

Billie, struck with the happy thought of hanging one of his chickies on the Christmas tree, caused them all to laugh at this moment. It was difficult to refuse to be generous on Christmas morning in the presence of the happy child!

"Well," said Talbot, a reluctant smile crossing his face, "I guess it's all in the family anyway."

The Hopper, feeling that his work as the Reversible Santa Claus was finished, was rapidly retreating through the dining room when Muriel and Roger ran after him.

"We're going to take you home," cried Muriel, beaming.

"Yer car's at the back gate, all right-side-up," said The Hopper, "but I kin go on the trolley."

"Indeed you won't! Roger will take you home. Oh, don't be alarmed! My husband knows everything about our conspiracy. And we want you to come back this afternoon. You know I owe you an apology for thinking—for thinking you were—you were—a—"

"They's things wot is an' things wot ain't, miss. Circumstantial evidence sends lots o' men to th' chair. Ut's a heap more happy like," The Hopper continued in his best philosophical vein, "t' play th' white card, helpin' widders an' orfants an' settlin' fusses. When ye ast me t' steal them jugs I hadn't th' heart t' refuse ye, miss. I wuz scared to tell ye I had yer baby an' ye seemed so sort o' trustin' like. An' ut bein' Chris'mus an' all."

When he steadfastly refused to promise to return, Muriel announced that they would visit The Hopper late in the afternoon and bring Billie along to express their thanks more formally.

"I'll be glad to see ye," replied The Hopper, though a little doubtfully and shamefacedly. "But ye mustn't git me into no more housebreakin' scrapes," he added with a grin. "It's mighty dangerous, miss, fer amachures, like me an' yer pa!"

X

Mary was not wholly pleased at the prospect of visitors, but she fell to work with Humpy to put the house in order. At five o'clock, not one, but three automobiles drove into the yard, filling Humpy with alarm lest at last The Hopper's sins had overtaken him, and they were all about to be hauled away to spend the rest of their lives in prison. It was not the police, but the young Talbots, with Billie and his grandfathers, on their way to a family celebration at the house of an aunt of Muriel's.

The grandfathers were restored to perfect amity, and were deeply curious now about The Hopper, whom the peace-loving Muriel had cajoled into robbing their houses.

"And you're only an honest chicken farmer, after all!" exclaimed Talbot, senior, when they were all sitting in a semicircle about the fireplace in Mary's parlor. "I hoped you were really a burglar; I always wanted to know a burglar."

Humpy had chopped down a small fir that had adorned the front yard and had set it up as a Christmas tree—an attention that was not lost upon Billie. The Hopper had brought some mechanical toys from town, and Humpy essayed the agreeable task of teaching the youngster how to operate them. Mary produced coffee and pound cake for the guests; The Hopper assumed the role of lord of the manor with a benevolent air that was intended as much to impress Mary and Humpy as the guests.

"Of course," said Mr. Wilton, whose appearance was the least bit comical by reason of his bandaged head,—"of course it was very foolish for a man of your sterling character to allow a young woman like my daughter to bully you into robbing houses for her. Why, when Roger fired at you as you were jumping out of the window, he didn't miss you more than a foot! It would have been ghastly for all of us if he had killed you!"

"Well, o' course it all begun from my goin' into th' little house lookin' fer Shaver's folks," replied The Hopper.

"But you haven't told us how you came to find our house," said Roger, suggesting a perfectly natural line of inquiries that caused Humpy to become deeply preoccupied with a pump he was operating in a basin of water for Billie's benefit.

"Well, ut jes' looked like a house that Shaver would belong to, cute an' comfortable like," said The Hopper; "I jes' suspicioned it wuz th' place as I wuz passin' along."

"I don't think we'd better begin trying to establish alibis," remarked Muriel, very gently, "for we might get into terrible scrapes. Why, if Mr. Stevens hadn't been so splendid about *everything* and wasn't just the kindest man in the world, he could make it very ugly for me."

"I shudder to think of what he might do to me," said Wilton, glancing guardedly at his neighbor.

"The main thing," said Talbot,—"the main thing is that Mr. Stevens has done for us all what nobody else could ever have done. He's made us see how foolish it is to quarrel about mere baubles. He's settled all our troubles for us, and for my part I'll say his solution is entirely satisfactory."

"Quite right," ejaculated Wilton. "If I ever have any delicate business negotiations that are beyond my powers I'm going to engage Mr. Stevens to handle them."

"My business's hens an' eggs," said The Hopper modestly; "an' we're doin' purty well."

When they rose to go (a move that evoked strident protests from Billie, who was enjoying himself hugely with Humpy) they were all in the jolliest humor.

"We must be neighborly," said Muriel, shaking hands with Mary, who was at the point of tears so great was her emotion at the success of The Hopper's party. "And we're going to buy all our chickens and eggs from you. We never have any luck raising our own."

Whereupon The Hopper imperturbably pressed upon each of the visitors a neat card stating his name (his latest and let us hope his last!) with the proper rural route designation of Happy Hill Farm.

The Hopper carried Billie out to his Grandfather Wilton's car, while Humpy walked beside him bearing the gifts from the Happy Hill Farm Christmas tree. From the door Mary watched them depart amid a chorus of merry Christmases, out of which Billie's little pipe rang cheerily.

When The Hopper and Humpy returned to the house, they abandoned the parlor for the greater coziness of the kitchen and there took account of the events of the momentous twenty-four hours.

"Them's what I call nice folks," said Humpy. "They jes' put us on an' wore us like we wuz a pair o' ole slippers."

"They wuzn't uppish—not to speak of," Mary agreed. "I guess that girl's got more gumption than any of 'em. She's got 'em straightened up now and I guess she'll take care they don't cut up no more monkey-shines about that Chinese stuff. Her husban' seemed sort o' gentle like."

"Artists is that way," volunteered The Hopper, as though from deep experience of art and life. "I jes' been thinkin' that knowin' folks like that an' findin' 'em humin, makin' mistakes like th' rest of us, kind o' makes ut seem easier fer us all t' play th' game straight. Ut's goin' to be th' white card fer me—jes' chickens an' eggs, an' here's hopin' the bulls don't ever find out we're settled here."

Humpy, having gone into the parlor to tend the fire, returned with two envelopes he had found on the mantel. There was a check for a thousand dollars in each, one from Wilton, the other from Talbot, with "Merry Christmas" written across the visiting cards of those gentlemen. The Hopper permitted Mary and Humpy to examine them and then laid them on the kitchen table, while he deliberated. His meditations were so prolonged that they grew nervous.

"I reckon they could spare ut, after all ye done fer 'em, Hop," remarked Humpy.

"They's millionaires, an' money ain't nothin' to 'em," said The Hopper.

"We can buy a motor-truck," suggested Mary, "to haul our stuff to town; an' mebbe we can build a new shed to keep ut in."

The Hopper set the catsup bottle on the checks and rubbed his cheek, squinting at the ceiling in the manner of one who means to be careful of his speech.

"They's things wot is an' things wot ain't," he began. "We ain't none o' us ever got nowheres bein' crooked. I been figurin' that I still got about twenty thousan' o' that bunch o' green I pulled out o' that express car, planted in places where 'taint doin' nobody no good. I guess ef I do ut careful I kin send ut back to the company, a little at a time, an' they'd never know where ut come from."

Mary wept; Humpy stared, his mouth open, his one eye rolling queerly.

"I guess we kin put a little chunk away every year," The Hopper went on. "We'd be comfortabler doin' ut. We could square up ef we lived long enough, which we don't need t' worry about, that bein' the Lord's business. You an' me's cracked a good many safes, Hump, but we never made no money at ut, takin' out th' time we done."

"He's got religion; that's wot he's got!" moaned Humpy, as though this marked the ultimate tragedy of The Hopper's life.

"Mebbe ut's religion an' mebbe ut's jes' sense," pursued The Hopper, unshaken by Humpy's charge. "They wuz a chaplin in th' Minnesoty pen as used t' say ef we're all square with our own selves ut's goin' to be all right with God. I guess I got a good deal o' squarin' t' do, but I'm goin' t' begin ut. An' all these things happenin' along o' Chris'mus, an' little Shaver an' his ma bein' so friendly like, an' her gittin' me t' help straighten out them ole gents, an' doin' all I done an' not gettin' pinched seems more 'n jes' luck; it's providential's wot ut is!"

This, uttered in a challenging tone, evoked a sob from Humpy, who announced that he "felt like" he was going to die.

"It's th' Chris'mus time, I reckon," said Mary, watching The Hopper deposit the two checks in the clock. "It's the only decent Chris'mus I ever knowed!"

TWO PIECES

Ambrose Bierce

From *The Devil's Dictionary*:

CHRISTMAS (*n*): A day set apart and consecrated to gluttony, drunkenness, maudlin sentiment, gift-taking, public dullness, and domestic misbehavior.

> *What! not religious? You should see, my pet,*
> *On every Christmas day how drunk I get!*
> *O, I'm a Christian—not a pious monk*
> *Honors the Master with so dead a drunk.*

From a letter to his friend (collected in *A Much Misunderstood Man: Selected Letters of Ambrose Bierce*):

Dec. 26, 1897

Dear Dr. Doyle,

How I hate Christmas! I'm one of the curmudgeons that the truly good Mr. Dickens found it profitable to hold up to the scorn of those who take such satisfaction in being decent and generous one day in 365. Bah! How hollow it all is! Always on Christmas, though, I feel my own heart soften—toward the late Judas Iscariot. Why, even Mrs. Martin has wished me a "merry Christmas." Great Scott! Who could want to be "merry"? Is one to grin through a horse-collar, or walk on one's hands, because a babe was born in Bethlehem?

Yours ever,
Ambrose Bierce

SHEPHERDS, WHY THIS JUBILEE?

Bryan Furuness

WHEN IT COMES TO CHRISTMAS EVE SERVICES, you can keep your megachurch inspire-a-thons, your Catholic pews jammed with the sweaty lapsed, your Lutheran sopranos keening like red-tail hawks on the descant in "Angels We Have Heard on High." For sheer production value, you can't beat the Episcopalians.

Trinity Episcopal, my church in Indy, is big on beauty. It's just that, for most of the year, the beauty is understated, almost austere. The building looks like it was airlifted from a village in Yorkshire. Think stone walls, oak doors with iron hinges, dark wooden pews on stone floors, all capped by rafters painted as brightly as a calliope.

Classy. Timeless. The church goes to work in a navy suit with a red tie. Until December, when the church leaves work and changes in a Speedway bathroom to head to a drag show.

The transformation starts with a process called "greening," which involves coiling about fifteen miles of evergreen boas around every knob and pole in the sanctuary. On Christmas Eve, these garlands bristle with candles, actual flaming candles (forget virgin birth; the real sacred mystery is how the church has avoided going up in a massive sap-fire). In their vestments of heavy brocade and tall pointy hats, the priests look like they wandered off the set of *Alice in Wonderland*. Trumpeters trumpet triumphantly while some dude in a crushed velvet hat whips around a censer of incense like he's the white Bruce Lee.

Pageantry? We're one torch song away from being a musical.

Or maybe the service is actually a musical. After all, it features several show-stoppers. "Adeste Fidelis" is the Anglican "Freebird." If you haven't heard "O Holy Night" sung by children twisting their hands and rocking up on the toes of their

Hush Puppies, then you have not heard "O Holy Night," my friend. And then there was the service a couple of years ago when the church pulled out all the stops during "We Three Kings." At first it seemed like a standard production, an excuse to let the men of the church let loose their most *profundo basso*, but then, lo! What was coming up the center aisle? Three kings! Dressed in shimmering robes made of mermaid scales and hats that looked like Jiffy Pop containers, post-pop. One of them had a service dog. And the dog *was wearing a Jiffy Pop hat, too.*

The congregation was moved, man. Episcopalians don't shout or flop around or anything so unseemly, but eyes were shining. Hands were squeezed. Glances were exchanged that could be translated as *Oh, man. This is really something. I'm feeling it hard.*

In my pew, I exchanged glances dutifully, but I was not feeling it. I mean, I liked it. I appreciated it. I cataloged it as Very Nice. But that was it.

By the time the last *star of wonder, star of night* faded, even the crusty verger was swiping at his eyes. Meanwhile I was wondering if my son, the acolyte, was in place to serve communion, and speaking of bread and wine, what were we going to eat after the service?

I wasn't always this way.

When I was a boy, church was full of ecstasies. I would stare at the eternal flame and tell myself *I am real, I am actual flesh that God has made, this life is not a dream* until I was thoroughly weirded out. All year I looked forward to the Good Friday service that ended in total darkness with the pastor slamming shut the Bible with a sound like the end of the universe, making my whole body prickle with goosebumps. At Easter, I would sing the Hallelujah Chorus with the choir, and we would whip ourselves into a frenzy near the end, gnashing at the words— *Forever! And ever! Hallelujah! Hallelujah!*—until it felt like we were all going mad.

Then it went away. I don't know when, exactly, but by the end of my teens, church didn't transport me anymore. And the loss went beyond church. I could no longer fall into a book like it was a dream. In a movie theater, I could no longer forget there were people around me, that I had a body, that I was separate from the screen.

"The first twenty years of life contain the whole of experience," wrote Graham Greene. "The rest is observation." I don't know if that's true for everyone, but by the time I went to that Christmas Eve service, the one with the three kings and the service dog, it seemed true for me.

Greene also said that sometimes his faith was that his faith would return. So I kept reading. I watched the screens. I warmed the pews. In cynical moments, I wondered if I was just going through the motions for a reminder of how these things used to make me feel, the way you might keep around an old girlfriend's shirt for an occasional sad sniff.

But even if I knew that to be true, I wouldn't stop. It's better than nothing. And in some burnt pit of my mind, an eternal flame burns a vigil for the return of awe.

Back to the service in question. Time for communion. My son must have been in the right place after all, because he ended up next to the priest, ready to hand out wafers. The two of them were working the drive-thru lane of communion—you walked up, got your body, got your blood, and you kept on walking. When I reached the head of the line, my son handed me the Eucharist and said, "This is my body, given for you," and then he smirked because that's what happens to his face when his lips are trying to smile while he's trying to stay serious. I know this because my face does the same thing. So there we were, smirking at each other until my wife nudged me to move along.

How much time passed before I heard the crash? Could have been two minutes, could have been ten. Communion was still going and I was trying to remember if we had the ingredients for skillet cornbread, but the clang of metal on stone brought me out of that daydream. Before I could tell what was happening, my wife climbed over me to get to the aisle. The church murmured. I stood stupidly.

I can still close my eyes and see the scene: my son laid out on the stone floor, looking woozily up at the rafters, his face as white as his alb, wafers scattered all around. The priest, a black woman, is kneeling next to him, cradling his head. My wife is on the other side, her fingertips on his chest as though telling him to stay down. The man in the crushed velvet hat looks on in concern. The dog whines. The congregation falls to a hush.

And there I am, standing. Gripping the pew in front of me like I'm being electrocuted and can't break away.

Then I did, of course. My hesitation only lasted a second or two. I made my way up the aisle and helped my son to his feet. My wife and I led him to the common room to get some orange juice and cookies. Within minutes, color was back in his face. After the service, he was treated like a minor celebrity, which he handled with embarrassed good humor. In short, the kid was fine. I wasn't so sure about myself. What happened to me when I saw him on the floor? In that electric second, I felt . . . something. Or maybe it's more accurate to say I felt everything, overloading my circuits.

Years later, I'm still wondering. What came over me? It's only now, as I close my eyes to picture that scene on the stone floor, that I see how much it looks like a tableau. Like art, or maybe theater. Like an accidental nativity scene. And the feeling that seized me—fear and unbearable love—seems a faint aftershock of the original.

PICTURES FROM A CLAPBOARD HOUSE

Jessamyn West

ELSPETH, GARD'S AND MATTIE'S DAUGHTER, WAS SPENDING Christmas with Jess and Eliza. The Christmas tree was already up. It stood in the parlor bay window, wild and shining, awaiting the harness of cranberry and popcorn ropes which would semi-domesticate it, quiet its outdoor cavortings and prancings. In the sitting room its harness was still taking shape. Cranberries and popcorn were being strung; gilded buts attached to cords, red paper bells, opened again for such ringing as the eye could apprehend. Grandma's hands were squeezing ropes of sparkling tinsel back to roundness.

The popcorn Elspeth was stringing squeaked a little now and then, and the lonely sound traveled up Elspeth's arm to her ear—which shuddered to hear it. Grandpa, who looked to be sleeping, with feet almost in the fire, heard it, too. When the squeaks were loudest his stockinged toes twitched uneasily. It was a sound, Elspeth thought, like a wind round a house corner, like the wind around the corners of Grandma's house, a house white in the windy night, square except for the balcony upstairs which projected like a watchtower or sentry box into the darkness and looked out across the great woods to her own home.

Elspeth thought of her mother. The clock ticked, slow, slow. It said, as Elspeth listened, For-ev-er . . . for-ev-er. The fire rustled and sighed; Grandma's tinsel made a scratchy sound. The popcorn squeaked.

"Grandpa," Elspeth asked, "what kind of trees are in the woods between here and home?"

Grandpa bent his toes comfortably back and forth, stared into the fire as if into a forest. "Oak," he said. "And honey locust. Shagbark hickory and but-ton-wood. Dogwood," he added. "And papaw and May-apple. But mostly farm," he said.

In the daytime Elspeth remembered the farms but at night only the long, black woods, dark even at midday. "Corn?" Elspeth asked.

"Yes, lots of corn," her grandpa said, "and timothy and clover."

All was quiet again, only the lonely sounds in the room: the fire, the wind, the clock.

"There's orchards, too."

"Yes," the old man said, rocking. "There's orchards. Summer Sweetings, Northern Spies, Grime's Goldens. Lots of orchards."

The fire curved like a wave; Grandma's tinsel crackled; the old house creaked. Elspeth's needle split a piece of popcorn, halved it so it was no longer a flower. The clock said, For-ev-er . . . for-ev-er.

"Grandma," Elspeth said suddenly, surprising even herself, "does thee love me?"

Grandma folded her strands of tinsel. "Of course, child. Thee knows I do. With all my heart."

Elspeth knew this. "Better than I did my own," Grandma often said. "Then I was too young," she'd say, "to know childhood wasn't enduring." She'd sorrowfully shake her head. "Better than thy mother Mattie or thy uncle Josh or Laban." But she never said, "Better than thy uncle Stephen," for not one could be better loved than Uncle Stephen.

The clock struck nine. "Time to call a halt," Grandma said and opened and shut her short plump hands, weary with the tedious squeezing. Elspeth looked at her grandma. Tidal wave and avalanche were nothing to her so long as Grandma was near at hand and well. But when Grandma's face grew sad, when, as sometimes happened, she would look far off and say, "Stephen, Stephen. My poor boy," then Elspeth's world was threatened. Tonight, Elspeth thought, Grandma's sad.

"Would thee like me to comb thy hair, Grandma, before thee goes to bed?"

"No, child, not tonight," Grandma said.

Then Grandpa asked, "How about a little music before we go upstairs, granddaughter?"

This was, in a way, a kind of joke, and Elspeth knew it—for she couldn't really play—but it was a joke she was glad to be a part of. The organ, which long ago had stood in the attic, was now in the sitting room open and dusted, awaiting someone's touch. The music Elspeth's mother, Mattie, had played, "Gala Water," "Evening Star," "Toll the Bell," had gone with her when she married, and Grandpa played by ear; but Grandma would not have the organ look bereft. On it she kept the red and gold atlas, larger and more beautiful than any songbook it had ever held, and Elspeth who could not play music played the maps.

"Now," she would say, "I will play Africa." Then she played all the pictures she had seen and all the tales she had been told of dark and distant Africa. She played the great winding rivers, the flash of tusks through leafy jungles, the black men with spears taller than their bodies.

Or she would open the atlas to a map of the arctic regions and play the North Pole, her hands hunting for sounds that said bareness and whiteness and icy winds and flashing northern lights.

And she could play China, too, whose sounds for her were all tiny: tiny bells, tiny feet, tiny chopsticks tinkling against the side of tiny bowls. But tonight Elspeth opened the atlas to a map of the United States and said, "Now, I will play California." She chose California because that was where Uncle Stephen had gone and because he wrote home of its great mountains, its sunshine like arrows, its oranges like gold. He wrote about the warm sea and the rivers with strange names: the Sacramento, the Yuba, the San Joaquin, the Feather. Tonight she would play the mountains, deep heavy sounds to show how big they were and thin high notes for the high, snow-covered peaks. And she would play the Feather River which must surely sound like a torrent of downiness.

But before the first mountain had been squeezed from the organ Grandma said once again, "No, child, not tonight."

Elspeth turned on the organ stool to look at Grandma who ordinarily liked all sounds which said California and reminded her of Uncle Stephen: but, "Not tonight," she repeated. "I can't bear the name tonight." Then she said something that had no meaning for Elspeth: "Oh, Jess, why'd he have to choose her? Marry outside the Meeting? What he need's a settled, sober-minded wife," but Grandpa only said,

"How about the North Pole, granddaughter? I like to hear that north wind whistle."

Elspeth played the North Pole, and for a while she thought that the cold air that swept about her dangling legs was music from the organ; but Grandpa had stopped pumping—there was no sound from the organ, and still the room grew colder.

"Shut the door," Grandpa said quietly. Elspeth turned and there in front of the closed door stood Uncle Stephen and Lidy Cinnamond, both tall, pink from the cold, and lightly dusted with snow.

"How did thee get over?" Grandpa asked and Elspeth saw he had known Uncle Stephen was home from California.

"Lidy's father brought us."

"He outside?" Grandpa asked.

"He went right back," Uncle Stephen told him and carried their luggage which he was still holding and set it by the door which led upstairs. "We plan to stay here until we go to Lidy's Christmas day." He spoke very clearly and loudly as if arguing with someone, but no one answered him.

Then he walked over to the organ, took Elspeth's hand, and slid her from the organ stool. "Lidy," he said, "this is Aunt Jetty."

Lidy Cinnamond spoke for the first time and her voice was the way Elspeth had remembered it, very low and soft with a sort of humming note in it. "Jetty?" she said.

"Because she's so black," said Uncle Stephen.

"Why is she aunt, Steve?"

"Oh, she's serious as an owl," Uncle Stephen explained. "Aunt Jetty, this is your aunt Lidy. Say hello."

Elspeth put out her hand. "I've seen Lidy before. Aunt Lidy," she corrected herself.

"Have you?" said Uncle Stephen. "Where?"

"At her house. And with Mr. Venters."

Nobody said a word for quite a long time and Elspeth, feeling responsible for the silence, broke it. "They were having a picnic down by Rush Branch."

"Mr. Venters and Lidy?" Grandma asked in a strange dry voice.

"Yes," Elspeth answered. "Mel Venters. They . . ."

But before she could say what she had seen, Uncle Stephen reached across and took his wife's hand. "Mel Venters almost beat my time," he said. "And who could blame him for trying?" he asked them all, but particularly his mother.

Elspeth looked at Lidy again. She could not think of her as beautiful, still it was hard not to stare at her; she was so black and gold and red, so tall and curving, so quiet. And so smiling too, as a bride should be, Elspeth knew.

"She's waiting to shake hands with thee, Lidy," Uncle Stephen said, and Lidy, as if recalling herself from some reverie, reached down and took Elspeth's hand.

Elspeth shook it gravely. "It's past thy bedtime," Grandma said to her—and to Lidy: "Take off thy coat. I'll heat thee and Stephen some milk as soon as I've put this child to bed."

Grandma held Elspeth's arm as they went up the cold stairs. "When did thee see Lidy and Mel?"

"Last summer," Elspeth said. "Picnicking. They were . . ."

"That will do," Grandma said and hustled her out of her clothes and into her cold bed, which stood anchored like a little boat at the foot of Grandma's great full-sailed four-poster.

On the ceiling next morning was a sea of light, a radiance like milk alive and dancing. It had snowed in the night and sunlight on snow was sweeping the room with waves of loveliness. Elspeth snuggled deeper into her covers. The snowlight so filled her room that it seemed as if, warmly wrapped about, she were bedded in snow itself. Then into the light something dark crowded; something dreamed, or imagined, or . . . remembered . . .

Grandma with a lamp in her hand and Uncle Stephen by her side: shining upward onto their faces the lamplight had made their mouths forbidding, their eyes shadowed. The light ate the flesh from their faces, made bones look down at her.

"While thee was away," Grandma was saying, "while thee was distant, sick, trying to get well, she not caring . . . carrying on."

The lamp in Grandma's hand trembled and Uncle Stephen took it and held it for her, as if he would patiently hear her out.

"It isn't that she isn't of thy faith . . . but holding herself so light, and her word given. And California's so far away."

Uncle Stephen steadily held the lamp. "Tell him," Grandma said, "with your own eyes . . . on Sandy Creek."

"There's no need," said Uncle Stephen. "No need. I know it all. Things work out one way and another. Not as thee'd always choose. This works out this way. Nothing to talk in the night about. I was away and Lydia was young. Did thee want her in widow's weeds?"

Uncle Stephen handed the lamp back to his mother and bent to kiss Elspeth. "Go to sleep now, Aunt Jetty," he said. "It's begun to snow."

Then, his arm about his mother's shoulders, he guided her toward the door and Elspeth heard his voice outside, diminishing, failing as they descended the stairs. "Love is more lasting than . . ." then his voice ceased, was swallowed by the narrow, echoing stairway, and then one more word came back . . . "fire." From a long way off, toward the bottom of the stairs, that word came back so emphasized that Elspeth heard it, though all else was lost.

"Love is more lasting than . . ." Elspeth was still thinking about it when she went into the sitting room after breakfast. The room was already tidied for the day. A holiday-sized log burned in the grate; an enormous bell of honeycombed red tissue paper hung from the suspended lamp and swayed with every movement in the room. Snowlight and firelight mingled on the rag carpet, gold and silver. Uncle Stephen sat by the fire, very fine in his good black suit, his light, curly hair dampened by water and still showing the marks of a comb.

"Hello, Aunt Jetty," he said. "Want to help?"

From a half dozen paper bags he was taking handfuls of candy, putting them in Grandma's best china and cut glass bowls. First a handful of chocolates, then one of gumdrops, then one of peanut brittle. "Have to mix them up," Uncle Stephen said. "Have to give everybody a fair chance."

"Is it for the Christmas tree?" Elspeth asked.

"No, no," said Uncle Stephen. "The shivaree. Thee knows what a shivaree is?"

She did not of course: the bride and groom surprised after they had gone to bed by sudden shots and shouts, by cowbells and horse fiddles and lard pails full of stones. And after that the party inside with cake and candy, hot coffee and cigars.

"Will it be tonight? Christmas Eve?"

"Yes," said Uncle Stephen. "Tonight, I figure. With us leaving tomorrow, tonight's about the only time for it."

The big log settled deeper in the fireplace, the red bell gently swayed.

"Love is more lasting than," Elspeth said and her voice asked her question.

"More lasting than the hills," answered Uncle Stephen.

"Fire," asked Elspeth. "What about fire?"

"Ask thy aunt Lidy about fire," Uncle Stephen said.

Elspeth saw Aunt Lidy then for the first time, in a chair by the far window, all in white. Not white like a bride, stiff and shining, but heavy and soft—like snow warmed and woven. She was looking out into the snow and she didn't look away from it as she answered in her low, humming voice. "Fire warms," she said.

Elspeth stared at her aunt. "Aunt Lidy looks like a snow queen," she said.

"She does, she does," Uncle Stephen answered her. "White and wintry and beautiful." Aunt Lidy, when he spoke, rose and walked to him and laced her hand, which was darker than his hair, in and out of her husband's curls.

The whole day was magic for Elspeth. Christmas Eve and the shivaree and in the parlor the waiting Christmas tree. Only at Christmastime did the parlor come truly to life: in summer a snowball bush, white as a cloud but noisier, tapped at the parlor window. In winter the snow was there, white too, but silent. But on ordinary days, now that the children had left home, it was empty of any eye to see or ear to hear. The tappings went unremarked. The snow-crystal pictures melted and in the common runoff of water at midday bore no sign of what they once had been.

Toward evening when the shadows of the pine trees along the driveway were already long and blue on the snow, Elspeth began to think with longing of the tree. There was no one about. Uncle Stephen was helping in the barn with feeding; Grandma was busy with supper, and Aunt Lidy had been nowhere to be seen for hours.

The tissue paper bell swayed a little, but was silent as Elspeth crossed the room toward the parlor door. The Christmas tree was secret, not to be really seen until Christmas morning when the presents were unwrapped, but the parlor door was unlocked and quick peeks not forbidden. It was as if Grandma knew that there must be a few stolen glances beforehand if the full sight of the tree's Christmas morning glory were to be endured.

But the opened door stayed open, and when it closed Elspeth was inside the parlor, close to the beautiful and shining tree, able to smell, to touch, to stroke. She stood with eyes closed for a minute, then opened them and the little parlor with its red carpet and stiff white curtains was alive. It was as if a flower had fallen into a dead shell, or a bee had crawled into a thimble. Or as if inside a marble clock that no longer ticked, a live butterfly fluttered. The tree had made the room alive. It was so beautiful Elspeth wanted now to be forever. And it was forever, only Aunt Lidy spoke and now came back again.

"Aunt Jetty," she said in her voice that had to Elspeth the sound of bees in it. She was sitting in her white dress by a window, just as she had sat that morning.

"I'm not supposed to be here," Elspeth said. "I oughtn't to be here," she whispered, feeling wicked to be in the parlor, talking the day before Christmas.

Aunt Lidy held out her arms and pulled Elspeth close to her so that she felt the soft warm springiness of the white wool dress. "Neither should I." Then she said, "Will you do something for me?"

"What is it?" Elspeth asked.

"Take a note down the road to Mel Venters? It's just a step really. It's stopped snowing and the wind's died down."

"Grandma'll never let me."

"I know. I'm sorry—but I'd fix it so you could go without Grandma's knowing."

It was all planned. She would take Elspeth upstairs after supper and instead of putting her to bed would bundle her in shawls. Six or seven, even. "You'll never feel the cold. I'll take you down the back stairs and start you on the road to Mel's myself."

"It's just a step," she said again. "The wind's gone, the snow's nice and dry, and you can see the lights of both houses all the way. It's—just—I wanted to say goodbye to Mel. The minute he reads the note he'll hitch up the sleigh and bring you home."

"Maybe he won't," Elspeth said.

"Oh, but he will. You just wait and see."

It was as easy as Aunt Lidy said. No one missed her, no one saw her leave. The night was dark, but quiet with a clear sky full of stars. The snow was dry and light, but hard to walk through. On any other night Elspeth might have been afraid—but what could harm her the night before Christmas?

The Venters opened their Christmas presents on Christmas Eve and they had a houseful of relatives, old folks and young, children and grandchildren. There were so many people and so much excitement Elspeth was scarcely noticed. She gave Lidy's note to Mel, who was sitting apart from his family warming his feet at a big stove. He read and reread the note. He put it deep in his pocket, then dug it out again as if he had forgotten what it said.

No one asked Elspeth to take off her many wrappings and she stood burning with warmth. Then the children gave her some candy, and she squatted in a corner, eating the candy and playing with an unclaimed jack-in-the-box. Grandma's sitting room, the organ with the atlas, the parlor and the Christmas tree seemed remote as a dream. She watched Mel read and reread his note and finally wad it into a ball and throw it into the open draft of the stove. She leaned against the wall, eating gumdrops, and drowsily frightening herself with the jack-in-the-box.

She was almost asleep when she heard from down the road the first shots of the shivaree, the banging of milk pans and the clanging of bells. Mel Venters looked away from the fire. "What's going on?" he asked. "Where's all that noise coming from?"

"From the shivaree," Elspeth told him. "They're shivareeing Uncle Stephen and Aunt Lidy."

Mel lifted her off the floor by one arm. "Come on," he said. "I got to get you home."

He took her without time for explanations or goodbye to the barn and clapped her into the front seat of the sleigh to wait while he hitched. He was a fast hitcher—before the cold had fairly awakened Elspeth he was beside her in the front seat, slapping the reins over the back of his horse.

"They'll stand out on the balcony," Elspeth told him, "and bow to the people. Then," she said, clutching her jack-in-the-box, which she had forgotten to put down, "they'll bow to each other and kiss."

"The hell they will," Mel Venters said. "The hell they will."

The sleigh felt as if it didn't even touch the snow—as if it flew. Mel's big black horse was a part of the dark night. Elspeth touched the latch of the box in her excitement and the jack sprang out with a whir and rapped her under the chin.

"Oh," Elspeth said.

"Be still, be still, can't you," Mel rasped. "Hush your noise."

There was a blaze of light from the torches and lanterns of the people who had come for the shivaree, but the house itself was still dark, the balcony empty. Mel's sleigh cut hissing up the driveway and the crowd, seeing who had arrived, shouted and pounded louder than before.

"Hi, Mel, come to have your last look at the bride?"

Mel said nothing, either to Elspeth or the shivaree-ers, but brought up his sleigh, sharply and deftly, in their midst.

"She ain't here," someone yelled to him. "Neither one's here. They've flown the coop."

"Go on, Mel, you ask the bride to come out," they shouted. "You got a way with women. She'll do it for you, Mel."

They seemed to know what they were talking about; lights showed through the upstairs windows while they were still calling on Mel to ask the bride to come out. They redoubled their shouting then and in a minute or two Elspeth saw Uncle Stephen open the door onto the balcony, then turn back, give his hand to Aunt Lidy who stepped out and took her place beside him. Uncle Stephen had on his black suit, but Aunt Lidy was in a long red dress, a dressing gown, perhaps; something that in the flicker of light from torches and lanterns looked to Elspeth like a dress which might have had a crown above it, or a garland of flowers. Aunt Lidy's dark hair was uncoiled and hung about her face and down her shoulders in rippling tongues of black.

Uncle Stephen called out, "Hello, folks," and waved and said, "I sure did," to somebody who yelled, "You sure picked a looker, Steve," but Aunt Lidy said nothing. She simply stood there very quietly with the red-gold of the torches and lanterns on her face, looking down at the crowd sometimes, but more often smiling and watching Uncle Stephen as he and the shivaree-ers shouted back and forth to each other.

Elspeth turned to look at Mel. She had supposed Aunt Lidy's note had said, "Farewell, Mel. I love another. We must part forever." That is what she would have written—and she supposed, too, that Mel would bow, throw a kiss, and drive away heartbroken through the snow. But Mel was neither bowing nor throwing kisses. He was leaning far back in the sleigh, head lifted, eyes narrowed. Elspeth watched his small, soft mouth lengthen and thin as he returned Aunt Lidy's gaze.

Once again somebody yelled, "Here's Mel, Lidy, come to have a last look at you. Feast your eyes, Mel. It's your last chance. They're headin' back to Californy."

Then Aunt Lidy did what Elspeth said she would: she made toward the crowd beneath her a slight bowing movement, then laid her arms, very solemnly and slowly, as if thinking what she was doing, about Uncle Stephen's neck and kissed him, just as seriously and just as slowly. No one of all the shivaree-ers yelled or hooted—because the kiss did not seem playful, but almost a part of the wedding ceremony, dignified and holy.

The first movement, the first sound came from Mel. "Take her and welcome," he yelled. Then he pushed Elspeth into the snow like a bundle of rags, laid the whip across his horse's back, and cut across the front yard and onto the north driveway with runners hissing. He pulled out onto the pike, slowing up for an instant to yell back, "Merry Christmas," and to add in a voice that was both sharp and bellowing, "and a Happy New Year."

Elspeth turned from where she had been dropped in the snow to gaze after him—but Mel, his sleigh and black horse, were lost in the night. When she looked back at the balcony Aunt Lidy was standing as before and Uncle Stephen had his arm about her shoulders. He leaned over the balcony and spoke in a matter-of-fact way. "There's food in the house, folks, and warm drinks. Come in and welcome."

Elspeth came in with the shivaree-ers, but Grandma hustled her upstairs before the eating and drinking started. In bed she lay listening to the night's many sounds. The sounds, at first from below stairs: the shouting and talking and singing, then the pawing and neighing of horses and the sound of sleigh bells growing fine and thin as the bells of China in the frosty air, and finally the sounds of Grandpa's and Grandma's talking. Talking, talking, their voices murmuring, rising and falling, until at last the bedroom door was flung wide and Uncle Stephen came in. He held the big china lamp in his hands and his black coat was off so that the fine pleated front of his white groom's shirt showed. He put the lamp on the bureau and leaning against the bureau's edge looked down on his father and mother who lay wide-eyed and unsleeping. Uncle Stephen looked buoyant and well, serene and happy.

"Give over fretting," he said to them. He pushed himself up very tall against the tall dark bureau. "It's my marriage and I'm content. I couldn't love except where there's a core of wildness. It's not in me. It'll be a happy marriage."

Uncle Stephen ran his fingers through his light, curly hair, which was no longer neat or combed. His face was calm but his eyes blazed. He leaned over to blow out the light, decided not to and picked it up again. The light fell on his shining face so that Elspeth thought, He looks like an angel of the Lord. He stood on the threshold for a minute, lamp in hand, as if hunting for some word to say. What he finally said reminded Elspeth that Christmas day had come. "Wise men came bearing gifts of frankincense and myrrh," he said and closed the door softly behind him.

Elspeth went to sleep thinking of those words and they were still in her mind when she awakened next morning. But before she went down to see the tree again, she wanted to stand out on the balcony where Uncle Stephen and Aunt Lidy'd stood and to think if what she'd seen and heard the night before could be true.

She stood on the balcony, looking out into the fresh, sparkling morning across the front yard. New snow had fallen in the night, hiding the footprints, the sleigh tracks, the charred splinters from the blazing torches. No, it could not be true. She lifted her arms as Aunt Lidy had done, slowly and seriously—but it was unreal. What she had seen and heard could not be true.

Then she saw something in the snow, red and silver and blue, partially covered, but still, shining in the sun, brilliant as a flower. It was the jack-in-the-box. It was true, it was true. The black horse had gone down the road in darkness; Aunt Lidy's face had shone, gold, with the blaze of torches on it; Uncle Stephen had held the lamp so that he looked like a Christmas angel. Elspeth gazed far away, across the glittering woods toward her home. "Oh, mamma," she said, "it was all true."

TOO COLD

Jayne Marek

The deep cold approaches us
Like the threat of greatest loss.
Floorboards cannot resist it
And exhale its coming.
The pond shudders, diminishes,
As its muscles tighten in rigor.
The hours will pass.

Night barks once, then again,
In a sad dog voice. Darkness
Can be taken inside,
Where it will sit alert to watch
The frost-edged door,
Hoping it will stay shut,
Knowing it might not,

If the wind looks up
And hears the crackling sky
Tell it to pounce.

WINTER RUNES

Jayne Marek

This snow will stop
as it began.
Now wind rises to speak.

A young sparrow, left behind,
utters a sharp cry
over and over.

Black seeds fragrant as past summer
fall from my hands.
Everywhere particles of white

gather to hide
narrow tracks where juncos hopped
and shadows where the seeds dived.

TRIFLES

Lori Rader-Day

THE DAY WE MOVE IN, A DEFLATED orange basketball—punched into a bowl and cupping several handfuls of rice—sits on the parkway of the bungalow next door. *Parkway*, a word I had learned from going to a thousand open houses all over Chicago: the little patch of grass by the street that you must care for but that never belongs to you. Sam and I have learned a new vocabulary: *earnest money, contingency, escrow*. I don't mind *parkway*. I don't mind that I have to care for it. Mow it, weed it. The parkway looks like it belongs to me, and so it does.

Sam's brother Jeremy steps out of the moving van and onto the lip of the basketball bowl. It flips and dumps wet, cooked rice onto his tennis shoe. "Did you guys vet the neighbors before you signed?" he says, not as quietly as he should. "I mean. What are we dealing with?"

"It's probably for the birds," I say. I had already pictured the birdbath I would set up in our new backyard. Finches, cardinals, mean little sparrows. The backyard was perfect. We had a huge maple tree that you could see in the aerial maps online. I had been studying the neighborhood from above, like a god, since our offer was accepted. No one else on the block has a tree quite as big as our tree. It rises over the top of our roof, the leaves turning candy yellow.

"It's for the birds, all right," Jeremy says, shaking the rice off his foot. Jeremy is older than Sam. He's divorced, not dating anyone, though he's tall and good-looking in a way that makes waitresses blush. He lives in an apartment in a building owned by their parents. I think he does his own laundry, but I wonder. Until yesterday, we also lived in the building. "Our independence day," Sam said yesterday after we signed our names to forms and thirty-year promises until our hands ached. Sam assures me his family is happy for us, no matter how often his mother reminds us that home is still out in Clarendon Hills, out where she is, and that we should remember to come visit. It's less than thirty miles from our house to the suburbs, but we might as well be moving to the lunar surface, to listen to Sam's family. My mother-in-law has her half-acre, her garage opener, her *properties*, her two boys raised, but she would begrudge us the chance to start our own lives. My family lives safely and quietly in California. We have an open invitation to visit, but all of us are content to let the invitation stay open. I talk to my mother once a month; she always puts my father on for a few minutes. "How's my girl?" he asks, something he would never ask in person. We have found the right distance.

The right distance for Sam's family is none at all. Jeremy can't understand why we're leaving. "The rent is cheap," he keeps saying. "Who is going to watch your back in the city?" He means: Who is going to let themselves in when you're not home to make sure you're living right? Who is going to use their key to borrow stuff and forget to return it?

"Jolie, don't you have a paper towel or something?" Jeremy says now.

"It's just some rice," Sam says, coming around from the driver's side. He un-latches the back of the van and stretches to raise the door quietly, already thinking of the neighbors. He would have hired a service to move us, but his father gave him hell for the waste of money. Jeremy can help you, he said. And, changing his mind, "He needs the money." There's not much to move anyway. We have purged all the pressed cardboard furniture of our youth, all the ragged paperbacks we said we'd read someday. No clothes that do not fit, no dishrags with stains. This is a clean start. Not because we have something sordid in our pasts—we don't. It's just that our other start was so messy. All those *things* stacked around us, all those relatives living too near.

In the move, Sam put up a fight over a box of old baseball cards and some old G. I. Joe action figures still in the packages, which cracked a narrow opening for a few things I wanted. Like: no extra sets of keys to this place. Sam agreed. No more layers of relatives dropping by unannounced. We want to rely on one another. We want to do this alone.

The next summer, the basketball is full of rice, topped with browning pineapple rings. Fat, languid bees twirl around the plate, drunk on their luck.

When I open the door, Jeremy and his girlfriend are there. He says, "So the rice—is it for the birds or for the bees?"

"The birds *and* the bees," Shana says. I haven't decided whether or not I like Shana. She's unabashed that she's sleeping with Jeremy, as though sex is something she invented. She seems to think that she's somehow closer to the core of the family because she's dating the older brother. Or maybe it's because she lives out in the hills with them, went to the same high school a few years behind Sam. Fitting into the family on the basis of her résumé, rather than having to wed in, like me. I guess I have decided: I don't like her.

"Everybody's in back," I say, and lead them through the house. The light is coming through all the windows on the north side, lighting up the new, cherry electronics cabinet in the living room, the stainless steel in the kitchen. I am *house-proud*, that's what I heard my mother-in-law say on Christmas Eve, as though house-proud was a terrible thing to discover in a woman. She thought I was upstairs wrapping presents, but I had finished and had come to the kitchen to claim the last of the wine we'd brought. I hadn't dared walk in. Had to skip the wine. Clear-eyed, I spent the rest of the evening alert to slights. I received an old-fashioned Laura Ingalls nightgown that year and a Sinatra CD because my father-in-law couldn't believe anyone disliked Frank. Though we'd planned on staying the night in Sam's old room, I talked him into driving home to spend the holiday together, just the two of us. New traditions, I said to him, avoiding the argument that was itching under my skin. This thing with his mother—I believed I could win it.

"No, seriously," Shana says as we pass through the sliding doors to the patio after Jeremy leaves her to go greet some of the guys he knows out by the grill. The teasing tone goes out of her voice as soon as there are no men to hear it. "Who is the basketball thing feeding? Flies?"

I decide not to mention the people down the street who use dried blood fertilizer on their roses. "Gods, I think."

Shana snorts.

"You should go meet some of the guys," I say, nodding to where Jeremy and Sam are holding court, and turn toward the house. I'm neighborhood-proud, too, though I barely know anyone. All around us are families with working moms and dads that push strollers and young children who have been raised on manners. People close their blinds at the appropriate times and mow their grass on a regimented schedule. We have nodding and smiling relationships with everyone on the block. Everything is as suburban as Sam's mother could imagine, except for the basketball on the lawn. But it's my prerogative to hate the basketball bowl, not Shana's.

The rice people are an elderly Asian couple. Chinese. Maybe. We have opportunities to nod, to wave over the fence that separates our yards. Their son has come to stay. His large black truck has been parked in front of our house, unmoved, since his arrival. It's my prerogative to have a problem with the truck.

In the kitchen, I rinse a beer bottle for recycling and glance out the window. There he is, sitting half in the shade of the flowering tree in their backyard, bare-chested and pale. His black hair is shaggy, a style too young for how old he probably is.

He's at least partly responsible for the state of the basketball. It's been robust all spring, since the day he arrived. I've come to understand the ball's palm to be a barometer of luck, but I can't read its message. Is the heap of rice and fruit cocktail on the grass a request for favors or a thank-you for blessings? It's like trying to read headlines in a foreign newspaper; things are happening, but I don't know what they are.

When the food is off the grill, I bring out the potato salad, the baked beans. There's a deep bowl of fruit salad for dessert. As soon as I place it on the checkered cloth of the patio table, a bee begins to figure-eight above it. Sam tries to swat it away from the table. "Come on, buddy," he murmurs. Jeremy grabs a magazine from the deck, rolls it up, and slams the bee against a deck railing. "You've got a real bee problem here," he says.

When Jeremy and Shana break up that summer, Sam's parents decide to have a party in their backyard. "I guess they didn't like her, either," I say to Sam on the drive out. "Hush," he says, putting his hand on my knee. "Jeremy liked her. Mom's just trying to cheer him up."

And celebrate that he's back in his old room, where model airplanes still hang by fishing line from the ceiling. The house where nothing changes.

But I'm wrong there. The backyard is lit with shining copper lanterns that I've never seen. I count backward in my head to Memorial Day; we haven't been out to their house in three months. The lanterns will be the way she reminds me.

"When am I going to find a girl like you?" Jeremy asks, poking burgers on the grill as if he means to hurt them. He might have used a different tone, joking, once, but now he is serious. I don't know what to say. I don't think he wants an answer. I don't think he wants a girl like me.

Sam stays to console him. Inside, the women are at work: casseroles, pitchers of mixed drinks, vegetable platters. "Jolie, there you are," Sam's mother cries. She always likes me better when her friends are watching. I recognize a few of them from our wedding, silver- and golden-haired women who wear *outfits*, little plaid pants and sweater sets. They flutter over my arrival like pigeons over breadcrumbs. Sam's mother says, "I've saved a special assignment for you. You brought the whipping cream? It's for the trifle."

Trifle. It's a good name—trifle, just a little bit. The Midwestern potluck dessert so rich that you don't want more than a trifle. The sort of over-the-top recipe I wouldn't normally trifle *with*. Her friends are all listening, up to their knuckles in cold ground beef and seven-layer salad. "Sure," I say. Someone else will have baked the cake and let it cool, perhaps even soaked it in sherry or pineapple juice. I can open cans of fruit in heavy syrup and jars of cocktail cherries. I can dump custard and jelly and every sweet thing I can find on top of the cake and be back outside with Sam in ten minutes. Whip the cream, ladle it on. Fifteen.

Sam's mother places the glass pedestal dish in front of me. The cake is cool, soaked, and already covered in a layer of pineapple rings.

"You remember where everything is? It's been *a while*."

Ah, there it is, I think, heading for the pantry. I've stolen her son away and now I keep him prisoner in his own home. In the pantry, I shake my head clear, find the cherries and cans of fruit cocktail. I find a jar of lemon curd—a contribution we'd brought to brunch one Sunday that has never been touched. I resolve to make a trifle not soon forgotten. I will pour sugar into this trifle until no one can think my name again without thinking *sweet*. Back in the kitchen, Sam's mother and her friends are done with their chores, sipping wine spritzers and watching Sam's aunt Meg patting hamburgers. "I just buy those pre-patty ones," one of them says, as though she has solved a real problem.

"I wish you'd come out the other night, Jolie," Sam's mother says. "Jeremy was in a bad spot."

The other women turn to look at me.

"Sam had to work early the next morning. You know how tiring that drive is." I've got her; she's always complaining about the drive. I'm only agreeing with her. In fact we hadn't gone to the hills to see Jeremy after the breakup because it had been a long, strange day where we were. That morning Sam had left for work in the middle of an argument—over what, I couldn't even remember—and then around three, I'd developed serious cramps. We'd been trying to get pregnant for a few months, but the cramps told me all I needed to know. One more month with no luck, but Sam's mother didn't know any of this. And then, as we had picked at our dinners, a siren wailed into the neighborhood and up the street until there were lights rolling across our wall. "It's next door," Sam said, coming back to the table. "The old guy, I bet." I went to the door and peered out the window until the gurney was eased down the sidewalk to the open door of the ambulance. The man lay with his eyes closed, his still-black hair stark against his ashen face. A week. He hadn't come back yet, and we hadn't seen the wife or the son. The rice in the basketball is there, hopeful, but the son's big truck is missing. Our wide-open view of the street seems vast, unnatural.

My trifle is an architectural wonder. I layer the fruit, the lemon curd, the custard, layer, layer, layer. Sam's mother comes over to check my progress and can't seem to find a flaw.

"Well," she says. "It still would have been nice if you'd made it out to see him."

"Yes," I say, because the other women are pretending not to listen. "It would have been." I lick the custard spoon.

Jeremy and Shana elope just before Thanksgiving. To cheer his mother, Sam tells her we are trying for a baby. He doesn't tell her how long we've been trying. She is so pleased we can have anything we want, so we ask his parents to come to Christmas Eve at our house. They arrive on our doorstep, their faces ruddy pink and their arms loaded with presents and a large, round dish of trifle.

"It won't be as good as yours," Sam's mother says, giving my cheek a kiss. Her lips are cool, almost minty. I know she could have brought the trifle to show me how I ruined the one at her house this summer. I did. But I am warm and benevolent. I am pregnant. Just barely—I haven't even told Sam. Every time I think about the baby, a nervous trill runs through my stomach and I think, *This is it*, and wait for the cramps again. A part of me wants to keep the news from Sam. Until it's safe. I'm superstitious about it. If I keep the baby safe until noon. If I make this green light. If I can be nice to his mother for the next four hours.

We have a lush dinner, Sam's mother complimentary of my mashed potatoes to the point of ridiculousness. We eat dainty portions of the trifle by candlelight. It's a Christmas trifle: cake soaked in a sweet, milky liqueur, and instead of fruit, chocolate. Hot fudge, cinnamon Santa cookies, and a drizzle of caramel across the top. It is much better than anything I have ever created. Yet.

We move to the front room to stare at the fireplace and the tree and to open presents. I have braced myself for another granny nightgown—it turns out a friend of the family makes them—but Sam's mother hands me a small box. Inside is a framed black-and-white photo, a candid of Sam as a baby, cradled in his mother's lap. I study his chubby baby fingers, look for the dimple in his left cheek. She's wearing a sleeveless dress, really charming, and the arm around Sam is fierce. I stare at them both as though they are not mere inches from me. I miss this baby. I never knew him, but I miss him. I feel the physical desire for this baby in my arms and reach out to show Sam the photo. "Aw," he says. "I was cute." Even in the heat of Sam's nearness, I am cold with fear. Mourning his loss even as his hip slides against mine. Mourning the baby that I still carry more in my heart than in my body. He is already gone. He does not belong to me. Someday he will grow up and leave me, and I know that I might die from it. "I love it," I say, and cannot think of another word. I understand the gift—all the gifts—this woman has given me. "I love it."

Sam and his dad sit down with coffee, but I refuse a cup. His mother watches me with bright eyes. She won't hear of me doing dishes. "But," I say, "I will have a *trifle* more dessert."

"You will?" She brings me a tureen of it, full, fresh whipped cream on top. I spoon some into my mouth. One bite for me, one for baby.

Out the front window, I see that it has started to snow again. I stand and eat my dessert by the tree.

"Didn't see your neighbor's big truck out front," Sam's dad says.

"He works nights now," Sam says. It is enough for his dad, who doesn't think to ask, Even on Christmas eve?

"His father is very sick," I say. "In the hospital."

"Oh?"

This is all I know. We've seen the neighbor's son get into his truck and leave every evening for months. His newfound resolve must be keeping his mother in her home and his father in the ICU. We still don't know their names or if they are Chinese. I'm shamed by how little I know, how incurious I've been, and not just about them. We still don't know anything about them but what they put in their yard.

I press my face to the window and shade my eyes from the glare of the tree lights. There it is. The deflated basketball is still by the curb. For a moment I don't notice, and then: Empty. The bowl of the ball is filling with snow. No rice. No sticky, rotting mandarin oranges or pineapple rings. I don't know what this means. I don't like it.

"I'll be right back," I say, slipping into my boots.

Sam looks over at me, frowning. "Are you crazy?"

"Just a minute." Snow swirls in when I swing open the door. I pull it closed again and walk back toward the couch.

"I told you," he says, smiling.

"Merry *Christmas*," I say, smiling back. I grab my trifle and spoon.

Outside the wind rushes up from the cold ground. Snow pellets land harsh across my face. I leave man-sized footprints across my lawn and into the neighbor's, and turn back to enjoy them and my house, the windows filled with tree lights. The neighbor's house is dark except for a quiet orange circle of light in a window upstairs.

I crouch down, grab the basketball, and shake loose the snow. I have to form it back into a bowl. For a moment I'm uncertain. This is a religious rite, but not my own. Surely it is selfish to bribe someone else's gods. But, I think, turning back to the orange circle of light in the neighbor's window, not everything I want is for me. Shaking snow from the ball again, I begin to think of spring, when my neighbor's flowering tree would bloom, and of how every morning when her son comes home from work, she meets him at the door and draws him in with her reedy arm. I think about holding our children tightly, and start to spoon trifle into the basketball's wide mouth.

DECEMBER BARNS OF DARKNESS

George Kalamaras

Sometimes there's a barn, in Fulton County,
in Tippecanoe. Down near Bloomington
or Boonville. Sometimes it's Christmas
or New Year's, or somewhere in between.
Snow, say, may pile up in our ears,
between neighboring mouths, as the space between
trees diminishes. Let's say there's a fireplace
burning slow cherry wood
for the holiday. The roads have been salted.
In the world of ground smoke and foggy breath-
blossom, no one is better than anyone else.

The barn needs repair. As does the springhouse.
The smokehouse. As you work on it, you realize
each hammer stroke is a way to fix
what is loose inside you. Still,
there is wind. *Still* wind. After all-night
drifting snow. And the cold that blows doesn't
blow but hangs there getting colder. It's Christmas
after all, you realize, because you are both
happy and sad at the same time.

You couldn't live, you are certain, without your hound dog.
Your mother left the body in June, and now you feel,
full-force. For sixty-two Christmases
you've always had a mother. You draw closer

to the fire, remembering the red-tailed hawk
that startled you just yards in front of your moving car
the exact hour your mother and her red hair
were cremated. There is order
in the blackbird's crawl across snow.
In the starling's strut. Lord knows the fur of your dog
is asking for wind, weathering the wind's ache
and all the primordial moanings of the mouth.

So the barns of Allen County suggest
a life. Loaded with animal debt
and oats. In this sliver
of northeast Indiana. They sit on the horizon, rising
and falling with snow. This is the way
Christmas glows and quiets the embers
that refuse to die. The way the solstice
darkness suggests light. The way we turn
from or toward one another and decide a life.

Your hound dog—yes—sleeps near the fire,
sipping warmth into its bones. Even as it dreams
of crushing hollow bird bones in a field
of cornstalk skeletons and evening mist.
Even as the snow crawls down from the hills,
speckling the starlings' dark. Even
as Christmas arrives just as it leaves us.

IN SUNSET AND MOONLIGHT, WHAT GATHERED OUR THOUGHTS WAS THE ADHESIVE DARK

George Kalamaras

CALL IT PIKE COUNTY. CALL IT CROTHERSVILLE. Call it Auburn or Fort Wayne, Indiana. Whether inside the moon or out, hound dogs crawl down the freshly fallen snow hills into a season of the darkest dark. The most moist light.

Say there were two ways to celebrate Christmas, as the yogi had said: the social one and the spiritual. Let's add one more and embrace a bawl-mouthed hound as a third.

What if I told you Edwin Way Teale was alive again and coming to my house for the holiday? That he'd sit by the fire and write yet another great book about the animal in things. What if he left the Port Aransas breakwater and brought *a brown pelican released from a fishhook embedded in the skin of its pouch*? Would we eat turkey or focus, instead, on the green bean casserole topped with crispy onions?

In sunset and moonlight, how many snowflakes did we see in the adhesive dark? Open the mouth of the hound and let yourself melt in just moments upon the lolling tongue.

The year passed, and we forgot all about the bitter wind. The way Halloween was just a short drive back there near our masked selves. How easily our mouths took to Thanksgiving and firelight and Chinese oolong tea. Was Christmas the holiday for which we'd waited all this time, or was it time itself we had wanted to flee, to feel slip away at the height of the winter solstice?

I drove from my home in Fort Wayne to Middlebury just to see the farmhouses rise out of the darkness like great lost animals fiercing the winter sky, the lights of Christmas unlit but worshipped here in Amish country in the flickering of a kerosene lamp.

When I think of Christmas, I think of a good Indiana hound asleep by the wood-stove, the iron belly of the stove holding the entire year before us, the hound dog's snout twitching in sleep as if time was not leaving us but was only yards ahead on the trail.

NANNY ANNE AND THE CHRISTMAS STORY

Karen Joy Fowler

RAIN LASHED THE HOUSE. FIONA HEARD IT, drumming on the roof and rushing through the gutters. A handful of drops hit the window so hard the glass shook. A sudden sheet of light, and there were the black trees at the end of the yard, their branches bare and tossing wildly about. Underneath the window, in the other bed, Dacey was crying, great gulps of agony because the thunder was scaring her and she couldn't find Moe Bear. Could there be any two twins so different from each other? Fiona's knees were bent, the covers tented, so that no one would see the lump that was Moe Bear under her legs.

She wasn't the only one taking things that didn't belong to her. Nanny Anne was wearing their mother's locket. The pendant was hidden under her bulky sweater, but she was kneeling now, looking under Dacey's bed, and Fiona could see the distinctive chain around the white back of her neck. When the time was right, Fiona would return Moe Bear, pretending to have just found him, saving the day. Fiona loved to save the day. She did it a lot. What was Nanny Anne's plan? No one was looking for her mother's locket.

"Nanny Anne is what makes it all work," Fiona's mother often said. Fiona and Dacey's parents were very particular about who took care of their children. "There's an old soul in that young body. I never worry for a minute. And she's got a playful nature. The girls adore her."

"We never planned on twins!" Fiona's father always said.

But sometimes women asked Fiona's mother if she didn't worry just a bit to have such a beautiful young woman in the house. At eight years old, Fiona was already very good at hearing what she wasn't supposed to hear.

Fiona's mother and father had both gone off to a conference to give a paper they had written together and they were both supposed to be home in plenty of time for Christmas. But yesterday their flight had been canceled and they hadn't been able to book another. Yesterday they'd called and they'd still promised to be home for Christmas, but now Fiona had her doubts. "Let me talk to Nanny Anne," Fiona's mother had said, and Fiona wanted to tell them that she didn't adore Nanny Anne anymore, that something was going on with Nanny Anne, but Nanny Anne took the phone away, so she couldn't.

Now Nanny Anne sat in the big chair between the beds. The light from the lamp fell on one side of her face, turning her hair from black to gold, making her eyes shine. She was giving up on finding Moe Bear and Dacey was slowly giving up on sobbing about it.

"Once upon a time," said Nanny Anne.

Fiona's mother and father read to them at night, *Frog and Toad* and *Mary Poppins* and *Amelia Bedelia*, but Nanny Anne said she was tired of those same old stories and would tell them some new ones. Thunder made the lights all flicker and Nanny Anne's voice was a little flickery, too. She was using the voice she used when she talked to Dacey.

"Make it a true story," Dacey said gamely. She was still sniffling and gulping.

"Once upon a time, in this very house."

"With no rain," said Dacey.

"Once upon a winter's day, it snowed and snowed and snowed," said Nanny Anne. "The cats, they huddled by the fire, the wind it fiercesome blowed."

"No wind either," said Dacey. "No storms."

"But this was just a little storm. A strange and little storm. It didn't snow in the town or the school you go to or the park you play in. The only place it snowed was right here, on this house and the yard right here and the little stand of woods behind. The rest of the town didn't even know it was snowing.

"But right here," said Nanny Anne, "the snow came all the way up to the nursery sill." She pointed to the window by Dacey's bed and the shadow of her hand swept across the wall.

"This isn't a nursery," said Fiona.

"Once upon a time it was.

"With a cradle gently rocking and a baby soundly sleeping and the snow it softly falling and the woods a silence keeping."

"Was the baby a boy or a girl?" Dacey asked.

"A girl. With a little wisp of brownish hair and long, dark eyelashes and tiny fingers. Her mother and father had waited a long time to have a baby, waited and wished and wished and waited."

One day a man in a knitted cap with a point like an acorn came out of the woods with a cradle to sell. He'd said he'd carved it himself, all from one block of oak, and it looked like a leaf and it rocked like a boat and he said that if they bought it, it would fill itself. It was a magic cradle. He asked for a lot of money for that cradle.

The mother told him to go away, her heart was that broken, she'd given up. Anyway, she knew they didn't have so much money. But the father followed the man into the woods and offered him the money they did have. And the man took that money and gave him the cradle. The father took it home and he didn't tell the mother what the man had said, that because the money was short, there'd be an owing later.

Soon even he forgot about it, because all the wishing came true and one day there was a baby. They had never been so happy.

"The end," Dacey suggested. Sometimes even *Frog and Toad* was too much for Dacey. There were lots and lots of parts of *Mary Poppins* that had to be cut. Fiona imagined that she herself would like those parts best of all if she ever got to hear them.

Nanny Anne paused.

"Keep going," Fiona told her and when Dacey didn't protest, Nanny Anne continued. But she switched over to the voice she used for Fiona, which was not so flickery. Before Fiona's mother and father had left for their conference, she'd had the same voice for both of them.

The baby was only six days old, when the mother and the father woke in the morning, surprised to have slept so long. They hurried to the nursery where the bedroom window was open with the wind whipping the curtains and the cradle full of snow. And then the father remembered the owing.

They fell to their knees and they dug with their hands, finding each other's fingers so they kept thinking the baby was buried there. But she wasn't. And their first thought was to be relieved.

And their second thought was to be afraid. They looked outside and they could see a shallow indent of footprints leading up to the window and away again into the woods.

They ran outside in their nightclothes. The snow fell on their hair and their faces and into their slippers; it came down fast and it filled in all the footprints, including their own, erased them as if they had never been. They never saw trace of the baby or the person who took her.

Deer and squirrel, fox and crow, left their prints atop the snow. Drifts came down, wind did blow, gone the prints atop the snow.

Dacey drew in a long, shuddering breath and Nanny Anne paused again. But Dacey didn't speak and Nanny Anne went on. "The police came and they looked, too, and never saw trace, so they didn't believe in this person who had come and taken the baby. They thought that someone in the house, either the mother or the father, had killed the baby and hidden her body."

"I don't want this story!" Dacey's voice was filled with panic. She was the one with the bed by the window.

"The baby isn't dead," Fiona told her impatiently. "The police just think that."

Dacey was crying again, even louder this time. "I want Moe Bear."

"Is this the end of the story?" Nanny Anne asked.

"No," said Fiona.

"Yes," said Dacey. "Please."

And because Dacey said please and Fiona didn't, Nanny Anne stopped telling it. She stood and came and kissed them, first Dacey and then Fiona, on the forehead. She smelled of their mother's perfume, lily of the valley.

"Sleep tight, Dacey. Sweet dreams, Fifi," she told them. Fiona's mother was the only one who called her Fifi. Fiona's father hated it. He said it was a name for a dog and a poodly-sort of dog at that. They both called Dacey "Dacey" or rarely "Oopsa" for Oopsa Dacey. Nobody called his dog Oopsa.

Nanny Anne had gone, shutting the door. Fiona could still feel the mark of her lips. The door always made a shushing sound as it scraped the rug, but the rain was too loud for Fiona to hear it. Right away, Dacey came and got in bed with her. Her feet were cold and her toenails scratchy. Fiona gave her Moe Bear since she was about to find him anyway. "I won't tell," she said. Dacey was the sort of girl who never told. Fiona was a different sort of girl.

The herb garden under the window, the one with the dead rosemary in it, was a pudding of mud and water. Fiona and Dacey went into the kitchen and Nanny Anne was already up, had already eaten.

"Today is a let's-pretend day," Nanny Anne told them. "Today, let's pretend I'm your mommy. I'll make you French toast just the way she does."

"I don't want to pretend that," Fiona told her.

Nanny Anne was pinning up her hair the way Fiona's mother did when she was going out. Fiona would have thought Nanny Anne's hair was too short to be pinned up like that. "Don't be silly, Fifi," Nanny Anne said. "It's just a game. It's not like you won't know the difference."

"I'll play," said Dacey. And sometimes, as the day went on, she remembered and called Nanny Anne Mommy and sometimes she forgot. They finished breakfast and got dressed and brushed their teeth. Nanny Anne played cards with them, Spit and Fish and Slap Down, which took five decks. Dacey sat in Nanny Anne's lap while they watched "Come-Again Mulligan" on television.

Their real mother called in the afternoon, but Fiona had her earbuds in, listening to music, and she didn't hear it. Nanny Anne didn't tell Fiona until later. "No plane yet," Nanny Anne said.

Fiona went upstairs and hid in her mother's closet, way in the back where the laundry hamper was. She cried a little because she hadn't gotten to talk with her mother and she was more and more sure they would be spending Christmas with only Nanny Anne. She found two sticker books under her mother's sweaters, sticker books that were probably presents for her and Dacey. She picked the one with jungle animals, and began to do it. The tiger went in the grasses. The giraffe in the trees. She fell asleep.

She woke up when Nanny Anne opened the closet door. Fiona had a strange feeling, as if she were doing something wrong and didn't want to get caught at it. She held as still as she could while Nanny Anne took a pair of her mother's shoes from the shoe rack and put them on her own feet. She put them back and tried another pair. She settled finally on Mother's silver ballet flats. Nanny Anne put her own shoes in their place on the shoe rack, closed the door and went away. Fiona's mother's feet were larger than Nanny Anne's. Fiona had walked around the house in both their shoes on many occasions, so she knew this.

She waited until the room was quiet and then she pushed open the door to her mother's closet. She saw Nanny Anne's shoes on the shoe rack and she took them down, hid them behind the little yellow curtain on her mother's vanity table. She went back downstairs, into the kitchen where Dacey and Nanny Anne were making cookies shaped like stars, decorating them with colored balls and sprinkles of sugar. "What have you been up to?" Nanny Anne asked her.

"Nothing." Fiona climbed up on a chair beside Dacey. It was very easy to tell which cookies Dacey had decorated and which ones were Nanny Anne's. She looked down at Nanny Anne's feet. "You shouldn't be wearing Mommy's shoes," she said.

"It's just to help with the game," said Nanny Anne.

"We won't tell," said Dacey.

The kitchen was warm and smelled of the baking. The sound of the rain was soft, windless. For just a moment, Fiona could see how it was almost like having her mother home. Only not. She climbed down and went to her room to finish her sticker book. As soon as her mother came back, she was absolutely telling on Nanny Anne.

That night they decorated the tree without Mommy and Daddy, but Nanny Anne said they'd told her to go ahead without them. Dacey fell asleep on the couch and Nanny Anne covered her with the knitted afghan. The Christmas lights bubbled and blinked and turned one wall and the photo on that wall, the photo of Dacey and Fiona when they were littler girls, red and then green and then white. Fiona sat on the floor and watched this. She had a horrible, abandoned feeling inside. Mostly sad, but a bit of outrage, too, that she should be made to be sad at Christmastime. "I'm afraid Mommy won't be home for Christmas," she said. She'd lost track of how many days were left. She'd lost track of how many times she'd said this. Rain on the roof. Wind in the trees.

"Don't be silly. She wouldn't miss it." Nanny Anne smiled and Fiona saw the tips of her teeth. She had come downstairs wearing their mother's party dress, the black one with leg slits and a heart-shaped bodice. The pendant to their mother's locket was now settled in the crease between Nanny Anne's breasts. The dress was just a little large for Nanny Anne so the straps kept falling off her shoulders.

"I could tell you the end of the story," Nanny Anne offered. "The part Dacey didn't want to hear," and Fiona knew she should say no, but Nanny Anne looked so pretty now she was all dressed up, so much like a princess in a movie, that no words came out of Fiona's mouth. The colored lights continued to stroke sleepily across the wall, across the faces of little Fiona and little Dacey.

"For two days after the baby had gone, the police kept coming back," said Nanny Anne, "and they tore the house apart, looking for the baby's body.

They emptied out the closets and they pulled the wood from the walls in the basement. And all the while, the cradle sat empty in the nursery. The father felt so guilty over the owing—that he'd agreed to it, that he'd concealed it from the mother. The police saw that guilt and it made them think he was the one had killed the baby.

But on the third day, a policeman was dusting for the prints on the nursery windowsill when he noticed that the cradle was rocking. He leaned over it and there was the baby, just waking up, stretching and yawning and looking at him with her infant-blue eyes.

He took her to the parents' bedroom where the father was weeping and the mother was wondering if it was possible she had married a man who would kill his own child. But when the policeman tried to hand her the baby, she screamed. She said that it wasn't her baby. Everyone wondered at that, because the baby looked exactly like her baby.

Eyes the same, same the hair, child of flesh, and child of air.

They all thought that grief and doubt had made her a little crazy. The father told her to nurse the baby, thinking that would bring her back to her right mind. Her breasts were so painful it wasn't hard to convince her. She opened her soggy blouse and gave the baby her breast. And all the while she said, this isn't my baby, this isn't my baby. This baby didn't smell right, didn't suck right. But she went on nursing and it did seem to calm her down.

When she had finished with one breast and was about to offer the other, a second policeman came into the room, carrying a second baby. He said he'd heard her crying in the nursery and gone in. The magic cradle had filled again. And this time the mother reached out, weeping with joy, because this one, she said, this one was her own little girl. The two girls were identical, one a perfect copy of the other.

Only the father said he couldn't be sure which was which and so the police went away and left them both babies. They couldn't figure out what to charge the parents with; there was no law against producing two babies where there should only have been one. And so they went away.

And the father and mother raised the two girls as if they were sisters. That was the owing the father had agreed to, though he didn't know it at the time. The owing was to raise the second child as if she were their own.

"And they lived happily ever after," said Nanny Anne, switching suddenly to her Dacey voice. Dacey had woken, was sitting up.

"And they lived happily ever after," she repeated sleepily.

"Let's get you to bed," said Nanny Anne. She picked Dacey up and took her to the bedroom, Dacey's arms and legs loose and flopping, as she was only half awake and almost too big for Nanny Anne to carry. Fiona followed behind, because Nanny Anne had Dacey. Fiona's feelings were all an unhappy blur, except for this sharp one—that she didn't want to be alone with Nanny Anne and she didn't want Dacey to be alone with Nanny Anne either.

"You *said* a true story," Fiona reminded her. It was her last hope, that Nanny Anne would admit she'd made the whole thing up.

"I did say that," Nanny Anne agreed. "Under the covers now, Fifi, and straight to dreamland." She leaned down, kissed Fiona on the forehead the way she always did at bedtime.

"Which one was the real child?" Fiona asked, knowing she wouldn't like the answer, whatever it was.

Nanny Anne turned the light off so Fiona couldn't see her face. "The real child was the one her mother has always loved best, of course." She moved in the dark like a shadow, back to Dacey's bed where she kissed her, too.

Dacey wasn't awake, but she wasn't asleep either. "Good night, Mommy," Dacey said.

Fiona woke up sometime later and it seemed to her that she could hear Nanny Anne singing even though Nanny Anne wasn't in the room. The rain came hard and the singing was soft. Fiona had to strain to hear it and even so words were lost. It was something about dreaming and something about the woods. It was something about a mother's love and a cradle and the snow. It was a lullaby that woke Fiona up. Or else it was another of those things Fiona wasn't supposed to hear.

Or else Fiona didn't wake up. Maybe she only dreamed this part. She had another dream that the window was open. It rained on Dacey and then grass grew under her on her bed and she was lying in a meadow with a cat curled under her arm. And then the grass grew over Dacey and Fiona couldn't see her anymore and she was frightened and calling for Dacey to come back.

When she woke up next, her head was in her mother's lap on the living room couch and it was early morning. The lights on the tree had all been turned off.

"I told you I'd be home for Christmas," her mother said and Fiona felt a rush of relief. She smelled her mother's lily of the valley perfume.

"When did you get here?"

"A few hours ago. You don't remember, but I went in and kissed you. And then you had a bad dream," her mother said. "You were so frightened. So we came down here to see the tree and you fell asleep again. Do you remember that part?"

Fiona didn't. She rested her cheek on her mother's terry-cloth bathrobe. She felt the nubs of the fabric, bumpy against her face. She started to tell on Nanny Anne. But before she spoke, something twisted the words back inside her. "Where's Daddy?"

"He'll be home later, maybe tonight, maybe tomorrow. I couldn't wait to see you so I took the only seat." I couldn't wait to see you and Dacey, is what her mother should have said, but didn't.

Fiona had a horrible feeling that if she lifted the hem of her mother's bathrobe, the black party dress would be underneath.

She was too frightened to do it. Instead she got up, carefully, and slower than she wanted. "I didn't hear you come home."

"No. You were a-roaming dreamland. Are you ready for breakfast? I'll make French toast."

Fiona followed her into the kitchen, and then, when her back was turned, went on through the kitchen and into the mudroom. She took Dacey's coat and Dacey's boots because they were the closest and put them on as quietly as she could, listening to the sounds of the skillet coming out of the cupboard, the eggs and milk from the refrigerator, the knife from the butcher's block.

When she was dressed, she ran out into the rain, which came in slanted under Dacey's hood and pelted her face and her hair. The door banged behind her.

"What are you doing?" her mother shouted. "Where are you going?" She stood on the porch under the eaves, her bathrobe tightly wrapped around her. "Fifi! Come back inside! You'll catch your death!"

Fiona turned back to look at her. She wiped the rain from her eyes with her dripping hands. Her mother looked exactly like her mother.

And then she ran for the trees, each step making its own squelching sound, some of the puddles so deep they splashed into Dacey's boots, turned Fiona's toes to ice. It was less wet, but more treacherous underfoot once she made the woods. She kept running, but she wasn't running away exactly. She wasn't thinking that she would never go back, that she would leave Dacey or miss Christmas. She just needed to see if it was a little storm, a strange and little storm. She needed to know if she could run to where it wasn't raining.

BLESSED RANCOR OF MUSIC

Curtis L. Crisler

—inspired by Cindy Cradler's #10 painting

The strings strummed in overture of Tchaikovsky
         plants dreams where a small child in me finds flight,
& fights for Decembers in a small house in Gary's

      suburb. How many houses since then have I lived
in? How many tapes & CDs have I bought to
        take me into a Russian man's mind of a ballerina's

perfect gift, one that protects her from danger?
      How those dangers get twisted up when in real life,
where we want to protect children from them, like how

        by the assimilation of the dance of the sugarplums
& the Arabian soldiers will save a child. A cold
      brings chill, makes me readjust under Mama's quilt.

I have traveled to worlds, to other children's dreams,
        in my drowsiness. I hear Nat King Cole singing
"tiny tots with their eyes all aglow," & hear that

      connection to us all, know too how a song from
one man belongs to many. Now the chubby-jawed
        jazz man, Mel Tormé, waves to me, along with

Ebenezer & Rudolph & Ralphie. They're things
        in my drowsiness—how I got here. The music
snuggles me into slumber. The tree's manipulation

                with lights. A decorative soldier, positioned
around strings of rainbow bulbs & garland, winks to
        me under blurried cacophony of family voices, as

I pursue a nap on the couch in the home my mother
                bought back in the 70s. How the home can save us
from what flurries life. How devout the beauty of voices

        that clamor with the smells of coming back.
I own the noise, that heartbeat reverberating against the body
                of the couch. That head space, & all its children.

WEALTH

Scott Russell Sanders

ONCE, NOT LONG AGO, THERE WAS A jack-of-all-trades named Gordon Milk who lived with his wife, their four children, and three grandparents in a city tucked away in the southern Indiana hills. Their old house, which fell apart as fast as Gordon could fix it, was packed with souls from foundation to rafters. Gordon slept in the basement with his wife, whose name was Mabel. His mother slept in a room he had tacked on beside the kitchen, and Mabel's parents slept in a room tacked on to the garage. The two daughters, prone to squabbling, occupied separate bedrooms on the second floor, while the two sons, far enough apart in age to avoid fighting, shared bunk beds in the attic.

They weren't exactly poor, since they never went hungry, but they also rarely had any spare dimes to rub together. Each month Mabel's parents received a tiny Social Security check, which they used to order surefire cures for old age from ads in the back pages of magazines. Gordon's mother drew an even tinier pension from the owner of a quarry where his father had been crushed by a slab of limestone. She spent much of her money on lottery tickets, without any luck. The older children worked odd jobs after school, but the few dollars they brought in went for clothes, music, and electronic gadgets. Mabel had her hands full running the household. That left Gordon to earn enough cash to keep food on the table and a roof over their heads. Most of the year, they managed to scrape by on his wages from working on the city maintenance crew.

But now here it was, less than two weeks before Christmas, and the Milk household was flat broke. Gordon learned this fact at bedtime on Friday from Mabel, who kept the checkbook. She often delivered bad news during the brief interval between when Gordon's head hit the pillow and when he began to snore, since it offered a rare chance to unload her worries without other ears listening in.

On Friday evenings, after a week of patching up streets and sewer pipes and other crumbling parts of the city, Gordon felt as if he had been pounded head to foot with a hammer. Sleep was the only relief. "Let's dip into savings," he suggested drowsily.

"We've already dipped in for Veronica's braces and Granny's new hip," Mabel reminded him. "There's zero in savings, and seven dollars in checking."

Gordon forced his eyes open and squinted into the glow of the reading lamp over Mabel's side of the bed. "Can't we borrow against my pension?"

"We borrowed up to the limit for Jeanne's tuition, and Lord knows how we'll pay for her next two years."

Giving up on sleep, Gordon started thinking about money, his least favorite subject. His paychecks never quite covered the family's expenses. In the warmer months he earned extra bucks in the evenings and on weekends by painting houses, cleaning gutters, laying bricks, or trimming trees. In winter, it was too dark to work outdoors in the evening, and on weekends about all he could do was shovel snow. But recent winters had been so warm, they brought little snow, and what little they brought soon melted. So far this year, midway through December, not a flake had fallen in southern Indiana.

"You could murder me and collect the insurance," he said.

"I thought of that," Mabel said. "But the cops would catch me and send me to prison. Then who'd look after the kids and the grandparents?"

"I figured you'd have the perfect crime scoped out, with all the mysteries you read."

It was true that Mabel had a taste for novels featuring blood and corpses on their covers. Her current bedtime book was called *Yuletide Gore*. Nobody in the story had been murdered yet, but there was one likely suspect—a glamorous, red-haired woman who played the piano and feigned holiday cheer but was clearly up to no good.

"Even if I could get away with it," Mabel said, "we'd spend all the insurance money on your funeral. No, no. I've invested too many years in civilizing you. I don't have the patience to train a new husband." She cuddled against him and twirled a finger in his chest hair, which was as wiry as steel wool. "Besides," she said, "I like having you around, even if we're broke."

Gordon laid his hand on top of hers, a weight as rough as a cheese grater. "We could skip presents this year," he said. "The kids have got too much stuff already."

"I'm not even thinking about presents. I'm thinking about groceries. I wanted to stock up before the blizzard, but I knew the next check would bounce."

"There's a blizzard coming?"

"A foot or more by morning."

A grin split Gordon's black beard. "Then ease your mind, sweetums. We'll be flush again by tomorrow night."

When his wheezing turned to snores, Mabel slid her hand out from under his callused paw and resumed reading *Yuletide Gore*. The next suspect to enter the story was a rugged guy with a booming voice and killer good looks. He played the guitar and claimed to be a folk singer, but Mabel could tell he was something less wholesome—a junk bond salesman, maybe, or an actor.

Sure enough, by dawn on Saturday, when Gordon opened the garage door to step outside, the snow reached nearly to the top of his sixteen-inch rubber boots. The storm had blown past, and the eastern sky was robin's-egg blue. His cheeks stung with cold. There would be no melting today. He should be able to earn a couple hundred bucks by nightfall, enough to fill the fridge and buy a few presents.

Without waiting for breakfast, he gassed up the snowblower. The machine had been a rusted hulk when he and his youngest child, Danny, had salvaged it from the town dump the previous summer. Since then, Gordon had overhauled it piece by piece—rebuilding the engine, replacing the drive chain and auger, greasing the gears, painting the chassis fire-engine red—and now the juiced-up contraption gleamed.

Eager to see how it would perform in its first real test, he put on ear protectors, cranked the engine, set the augur spinning, and went roaring down the driveway, clearing a swathe three feet wide. Snow streamed from the chute, light as feathers, forming a white veil as it fell to one side of his path. He continued on across the street to clear the front walk and driveway of the house belonging to Mrs. Westover, a retired librarian whose husband had recently died. When she appeared at the door holding her purse and waving at him, Gordon realized he couldn't accept money from a widow, so he waved back and chugged along the sidewalk.

He decided to clear snow for the other neighborhood widows first, and then he would move on to paying customers. So he proceeded to the home of Mrs. Hernandez, who flicked her Christmas tree lights off and on by way of thanks; then to the home of Mrs. McEwen, who blew him a kiss; and then to three other houses, always hurrying away before any of the women could offer him money.

Meanwhile, at her post in the kitchen, Mabel stole a few minutes between chores to read *Yuletide Gore*. Still no corpses, but a third suspect had appeared—a soft-spoken man who claimed to be a Quaker pastor, a champion of peace and kindness—surely one of the phoniest disguises she had ever come across in a mystery novel.

Thoughts of Gordon, out there in the cold earning money for the family, prompted her to close the book. She packed his lunch bucket with all the treats her depleted refrigerator and pantry could supply, and then she enlisted Danny to deliver it.

Gordon was finishing up the sidewalk for the last of the neighborhood widows when Danny came hustling along lugging the lunch bucket.

"Mom says you've got to eat, 'cause you're keeping bread on our table," Danny said.

While Gordon wolfed down an egg sandwich, a bagel with cream cheese, dill pickles, Vienna sausages, and a handful of chocolate chip cookies, Danny looked over the idling machine. "Can I drive it?" he asked.

"Sure, but only if you wear these." Gordon removed his orange earmuffs and clamped them down on Danny's black knit cap.

"I bet I look like a bug," Danny said, patting his head. "But what'll you wear?"

"My hearing's already ruined. I want to save yours."

With Danny walking between the handles, clinging to the rubber grips, and Gordon walking behind to guide the machine, they cleared snow at the house of the man who had taught all four Milk children in kindergarten, and naturally such a man could not be asked to pay, nor could the couple down the block who were expecting their first baby any day now, nor could the hairdresser whose daughter had leukemia, nor could the machinist who had lost his job, nor could the minister with the broken leg.

In fact, although the two of them kept plowing until sunset, Gordon couldn't bring himself to accept money from anyone, not even from strangers who came outside waving greenbacks and shouting thanks.

As they headed home, both encrusted in snow, Danny asked, "Where's the bread?"

"What bread?"

"For our table. Like Mom said."

Gordon was trying to think of an answer when Mrs. Westover toddled up, wearing her late husband's camouflage hunting coat and carrying a bundle wrapped in a pink dishtowel. "It's whole wheat," she said, "just out of the oven."

Gordon took off his gloves to accept the bundle, which was still warm. Mrs. Westover patted his cheek, patted Danny's head, and then toddled away.

"So here's the bread," Danny said.

"I guess so," Gordon said, handing him the bundle. "Now run on home and give it to Mom. Tell her I'll be along for supper as fast as this old machine and my old legs can go."

When Danny burst into the kitchen, shedding snow on her freshly scrubbed floor, blurted his message, plopped the bread on the counter, and then rushed back outside, Mabel looked up in a daze from *Yuletide Gore*. To her disappointment, there were still no dead bodies, but a likely victim had just turned up. He was a retired English professor who wrote satirical sketches about the three suspects and kept correcting their grammar, giving each of them ample motive to bump him off. She would have to wait until bedtime to discover who did him in.

She set Mrs. Westover's gift on the kitchen table beside those that had already arrived—a blueberry pie from Mrs. McEwen, a Three Kings fruitcake from Mrs. Hernandez, a plum pudding, two salads, three casseroles, canning jars filled with veggies and fruits, and enough other food to restock the pantry and refrigerator. The doorbell had been ringing all afternoon. It rang again now, and Mabel opened the door to find the children's kindergarten teacher, who presented her with a carton of eggs from his backyard chickens. As the teacher left, she was about to close the door when she spied Gordon trudging homeward, driving the bright red snowblower, his beard shaggy with icicles, and three neighbors trailing him, each bearing a gift.

THE CHRISTMAS LONG AGO

James Whitcomb Riley

Come, sing a hale heigh-ho
For the Christmas long ago!—
When the old log-cabin homed us
From the night of blinding snow,
Where the rarest joy held reign,
And the chimney roared again,
With the firelight like a beacon
Through the frosty window pane.
Ah! the revel and the din
From without and from within,
The blend of distant sleigh-bells
With the plinking violin;
The muffled shrieks and cries—
Then the glowing cheeks and eyes—
The driving storm of greetings,
Gusts of kisses and surprise.

A FEEL IN THE CHRISTMAS AIR

James Whitcomb Riley

They's a kind o' *feel* in the air, to me,
When the Chris'mas time sets in,
That's about as much of a mystery
As ever I've run ag'in!—
Fer instunce, now, whilse I gain in weight
An gineral health, I swear
They's a *goneness* somers I can't quite state—
A kind o' *feel* in the air.

They's a feel in the Chris'mas air goes right
To the spot where a man *lives* at!—
It gives a feller an appetite—
They ain't no doubt about *that*!—
And yit, they's *somepin'*—I don't know what—
That follows me, here and there,
And ha'nts and worries and spares me not—
A kind o' *feel* in the air!

Is it the racket the children raise?
W'y, *no*!—God bless 'em!—*no*!
Is it the eyes and the cheeks ablaze—
Like my own wuz, long ago?—
Is it the bleat o' the whistle and beat
O' the little toy-drum and blare
O' the horn?—*No ! no!*—It's jest the sweet—
The sad-sweet feel in the air.

A SONG FOR CHRISTMAS

James Whitcomb Riley

Chant me a rhyme of Christmas—
    Sing me a jovial song,—
And though it is filled with laughter,
    Let it be pure and strong.
    Let it be clear and ringing,
    And though it mirthful be,
Let a low, sweet voice of pathos
    Run through the melody.
Sing of the hearts brimmed over
    With the story of the day—
Of the echo of childish voices
    That will not die away.—
Of the blare of the tasseled bugle,
    And the timeless clatter and beat
Of the drum that throbs to muster
    Squadrons of scampering feet.
    But O let your voice fall fainter,
    Till, blent with a minor tone,
You temper your song with the beauty
    Of the pity Christ hath shown:
And sing one verse for the voiceless;
    And yet, ere the song be done,
    A verse for the ears that hear not,
    And a verse for the sightless one:

For though it be time for singing
A merry Christmas glee,
Let a low, sweet voice of pathos
Run through the melody.

BABY ALIVE

Melissa Fraterrigo

AS A CHILD, MY FAMILY CALLED ME little mama. The second of three children and first girl, I tried to do everything my mother did, from unpacking groceries to potty training my little sister by bringing her to the bathroom anytime I had to go.

By the time I was eight and Christmas neared, I was ready to become a mother in earnest. Baby Alive was the doll that would make this dream come true. She came with packets of food and a bottle, and after she was fed, she would wet herself. I loved the idea of mixing a baby's cereal, spooning it into her mouth until she was full, putting her down for a nap, changing her diaper upon waking, and then doing it all over again. What could be more real, more lifelike than that?

On Christmas morning I sprung out of bed, shook my sister awake, and then the two of us woke our brother and rushed toward the living room. The tree was heaped with presents, and soon Mom and Dad tumbled out of bed to join us. Mom drank coffee in her terry-cloth robe while Dad took photos with a flash so bright we saw stars. It didn't matter. Papers flew. There were yelps of delight and clapping; our stockings were filled with Hershey kisses, oranges, and new underwear.

But it was puzzling. I tore through every package addressed to me without finding Baby Alive. There was a doll for me, only she had short curled hair and was as large as a monkey with outstretched arms and blue eyes that closed when she was laid down.

I burst out crying.

"What's wrong?" Mom asked, wiping sleep from her eyes.

I held the new doll at arm's length and told her I wanted Baby Alive. "Santa must have made a mistake," I said.

"Santa doesn't make mistakes," she said, her voice as solid as cement.

138

I looked back at the new doll. She was big and bulky, and her arms were arranged as if something stuck her beneath the armpits.

My other doll clothes were too small on her, and after we cleaned up the wrapping paper and had breakfast, Mom lugged from the attic a box of clothes that we'd worn as infants.

There were sweaters of the softest wool, sleeveless jumpsuits and sundresses with embroidered flowers. I remember Mom holding up items exclaiming, "I haven't seen this in years!" I remember her placing my new doll on the kitchen table and carefully pulling the sleeves of a pink cardigan over its arms. There were pearl buttons that she fastened before lifting her upright ever so gently. "There you go," she said to the doll before easing her into my arms.

I patted the doll's back as if she'd been crying. It seemed like the right thing to do.

Even now I cannot tell you this doll's name. Unlike Baby Alive, she didn't eat food or drink from a bottle, but there was a surprising realness to her. Something in her turned Mom from the dirty dishes to our makeshift changing table where together we dressed a doll in our hand-me-downs.

When I look back at photos from my eighth Christmas, my face is red and splotchy from crying, my mouth a tight fist, but in my arms I'm holding the new doll.

She's propped awkwardly at my waist, looking at me with her blue plastic eyes, waiting to see what I might do.

SANTA CLAUS, INDIANA

Bryan Furuness

WHEN CHILDREN WRITE LETTERS TO SANTA CLAUS, where do those letters go?

To the post office in Santa Claus, Indiana, of course. For nearly ninety years, these letters have arrived by the sackful, and in 2015, the "elves" of the town collected some of the most compelling notes in a book called *Letters to Santa Claus*.

Here, for your enjoyment, are a few letters from that book. The careful reader may notice that some of the letter writers are *not* from Indiana—but I would say this feature is not about the point of origin. It's about the destination. When Christmas is coming, the hopes and dreams of children everywhere pour into Indiana.

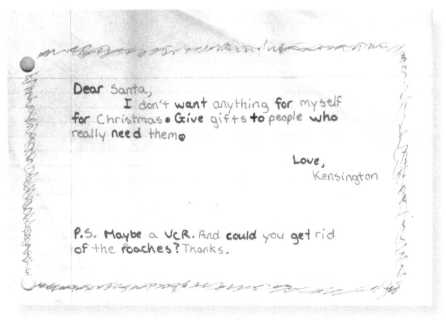

Dear Santa,
I don't want anything for myself for Christmas. Give gifts to people who really need them.

Love,
Kensington

P.S. Maybe a VCR. And could you get rid of the roaches? Thanks.

Annapolis, Mo.
Dec. 12th 1939

Dear Santa Claus

I am a pretty big boy 12 years old some of my pals say there is no Santa but I just have to believe in him and I'm hoping he will not forget me.

My dad was a soldier in the World War. He got shot when he was a deputy sheriff by gangsters after he come back.

I have a step dad but he is so mean he never buys me any thing. Some day I will be a man and I want to be brave. I like books better than any thing and I like boxing gloves + foot balls.

I hope you answer my letter.

Your friend
Wilson Castile Jr.
Annapolis, Mo.

Chgo, Illinois
Nov. 5, 1953

Dear Santa Claus:

You must help us this year Santa, our daddy still doesn't come home and mama cries at night when she thinks we are asleep, because she has no money for our coats and shoes and some dolls for Christmas

Sister says Santa Claus would help if he knew so I am writing you early so you can read this before Christmas.

Junior wants Gene Autry guns, he is 4 years old.

Duffy is the baby she is 2 she can't talk

Mechele wants a piano she is 5

Michael is 3, he wants a truck

Don't give me anything but give

2

my mother some shoes please
with the heels on like the other
ladies she wears sock and I
like stockings on the pretty
ladies I see. I am 8 years
old but if you can I would
like a pretty coat like the
other girls have on.
        Father William said pray
and I do, but do you think
he heard me.
                Shyrle

                Chicago, Illinois

P.s we go see you every year
     and I called you up
     once.

Dear Santa,

I would like skis, ski boots,
ski poles, ski harnesses, for
Christmas. I think of you every
day in school, I hope you will
send me the things I wrote on the
letter. Pleas send me skis,
ski boots, ski poles, and ski
harnesses. My arm is getting
tired. I guess I have to go
now. Good-by.

With love,
David

Santa Claves
North pole

Dec. 11, 1966

Dear Santa Clause,

I am not sure if I was a good girl this year. But if I get presents for Christmas I promise to be a good girl next year. Here is what I want. I would like to have some clothes, and anything you would want me to have. And if you want you can give other children more toys then me. But there are so many more things I want but I cant have. Like beatles records, doll, roller shakes and a record player. But you dont have to give me all these things.

Love Always
Jofrances.

5. I will love you even when I'll be 40 years old, and its not only because I want presents Its because I Love you

40 kisses

XXXXXXXXXX
XXXXXXXXXX
XXXXXXXXXX
XXXXXXXXXX

Dear Santa,

I have made out a Christmas list, but I can't find a doll I like. I would rather have a baby sister, but I know no matter how hard I wish I will never get one (ever). So if you will look in your workshops and others and see if you can find a doll you think I'd like I'd be happy. I would like to have a 1 or 2 year old floppy doll that looks just like a baby, kind of tall about 24 or 25 in. (heavy if you can find one) I want to thank you for all my gifts last year. I hope you wont stop bringing my family and me presents just because I'm in the 7th grade. Last year when I wrote you the letter in my stockings about the baby sister and you said "You never can tell" it pepped me up for about 6 months, then I began to think that I never would get one because when I mention it to my mother, she gets mad! If you write me a letter this year will you put in it if I will get a baby sister or not please?

P. S. I love you. (I want you to come this year even if you think I'm too old.)

XXXXXXX – 0000000   Love,
XXX   000   Gail

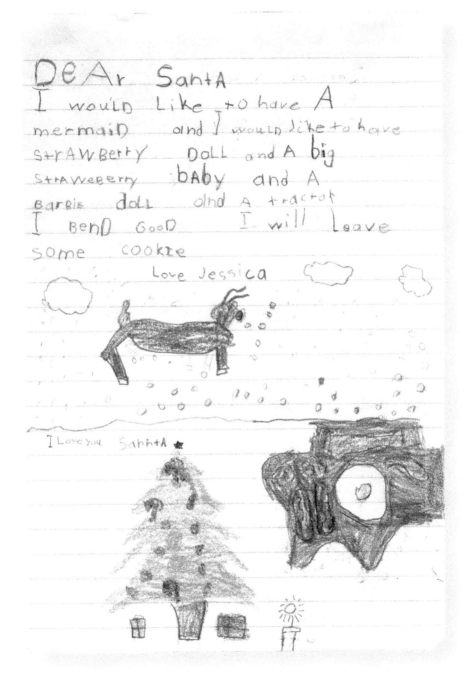

DEAr SantA
I would Like to have A
mermaiD and I would like to have
strAWBerry DoLL and A big
StraWeBerry bAby and A
Barbie doll and A tractor
I BenD GooD   I will Leave
some cookie
           Love Jessica

I Love you SahhtA

Dear Santa claus
I love you very much, I
whached a show about you
and thay sed thair was no
Santa claus. but I believ
in you. If you are really
Santa claus, could you get me
a baby alive. The boys in
my class sed that thair was
no Santa claus my mom sed
that thay will disappointed
when thay don't get anything.
You are my best friend I've
got

Your friend

Sarah

Dec. 2, 1994

Dear Santa,

How many houses do you have to visit? Do you get Christmas presentes yourself? I'm not trying to be mean but can I have a good present and i'll let you have some of my Holloween candy? Or, if you dont wont that you can have a cookey and your reindeer can have some carpites or anything they want even if they want somthing else they can have it. I wish you can bring me all the Power Ranger toys.

2nd grade

December 11, 1997

Dear Santa,
I what my dad to be smarter.

Love Robbie

From: Nick

FORT WAYNE IN 46806

Dear Santa,

I think YOU ARE A GREAT GUY

Your Friend,

NICK

HOWARD GARFIELD, BALLADEER

Edward Porter

MY TROUBLES BEGAN WHEN I WAS TEN and my parents spent the summer traveling, leaving me with my great-aunt in her decrepit gray Prairie School castle way out past the fairgrounds. This disconcertingly spry and moody octogenarian had a large collection of vinyl records, and out of desperate boredom one rainy afternoon, I took one at random, impaled it on the nub of her old Garrard SP25, and dropped the needle. A honeyed voice came pouring out of the speakers, crooning about a lumberjack drowned while freeing a logjam. It was Glenn Yarbrough, and I was lost.

It was music from a different era: The Weavers, The Limelighters, The New Lost City Ramblers, The New Christy Minstrels, The Brothers Four, The Stanley Brothers, The Carter Family, Richard Dyer Bennett, Eric von Schmidt, Dave Van Ronk, Buffy Sainte-Marie, The Kingston Trio, The Chad Mitchell Trio, The Clancy Brothers and Tommy Makem, Sonny Terry and Brownie McGhee, Blind Blake, Blind Willie Johnson, Blind Willie McTell, Blind Boy Fuller, The Blind Boys of Alabama, and many others. Probably she did not have all those records. It is partly my own present collection I must be thinking of.

I fell in love with those voices, singing gloriously on-pitch and in harmony. They sounded bold and manly. I wanted to be like that—to sing sea chanteys, murder ballads, love ballads, work songs, protest songs, rebel songs, songs of the frontier, union anthems, Celtic dirges, Mississippi field hollers, Appalachian hymns, Oklahoma war whoops, Cape Breton lullabies, and satirical topical political ditties. This was the life for me—I would make my fortune as a folk singer. Naturally, I would find some like-minded fellows, and we would travel and have adventures together as balladeers. If I craved love, my heartfelt interpretation of "Poor Wayfaring Stranger" would win the heart of any woman I desired.

But these things never happened.

Through years of enthusiastic practice, first in my cellar and later at the Fort Wayne Academy of Music, I developed my voice until it was unquestionably powerful. But when I sang in public, I discovered that my voice did not have a thrilling and seductive effect on my listeners. To judge by their facial expressions, the principle emotion I elicited was puzzlement. But was this a condemnation of my singing, or merely unfamiliarity with my musical genre of choice? So far as I could tell, I was Winesburg's lone folk enthusiast, let alone folk singer. Perhaps my auditors' confusion only revealed their ignorance and limitation. Sadly, I lacked even a single aficionado to offer a trustworthy judgment.

My teachers at Fort Wayne praised my hard work but did not offer me the introductions to the musical impresarios of Indianapolis that they gave to other students, so I returned to Winesburg and have been trying to make a go of it here for the last twenty years.

I teach music appreciation at the Richard Corey Technical Institute. It is an elective class. Not many students elect it. The metal lathe shop is next door to the room in which I teach. When I play records, it is often difficult for my students to appreciate music properly because of the loud sound of metal being lathed.

Christmas Eve this year, I went to the annual family gathering of Patches, Garfields, and Studemonts at the big Patch house on Ash Street. Because I am unmarried and have no children, and am no longer youthful, I was there in a role I do not like, that of the funny uncle. "Why don't you boys play a game with your funny uncle Howard?" Julia Patch or Annie Studemont will say when they want to drink Old Fashioneds and flirt with the clergy.

That night, after many tumblers of bourbon, brandy, and hard cider had been passed around, Selma Patch made everyone gather at the Christmas tree so we could hear her six-year-old daughter sing. Brittany Patch was, as my students would say, a hot mess: teased blonde hair in a red and green felt elf costume, thirsty for attention, and arrogantly confident she could command it. She sang "Oh Holy Night" a cappella, belting it aggressively, without any sense of dynamics or nuance, or, for that matter, the most basic understanding of the lyrics. When she sang, "The stars are brightly shining" it sounded as if "starzar" was one word. Nevertheless, because her voice had a kind of juvenile cuteness and clarity, there was an explosion of clapping and cheering, and calls for her to sing it again, which she did.

My ears pounded and my white Aran Islands sweater grew smotheringly hot. Toys and electronic gadgets littered the floor amidst torn wrapping paper. If I had known for sure that an individual Barbie or PlayStation had been Brittany's, I would have crushed it under the heel of my worn, saddle-soaped cowboy boots.

Instead, I excused myself, telling people that I was coming down with something, which in a sense, I was.

In my Prius, I raced dangerously through the streets, splashing slush on the walks, tearing past all the Lutheran versions of holiday extravagance—the raw wood crèches, the plain white lights outlining the front hedge, the undecorated wreaths, the daring, almost Catholic blue lights under the eaves and around the windows—mentally shaking my fist at all humanity, until I got tired of it and drove over to Biff's Bar and Grill down by the railroad tracks.

Biff's was serving one other customer, a short wiry old fellow in dark blue denim bib overalls, his tan Carhartt jacket draped over the stool next to him, a hard hat on top of it. We were both drinking Hamm's, which seemed reason enough to strike up conversation. He introduced himself as Walt and said he worked on the railroad. After I'd bought a couple of rounds, he began to talk a blue streak about couplings, sidings, crummys, frogs, points, tie plates, grades, and lag bolts. He used his hands a lot as he spoke, showing me the way a knuckle-coupling fit, or how a shunt worked. His hands were hard and red, with thick yellowing pads of callous on the flats of his palms, and ridges of gray callous along the edges of his crooked fingers, even up to the quick of his short blunt flat fingernails. Watching those hands, it occurred to me that I'd stumbled into someone who was actual folk, maybe the only genuine folk person in Winesburg. My students were hardly folk, nor were the other teachers, or my relatives. Brittany Patch was probably the perfect mathematical inverse of folk. But this guy was unquestionably, unarguably unmitigated folk, and it felt like I'd been searching for him my whole life without knowing it.

By the time Biff kicked us out, we'd had more than a few, and it had turned Christmas. We stood there, beer-sodden in the raw foggy moistness of the new global-warming Midwest winter, not knowing what to do. "I think I'm going to walk my line," Walt announced. He settled his hard hat firmly with both hands and headed down the slope towards the railroad track. After a moment, I followed him, a helpless, shambling schoolboy to his diminutive Pied Piper.

He'd perfected a kind of rolling trot that put his feet naturally on one tie after another. I tried to imitate it to keep pace behind him, but I kept hitching my gait, stepping on the gravel and tripping on the tie. A half-moon the color of dirty milk blinked at us from between the low, fast-moving clouds and shone on the silver rails, making them glint intermittently in a slow, hopeless SOS for the world itself. We said nothing, for nothing needed to be said.

Then came what I took ever so briefly to be a Christmas miracle. Walt began to hum a tune, one I knew well. It was "On the Banks of the Ohio." After passing through it once, he began to sing the first verse softly, as if afraid to disturb the delicate atmosphere he'd created with his humming. I understood him completely: the moonlight, the tracks, Christmas Eve with a stranger, it all cried out with an unspeakable sadness. His folkish heart, like mine, instinctively craved the melancholy relief that only a murder ballad could provide. I held my breath, not wanting to spoil things, until he came to the chorus and I joined in, quietly harmonizing a third above him on, "And only say that you'll be mine." He glanced at me, surprised, I thought, that I was privy to the signs and countersigns of his tribe. I started in on the second verse, and for a moment, we sang in a tempered, restrained unison. Then I couldn't help myself. I had a song to sing, and I was going to sing it all over this land. I let my voice swell to its fullest until it resonated in the natural echo chamber of the high dark embankments on either side of us. I charged into the chorus again, and then into the third verse, and "Willie dear, don't murder me." Then I realized he'd stopped singing, stopped trotting, and stood silently staring at me. On his face was the unmistakable expression of pure puzzlement.

Then he smiled a gentle, terrible smile, the kind you give your sick dog just before you put him to sleep. He patted me on the shoulder. "Thanks for the beers," he said. "You'll be okay. Sure you will." And with that, he turned and walked away. The moon was smothered in cloud for a long moment, and when it shone again, he had disappeared. He must have taken some secret railroad way known only to him.

I'd gotten my answer, one I couldn't deny or ignore. Of all the people in Winesburg, or Indiana, or the world, he was the one whose appreciation might have redeemed me, and I had seen plainly in his face that he preferred to let the earth and the mists swallow him whole than to listen to one more bar of my grotesque singing. There in the dank, frigid shadows, on the tracks behind the back wall of the Business Athenaeum, its painted diploma and mortarboard blazoned as if to mark the exact spot of this graduation from my vainglorious dreams of becoming the thing I loved, I felt death inside me and knew that nothing would ever be the same.

Lost in despair, several sheets to the wind, I could have missed the rattle and hum of the rails, the trembling in the ground, the subtle but ominous change of pressure in the air, until it was too late. But I had enough presence of mind to look up as the single eye of light emerged from around a bend, rushing at me with murderous speed—an express freight on an inside through track. I jumped from the ties into the gravel culvert. A moment later the locomotive passed with a buffet of air that almost shoved me off my feet and a piercing scream of steel wheel against steel rail, like a thousand metal lathes. I yelled in surprise and fear but could not hear my own voice over the rattling cacophony, could not even feel it vibrate in my throat. I fell on my knees, threw my head back and sang the last verse, about killing the only woman I loved because she would not be my bride—sang it unheard by any human ear, including my own, without any art or technique, forgetting everything I'd ever learned, sang only for the sake of singing. The train was long, the black hulks of the boxcars roared past me endlessly, as I sang to them beneath that lonely moonlit Athenaeum, sang to them of my despair, my longing, and my failure. When the train finally passed, I was left in the darkness, silent, trembling, and shaken, and I realized that only then could I even begin to think of myself as a folk singer.

THE FIVE LITTLE SYKESES

EXCERPT FROM *MR. BINGLE*

George Barr McCutcheon

A COAL FIRE CRACKLED CHEERILY IN THE little open grate that supplied warmth to the steam-heated living room in the modest apartment of Mr. Thomas S. Bingle, lower New York, somewhere to the west of Fifth Avenue and not far removed from Washington Square—in the wrong direction, however, if one must be precise in the matter of emphasizing the social independence of the Bingle family—and be it here recorded that without the genial aid of that grate of coals the living room would have been a cheerless place indeed. Mr. Bingle had spent most of the evening trying to coax heat from the lower regions into the pipes of the seventh heaven wherein he dwelt, and without the slightest sign of success. The frigid coils in the corner of the room remained obdurate. If they indicated the slightest symptom of warmth during the evening, it was due entirely to the expansive generosity of the humble grate and not because they were moved by inward remorse. They were able, however, to supply the odor of far-off steam, as of an abandoned laundry; and sometimes they chortled meanly, revealing signs of an energy that in anything but a steam pipe might have been mistaken for a promise to do better.

Mr. Bingle poked the fire and looked at his watch. Then he crossed to the window, drew the curtains and shade aside, and tried to peer through the frosty panes into the street, seven stories below. A holly wreath hung suspended in the window, completely obscured from view on one side by hoar frost, on the other by a lemon-colored window shade that had to be handled with patience out of respect for a lapsed spring at the top. He scraped a peephole in the frosty surface, and, after drying his fingers on his smoking jacket, looked downward with eyes a-squint.

"Do sit down, Tom," said his wife from her chair by the fireplace. "A watched pot never boils. You can't see them from the window, in any event."

"I can see the car when it stops at the corner, my dear," said Mr. Bingle, enlarging the peephole with a vigor that appeared to be aggravated by advice. "Melissa said seven o'clock, and it is four minutes after now."

"You forget that Melissa didn't start until after she had cleared away the dinner things. She—"

"I know, I know," he interrupted, still peering. "But that was an hour ago, Mary. I think a car is stopping at the corner now. No! It didn't stop, so there must have been someone waiting to get on instead of off."

"Do come and sit down. You are as fidgety as a child."

"Dear me," said Mr. Bingle, turning away from the window with a shiver, "how I pity the poor unfortunates who haven't a warm fire to sit beside tonight. It is going to be the coldest night in twenty years, according to the—there! Did you hear that?" He stepped to the window once more. The double ring of a streetcar bell had reached his ears, and he knew that a car had stopped at the corner below. "According to the weather report this afternoon," he concluded, recrossing the room to sit down beside the fire, very erect and expectant, a smile on his pinched, eager face. He was watching the hall door.

It was Christmas Eve. There were signs of the season in every corner of the plain but cozy little sitting room. Mistletoe hung from the chandelier; gay bunting and strands of gold and silver tinsel draped the bookcase and the writing desk; holly and myrtle covered the wall brackets, and red tissue paper shaded all of the electric light globes; big candles and little candles flickered on the mantelpiece, and some were red and some were white and yet others were green and blue with the paint that Mr. Bingle had applied with earnest though artless disregard for subsequent odors; packages done up in white and tied with red ribbon, neatly double-bowed, formed a significant centerpiece for the ornate mahogany library table—and one who did not know the Bingles would have looked about in quest of small fry with popping, covetous eyes and sleekly brushed hair. The alluring scent of gaudily painted toys pervaded the Christmas atmosphere, quite offsetting the hint of steam from more fortunate depths, and one could sniff the odor of freshly buttered popcorn. All these signs spoke of children and the proximity of Kris Kringle, and yet there were no little Bingles, nor had there ever been so much as one!

Mr. and Mrs. Bingle were childless. The tragedy of life for them lay not in the loss of a firstborn but in the fact that no babe had ever come to fill their hungry hearts with the food they most desired and craved. Nor was there any promise of subsequent concessions on their behalf. For fifteen years they had longed for the boon that was denied them, and to the end of their simple, kindly days they probably would go on longing. Poor as they were, neither would have complained if fate had given them half a dozen healthy mouths to feed, as many wriggling bodies to clothe, and all the splendid worries that go with colic, croup, measles, mumps, broken arms, and all the other ailments, peculiar not so much to childhood as they are paramount to parenthood.

Lonely, incomplete lives they led, with no bitterness in their souls, loving each other the more as they tried to fill the void with songs of resignation. Away back in the early days, Mr. Bingle had said that Christmas was a bleak thing without children to lift the pall—or something of the sort.

Out of that well-worn conclusion—oft expressed by rich and poor alike—grew the Bingle Foundation, so to speak. No Christmas Eve was allowed to go by without the presence of alien offspring about their fire-lit hearth, and no strange little kiddie ever left for his own bed without treasuring in his soul the belief that he had seen Santa Claus at last—had been kissed by him, too—albeit the plain-faced, wistful little man with the funny bald spot was in no sense up to the preconceived opinions of what the roly-poly, white-whiskered, red-cheeked annual visitor from Lapland ought to be in order to make dreams come true.

The Bingles were singularly nephewless, nieceless, cousinless. There was no kindly disposed relative to whom they could look for the loan of a few children on Christmas Eve, nor would their own sensitiveness permit them to approach neighbors or friends in the building with a well-meant request that might have met with a chilly rebuff. One really cannot go about borrowing children from people on the floor below and the floor above, especially on Christmas Eve when children are so much in demand, even in the most fortunate of families. It is quite a different matter at any other time of the year. One can always borrow a whole family of children when the mother happens to feel the call of the matinee or the woman's club, and it is not an uncommon thing to secure them for a whole day in mid-December. But on Christmas Eve, never! And so Mr. and Mrs. Bingle, being without the natural comforts of home, were obliged to go out into the world searching for children who had an even greater grudge against circumstances. They frequently found their guests of honor in places where dishonor had left them, and they gave them a merry Christmas with no questions asked.

The past two Christmas Eves had found them rather providentially supplied with children about whom no questions had ever been asked: the progeny of a Mr. and Mrs. Sykes. Mr. Sykes being dead, the care and support of five lusty youngsters fell upon the devoted but far from rugged shoulders of a mother who worked as a saleswoman in one of the big Sixth Avenue shops and who toiled far into the night before Christmas in order that forgetful people might be able to remember without fail on the morning thereafter. She was only too glad to lend her family to Mr. and Mrs. Bingle. More than that, she was ineffably glad, on her own account, that it was Christmas Eve; it signified the close of a diabolical season of torture at the hands of a public that believes firmly in "peace on earth" but hasn't the faintest conception of what "goodwill toward men" means when it comes to shopping at Christmastime.

Mrs. Sykes's sister Melissa had been maid-of-all-work in the modest establishment of Mr. and Mrs. Bingle for a matter of three and a half years. It was she who suggested the Sykes family as a happy solution to the annual problem, and Mr. Bingle almost hugged her for being so thoroughly competent and considerate!

It isn't every servant, said he, who thinks of the comfort of her employers. Most of 'em, said he, insist on going to a chauffeurs' ball or something of the sort on Christmas Eve, but here was a jewel-like daughter of Martha who actually put the interests of her master and mistress above her own and complained not! And what made it all the more incomprehensible to him was the fact that Melissa was quite a pretty girl. There was no reason in the world why she shouldn't have gone to the ball and had a good time instead of thinking of them in their hours of trouble. But here she was, actually going out of her way to be kind to her employers: supplying a complete family for Christmas Eve purposes and never uttering a word of complaint!

The more he thought of it, the prettier she became. He mentioned it to his wife, and she agreed with him. Melissa was much too pretty, said Mrs. Bingle, entirely without animus. And she was really quite a stylish sort of girl, too, when she dressed up to go out of a Sunday. Much more so, indeed, than Mrs. Bingle herself, who had to scrimp and pinch as all good housewives do if they want to succeed to a new dress once a year.

Melissa had something of an advantage over her mistress in that she received wages and was entitled to an afternoon off every fortnight. Mrs. Bingle did quite as much work about the house, ate practically the same food, slept not half so soundly, had all the worry of making both ends meet, practiced a rigid and necessary economy, took no afternoons off, and all without pecuniary compensation—wherein rests support for the contention that Melissa had the better of her mistress when all is said and done. Obviously, therefore, Mrs. Bingle was not as well off as her servant. True, she sat in the parlor while Melissa sat in the kitchen, but to offset this distinction, Melissa could sing over her pans and dishes. Mr. Bingle, good soul, insisted on keeping a servant, despite the strain on his purse, for no other reason than that he couldn't bear the thought of leaving Mrs. Bingle alone all day while he was at the bank. (Lest there should be some apprehension, it should be explained that he was a bookkeeper at a salary of one hundred dollars a month, arrived at after long and faithful service, and that Melissa had but fifteen dollars a month, food, and bed.) Melissa was company for Mrs. Bingle, and her unfailing good humor extended to Mr. Bingle when he came home to dinner, tired as a dog and in need of cheer. She joined in the table talk with unresented freedom, and she never failed to laugh heartily over Mr. Bingle's inspired jokes. Altogether, Melissa was well worth her wage. She was sunshine and air to the stifled bookkeeper and his wife.

And now, for the third time, she was bringing the five rollicking Sykeses to the little flat beyond Washington Square, and for the thousandth time Mr. and Mrs. Bingle wondered how such a treasure as Melissa had managed to keep out of heaven all these years.

Mr. Bingle opened the front door with a great deal of ceremony the instant the rickety elevator came to a stop at the seventh floor and gave greeting to the five Sykeses on the dark, narrow landing. He mentioned each by name and very gravely shook their red-mittened paws as they sidled past him with eager, bulging eyes that saw only the Christmas trappings in the room beyond.

"Merry Christmas," said the five, not quite in one voice but with well-rehearsed vehemence, albeit two tiny ones, in rapt contemplation of things beyond, quite neglected their duty until severely nudged by Melissa, whereupon they said it in a shrill treble at least six times without stopping.

"I am very pleased to see you all," said Mr. Bingle, beaming. "Won't you take off your things and stay awhile?"

It was what he always said to them, and they always said, "Yes, thank you," following out instructions received on the way downtown, and then, in some desperation, added, "Mr. Bingle," after a sententious whisper from their aunt.

They were a rosy, clean-scrubbed lot, these little Sykeses. Their mother may not have fared overly well herself, but she had contrived to put flesh and fat on the bones of her progeny, and you would go a long way before you would find a plumper, merrier group of children than those who came to the Bingle flat on Christmas Eve in their very best garments and with their very best appetites. The eldest was ten, the youngest four, and it so happened that the beginning and the end of the string were boys, the three in between being Mary, Maud, and Kate.

Mrs. Bingle helped them off with their coats and caps and mufflers, then hugged them and lugged them up to the fire, while Melissa removed her skunk tippet, her pony coat, and a hat that would have created envy in the soul of a less charitable creature than the mistress of the house.

"And now," said Mr. Bingle, confronting the group, "who made you?"

"God, Mr. Bingle," said the five Sykeses, very much after the habit of a dog that is ordered to "speak."

"And who was it that said, 'Suffer little children to come unto me?'"

"Jesus, Mr. Bingle," said the five Sykeses, eyeing the pile on the table.

"And where do you expect to go when you die?" demanded Mr. Bingle with great severity.

"Heaven!" shouted the perfectly healthy Sykeses.

"How is your mother, Mary?" asked Mrs. Bingle, always a rational woman.

Mary bobbed. "She's working, ma'am," said she, and that was all she knew about her mother's state of health.

"Are you cold?" inquired Mr. Bingle, herding them a little closer to the grate. "Yes," said two of the Sykeses.

"Sir," admonished Melissa. "Sir!" said all of the Sykeses.

"Now, draw up the chairs," said Mr. Bingle, clearing his throat. "Mary, you'd better take Kate and Georgie on your lap, and suppose you hold Maud, Melissa. It will be more cozy." This was his way of overcoming the shortage in chairs.

Now, it was Mr. Bingle's custom to read *A Christmas Carol* on Christmas Eve. It was his creed, almost his religion, this heartbreaking tale by Dickens. Not once, but a thousand times, he had proclaimed that if all men lived up to the teachings of *A Christmas Carol* the world would be sweeter, happier, nobler, and the churches could be put to a better use than at present, considering (as he said) that they now represent assembling places for people who read neither Dickens nor the scripture but sing with considerable intelligence. It was his contention that *A Christmas Carol* teaches a good many things that the church overlooks in its study of Christ and that the surest way to make good men out of *all* boys is to get at their hearts while their souls are fresh and simple. Put the New Testament and *A Christmas Carol* in every boy's hand, said he, and they will create a religion that has something besides faith for a foundation. One sometimes forgets that Christ was crucified, but no one ever forgets what happened to Old Scrooge, and as Mr. Bingle read his Bible quite assiduously, it is only fair to assume that he appreciated the relativeness of *A Christmas Carol* to the greatest book in all the world.

For twenty years or more, he had not once failed to read *A Carol* on Christmas Eve. He knew the book by heart. Is it any wonder, then, that he was a gentle, sweet-natured man in whom not the faintest symptom of guile existed? And, on the other hand, is it any wonder that he remained a bookkeeper in a bank while other men of his acquaintance went into business and became rich and arrogant? Of course, it is necessary to look at the question from both directions, and for that reason I mention the fact that he remained a bookkeeper while those who scorned *A Christmas Carol* became drivers of men.

Experience—and some sage conclusions on the part of his wife—had taught him, after years of unsatisfactory practice, that it was best to read the story *before* giving out presents to the immature guests. On a great many occasions, the youngsters—in those early days they were waifs—either went sound asleep before he was halfway through or became so restless and voracious that he couldn't keep his place in the book, what with watching to see that they didn't choke on the candy, break the windows or mirrors with their footballs, or put someone's eye out with a pop-gun.

Of late he had been reading the story first and distributing the "goodies" and toys afterward. It was a splendid arrangement. The "kiddies" kept their eyes and ears open and sat very still while he read to them of Tiny Tim and his friends. And when Mr. Bingle himself grinned shamefacedly through his tears and choked up so that the words would not come without being resolutely forced through a tightened throat, the sympathetic audience, including Mrs. Bingle and Melissa—and on one occasion an ancient maiden from the floor above—wept copiously and with the most flattering clamor.

A small reading lamp stood on the broad arm of his chair, which faced the expectant group. Mr. Bingle cleared his throat, wiped his spectacles, and then peered over the rims to see that all were attending. Five rosy faces glistened with the sheen of health and soap lately applied with great force by the proud but relentless Melissa.

"Take off your earmuffs, James," said Mr. Bingle to the eldest Sykes, who immediately turned a fiery red and shrank down in his chair bitterly to hate his brothers and sisters for snickering at him. "There! That's much better."

"They're new, Mr. Bingle," explained Melissa. "He hasn't had 'em off since yesterday, he likes 'em so much. Put 'em in your pocket, Jimmy. And now listen to Mr. Bingle. Are you sure they ain't too heavy for you, ma'am? Georgie's getting pretty big—oh, excuse me, sir."

Mr. Bingle took up the well-worn, cherished book and turned to the first page of the text. He cleared his throat again—and again. Hesitation at a time like this was unusual; he was clearly, suddenly irresolute. His gaze lingered for a moment on the white knob of a door at the upper end of the room and then shifted to his wife's face.

"I wonder, my dear, if Uncle Joe couldn't be persuaded to come in and listen to the reading," he ventured, a wistful gleam in his eyes. "He's been feeling better the last few days. It might cheer him—"

"Cheer your granny," said Mrs. Bingle scornfully. "It's no use. I asked him just before dinner, and he said he didn't believe in happiness, or something to that effect."

"He is the limit," said Melissa flatly. "The worst grouch I've ever seen, Mr. Bingle, even if he is your own flesh-and-blood uncle. He's almost as bad as Old Scrooge."

"He is a sick man," explained Mr. Bingle, lowering his voice, "and he hasn't known very much happiness in his lifetime, so I suppose we ought to overlook— er, ahem! Let me see, where was I?" He favored young Mary Sykes with a genial grin. "Where was I, Mary?"

Mary saw her chance. Without a trace of shame or compunction, she said page seventy-eight, and then the three grown people coughed in great embarrassment.

"You sha'n't come next Christmas," whispered Melissa very fiercely into Mary's ear, so ominously, in fact, that Mary's lip began to tremble.

"Page one," she amended, in a very small voice. James moved uneasily in his chair, and Mary avoided his gaze.

"I believe I'll step in and ask Uncle Joe if he won't change his mind," said Mr. Bingle. "I—I don't believe he has ever read A Christmas Carol. And he is so lonely, so—er—so at odds with the world that—"

"Don't bother him, Tom," said his wife. "Get on with the reading. The children are impatient." She completed the sentence in a yawn.

Mr. Bingle began. He read very slowly and very impressively at first but gradually warmed up to the two-hour task. In a very few minutes he was going along rapidly, almost monotonously, with scant regard for effect save at the end of sentences, the ultimate word being pronounced with distinct emphasis. Page after page was turned; the droning sound of his voice went on and on, with its clock-like inflections at the end of sentences; the revived crackle of coals lent spirit to an otherwise dreary solo, and always it was Melissa who poked the grate and at the same time rubbed her leg to renew the circulation that had been checked by the limp weight of Katie Sykes; the deep sighs of Mrs. Bingle and the loud yawns of the older children relieved the monotony of sound from time to time, and the cold wind whistled shrilly round the corners of the building, causing the youngsters to wonder how Santa was enduring the frost during his tedious wait at the top of the chimney pot. Mrs. Bingle shifted the occupants of her lap more and more often as the tale ran on, and with little attempt to do so noiselessly; Mary's feet went to sleep, and James fidgeted so violently that twice Mr. Bingle had to look at him. But eventually he came to the acutely tearful place in the story, and then he was at his best. Indeed, he quite thrilled his hearers, who became all attention and blissfully lachrymose. Mrs. Bingle sobbed, Melissa rubbed her eyes violently, Mr. Bingle choked up and could scarcely read for the tightening in his throat, and the children watched him through solemn, dripping eyes and hung on every word that told of the regeneration of Scrooge and the sad happiness of Tiny Tim. And finally Mr. Bingle, as hoarse as a crow and faint with emotion, closed the book and lowered it gently to his knee.

"There!" he said. "There's a lesson for you. Don't you feel better for it, young ladies and gentlemen?"

"I always cry," said Mary Sykes with a glance of defiance at her eldest brother, who made a fine show of glowering.

"Everybody cries over Tiny Tim," said Melissa. "As frequent as I've heard Mr. Bingle read that story I can't help crying, knowing all the time it's only a novel. It seems to me I cry a little worse every time it's read. Don't you think I do, ma'am? Didn't you notice that I cried a little more this time than I did last year?"

"It touches the heartstrings," said Mr. Bingle, blowing his nose so fiercely that Georgie whimpered again, coming out of a doze. "I'll bet my head, dear, that Uncle Joe would sniffle as much as any of us. I wish—er—I do wish we'd asked him to come in. It would do him a world of good to shed a few tears."

"He hasn't a tear in the whole hulk of him," said Mrs. Bingle, sorrowfully.

"Poor old man," said Melissa, relenting a bit.

"I bet I know what he's doing," said James brightly.

"Doing? What is he doing, James?" demanded Mr. Bingle, surprised by the youngster's declaration.

"You can't fool me. I bet he's out there dressing up to play Santa Claus."

"Dear me!" exclaimed Mr. Bingle, blinking. The thought of crabbed Uncle Joe taking on the habiliments of the genial saint was too much for his imagination. It left him without the power to set James straight in the matter, and Uncle Joe was immediately accepted as Santy by the expectant Sykeses, all of whom revealed a tremendous interest in the avuncular absentee. They even appeared to be properly apprehensive and crowded a little closer to the knees of the grown-ups, all the while eyeing the door at the upper end of the room.

Melissa's involuntary snort was not enlightening to the children, but it served as a spur to Mr. Bingle, who abruptly gave over being sentimental and set about the pleasant task of distributing the packages on the table. Hilarity took the place of a necessary reserve, and before one could say "Jack Robinson" the little sitting room was as boisterous a place as you'd find in a month's journey, and no one would have suspected that Mr. and Mrs. Bingle were eating their hearts out because the noisy crew belonged to the heaven-blest Mrs. Sykes and not to them.

Ten o'clock came. Mr. and Mrs. Bingle sat side by side in front of the fireplace, her hand in his. The floor was littered with white tissue paper, red ribbons, peanut hulls, and other by-products of festivity; the rugs were scuffled up and hopelessly awry; chairs were out of their accustomed places—two or three of them no longer stood upon their legs as upright chairs should do—and the hearth was strewn with coals from an overturned scuttle. Candle grease solidified on the mantelpiece and dripped unseen upon the mahogany bookcase—all unnoticed by the dreamy, desolate Bingles. They were alone with the annual wreck. Melissa and the five Sykeses were out in the bitter night, on their frolicsome way to the distant home of the woman who had so many children she didn't know what to do for them, not with them. They had gone away with their hands and pockets full, and their stomachs, too, and they had all been kissed and hugged and invited to come again without fail a year from that very night.

Mr. Bingle sighed. Neither had spoken for many minutes after the elevator door slammed behind the excited, shrill-voiced children. Mr. Bingle always sighed exactly at this moment in his reflections, and Mrs. Bingle always squeezed his hand fiercely and turned a pair of darkly regretful eyes upon him.

"I am sorry, dear heart," she murmured, and then he kissed her hand and said that it was God's will.

"It doesn't seem right, when we want them, need them so much," she said, huskily.

And then he repeated the thing he always said on Christmas Eve: "One of these days I am going to adopt a—er—a couple, Mary, sure as I'm sitting here. We just can't grow old without having some of them about us. Someday we'll find the right sort of—"

The bedroom door opened with a squeak, slowly and with considerable caution. The gaunt, bearded face of a tall, stooping old man appeared in the aperture; sharp, piercing eyes under thick gray eyebrows searched the room in a swift, almost unfriendly glance.

"The infernal brats gone, Tom?" demanded Uncle Joe harshly.

Mr. and Mrs. Bingle stiffened in their chairs. The tall old man came down to the fireplace, disgustedly kicking a stray, crumpled sheet of tissue paper out of his path.

"Oh, they are perfect dears, Uncle Joe," protested Mrs. Bingle, trying her best not to bristle.

"I wish you had come in for a look at 'em—" began Mr. Bingle, but the old man cut him off with a snort of anger.

"Cussed little nuisances," he said, holding his thin hands to the blaze.

"I don't see how you can say such things about children you don't know and can't—" began Mrs. Bingle.

He glared at her. "You can't tell me anything about children, Mary. I'm the father of three, and I know what I'm talking about. Children are the damnedest curse on earth. You ought to thank God you haven't got any."

THE *SCHNEEBRUNZER*

Norbert Krapf

There was a boy you may
have known who came
into his own when it snowed.
His art was so private no one
saw him practice it but he left
his artifacts for all to enjoy
so long as they did not melt.
You might turn a corner
downtown and find a yellow
I in the gutter. A big U
would be burned behind a tree.
Sometimes when ambition
filled him like a balloon
he would etch the outline
of a yellow rabbit against
sparkling white or wriggle
a snake that disappeared
into a steaming manhole cover.
They say that once after he
got into his father's cache
of beer in the refrigerator
he left his signature

on the sidewalk behind
the church: The Schneebrunzer
lives! Mothers and fathers
would point, children would
giggle, and the mayor offered
a reward to anyone who would
reveal his identity, but the Schneebrunzer kept his name and his
art to himself. He came to
understand that his tenure
as artist on this earth was finite
and that all things must pass.

THE MYTH OF THE PERFECT CHRISTMAS PHOTO FAMILY

Kelsey Timmerman

THERE'S A STORY BEHIND EVERY CHRISTMAS CARD photo. This is ours.[1]

Our car looks like something Santa would drive. It has a red body, capped with a white top. Soon that white top will have a green tree strapped to it. At least that's the plan. We're on our annual trip to the Christmas tree farm where we also hope to get the perfect family picture for our Christmas card.

I tune the radio to the Christmas channel. I've become that cheesy Chevy Chase dad who tries too hard to build unforgettable childhood memories.

I'm about to join the chorus when a little voice in the back starts to sing, "Jingle bells, jingle bells, jingle all the way." It's our four-year-old son, Griffin. I slowly turn to make eye contact with my wife, Annie, sitting in the passenger seat.

This is a moment.

I take a hand off the steering wheel and put it over my heart like I'm an eighty-year-old grandma, acknowledging the moment without interrupting it. A four-year-old singing along with the radio might not seem like a big deal, but this is a big deal. Griffin is on the autism spectrum. He sings plenty, but not with the radio.

None of us move or speak. It's just Griff singing and the sound of our car dodging potholes on a rural Indiana road.

---

1. Author's note: Our imperfect photos from the outing are here: http://whereamiwearing
.com/2015/12/the-myth-of-the-perfect-christmas-photo-family/.

We're five minutes into a month of Christmas celebrations, and I can't think of a better gift. Christmas is off to a great start.

But things take a turn when we pull up to the Christmas tree farm. It's closed. Not just temporarily, but devoid of life, like it's a set from *The Walking Dead*.

A cry breaks the silence, bringing an abrupt end to any Christmas magic. Harper, our six-year-old daughter, cannot deal with this.

"What are we going to do?" she whimpers.

We've come to this farm since she could remember. There was nothing fancy about it. The trees were only twenty bucks regardless of size. You cut it, you carried it, you tied it to your car, all without the first note of Christmas music or whiff of hot chocolate to be enjoyed.

Damn it! We're going to make a new Christmas tradition, I think. I ask Siri for the directions to the nearest tree farm. It's forty minutes away.

Whatever is the opposite of Christmas magic fills the car.

A cartoon Christmas tree points the way to the new farm. There are lights, music, people full of Christmas cheer. A retired grandpa, who looks and acts like he's taken time off from whittling toys for orphans to spread peace on Earth and goodwill to men, greets us. He gives us a shiny new saw and a Christmas tree cart.

Griffin wants to ride on the cart. He sits on one of the crossbars and smiles until one of his new boots catches on the ground and he nearly falls off. I take him off the cart, and he looks like a drunken cowboy as he tries to walk in the boots, which might fit next Christmas.

He wants back on the cart. We try it again, and again it doesn't work. He doesn't understand why he can't ride. But I'm out of patience and run with the cart so he can't get to it. He runs after me. At first he thinks it's funny, but then he starts to get upset and cries as he pursues me. I keep running anyhow.

We stop at a tree that's nice but way too big.

"Let's do the picture here," Annie says.

For some reason the cuteness of kids' faces is multiplied by ten if they wear a hat. Annie pulls out Griff's hat and shoves it down over his ears. At his therapy, he will wear his hat for thirty seconds before he pulls it off. Annie has him stand next to Harper and then steps back to snap the photo.

I make funny faces and dance like an idiot behind Annie.

"Smile, Harper! Look here, buddy!"

Griff pulls at his hat.

"It hurts to smile!" Harper cries. She's been dealing with a canker sore for the last few days.

Only half of her upper lip moves. The other half droops into a pirate grimace.

I keep dancing and Griffin looks at me as if wondering, "What is wrong with my father?"

Annie stops trying and gives me the "let's get a damn tree and get out of this Christmas wonderland hell hole" nod.

I run ahead with the cart, pursued by my crying autistic son.

Remember those scenes from *The Lord of the Rings* where the fellowship is crossing some high mountain pass? In these scenes there is epic music as the camera zooms in on the travelers' faces, which reflect all the trials and tribulations, the wear and tear that led them to this—yet another—painful moment. That's our family looking for a Christmas tree.

I'm running. Harper is holding her swollen mouth as if one of her horrible parents just slapped her. Annie is trying to grab Griffin's hand to keep him from escaping our family to join another. I don't blame him. All the other families look so happy.

"What's your name?!" Griffin shouts, pointing at a family who've found a tree. They're all wearing Santa hats. Even their freaking tree is wearing a Santa hat and tinsel.

They introduce themselves, and then the perfect mother asks, "Do you like to take pictures, buddy?"

Griffin doesn't answer. But what four-year-old would be like, "Yes, ma'am, I'd be happy to take a photo of your family"?

"I'll take it," I say.

The perfect mother and father put their arms around their two perfect daughters and they all smile perfect smiles. Not one of them looks like a pirate. Each picture I snap is more perfect than the one before.

I want to take the phone and throw it into the row of blue spruce behind us. Instead, I hand her the phone, and they wish us a Merry Christmas. We walk away to the sound of the father's battery-powered saw firing up. That's right, he brought his own saw.

Once we're out of earshot, Annie and I start laughing. It's either that or crying.

And then Harper finds "our" Christmas tree, which makes her mouth hurt less. We take an imperfect selfie with the tree and get a "good enough" picture of the kids to work for our card.

It's a picture where the smiles are genuine, partly because the kids are excited about the tree and partly because I've added singing to my dancing while Annie snapped the shot.

Weeks from now, a hundred or so people will open a Christmas card from the Timmerman family. They'll add it to the pile of other smiling families, made up of people with canker sores, moments of joy, autism, unreasonable expectations, and a whole host of other things that make life interesting. But are they all perfect?

We try to make our family photos look like perfect moments, as if those are the only moments worth capturing. Maybe so, but without imperfect moments there would be no perfect moments. They're all worth remembering.

Years from now, when I look at our 2015 Christmas card, I'll remember Griffin singing and crying, Harper's pathetic little pirate mouth and the light in her eyes when she found our tree. I'll remember Annie's look of impatience and the laugh we shared as we drove away from the farm with a green tree on our Santa car filled with Christmas music and Griffin shouting, "Turn it off! Turn it off!"

TREASURE!

Eliza Tudor

IT WAS THE FIRST CHRISTMAS AWAY FROM my children. Their father's new wife paid for them to go skiing in Colorado. My children would stay in a condo on a bunk bed with brand new flannel Christmas tree sheets, their names embroidered on the pillowcases. A hot tub was offered, a chocolate fountain planned. And Santa would come just as he had the weekend before when *we* celebrated at our house, early. It was the year my children turned thirteen and ten. The next year, their father would have a new baby.

My parents invited me to spend Christmas with them. Kind, but I couldn't think of anything more depressing. Some friends invited me to go with them to Mexico. "I wish I could be there," I told them.

I'm from Indiana. We flatlanders lie to our closest friends, not out of kindness, but a mix of self-preservation and untreated anxiety. We are the people who save our friendliest waves for strangers.

The days felt dark at 10 a.m. At least we had sports, a near constant flow of sugar, and Christmas lights to sustain us in the early gloom. Otherwise, we would just be people with lying smiles that didn't extend past our lips. We'd be the people who cry alone in the car whenever the opening bars of that horrific John Lennon Christmas song come on the radio: *And what have you done? Another year over and a new one just begun.*

You shouldn't ask those questions of Midwesterners in December, John. Especially one who just dropped off her kids at the airport on the day before Christmas Eve. I was cheerful, kissing away their worry. They were children. It was Christmas. *You're going to have so much fun*, I said on repeat. Only gone for a few days, I told myself. Back before the New Year, I told the radio.

Then I got on the interstate and headed for Ubique.

Ubique, Latin for *everywhere*, was the first female utopia on American soil, and like several earlier utopias, it found a home in a fertile valley among the hills of southern Indiana. Southeast of Bloomington, northwest of Seymour, Ubique came about because women wanted to learn from mistakes made at other failed utopias, to give it a shot for themselves. Ubique was also the subject of my yet-to-be-completed dissertation.

My plan was to spend two days in a drafty, mousetrap-filled, one-story frame dwelling in need of a paint job. The Mary Bedford Coffin House, just off the tiny town square in historically preserved Ubique, would be my home for Christmas. Though I'd waited until the last minute, the house was still easily reserved. Who else would want to spend Christmas in an empty feminist utopian ghost town?

As soon as I got off I-65 and onto the back roads, I pulled into a gas station and purchased everything I would never consume in front of my kids. Monster-sized cola with ice pellets. Doritos, packs of orange crackers with peanut butter, and a Biggie KitKat, all in an ocean-clogging plastic bag. Also a large bottle of water, a can of V8, and three of Oliver Winery's easiest reds for medicinal purposes.

Maybe I was ready.

When the historical marker for Ubique appeared on my right, I pulled over to take a picture. This was tradition. I had maybe twenty of these pictures saved in my phone. This time, the background was gray and the sky insulated. I parked in front of the wide two-story Meeting House and turned off my car.

I've tried to capture in words what Ubique feels like, and I'm not sure I'll ever truly succeed. At one time, to its inhabitants, it must have felt like the realization of every dream they'd ever had. The large two-story Meeting House was matched across the village garden by an identical building that had once served as the living quarters for seventy-two women at the height of Ubique's success. To some, that number might seem small and the term *success* a misnomer, but for Ubique, that brief moment in time must have felt heady. Women of all ages helping each other, sisters doing it all for themselves (once a dissertation title I'd loved and then tossed aside). Women blacksmithing, women baking the daily bread, women designing the buildings, women repairing the fences, women healing the sick, women farming, women making decisions for their bodies and their community decades before the government of the United States gave them the right to vote.

The money came from Mary Bedford Coffin. The widow of a wealthy Scottish factory owner, Mary was a student of utopian-socialists Charles Fourier and Robert Owen. She asked feminists Anna Wheeler and Frances Wright to help her establish a "radical gathering place for women to organize themselves . . . a world of their own." Many believe it was Mary's words that inspired Virginia Woolf's own phrasing. But creating a community took more than one woman's money and several women's ideals. It took the right kind of inhabitants.

Owenite communities like New Harmony often failed because the wrong kind of people joined—people with great ideas, but no tangible skills, no abilities to take care of themselves or each other. Ubique lasted longer because most of the women who came had already learned what it took to keep an intentional community going because they'd been part of the previous failures. But, in the end, Ubique met the same fate.

I walked from building to building, thinking of the women who arrived after Ubique's founding. Some joined wanting a life of study, community, and ritual, but outside the auspices of religious institutions. Others were lesbians creating a new world order because the old one chose to persecute them. Still more came for short periods of time, using the community of Ubique as a place of safety for themselves and their families. They were wives running from abuse, the pregnant, disavowed young, or spinsters, sisters turned out when their nursing was no longer required, when someone more important was in want of a home. What did I believe the ghosts of Ubique offered me, now? I wasn't certain, but I opened every door.

By 1900, Ubique was almost empty. Many of its original founders had died, and the younger generation wanted something else, somewhere else. Why did Ubique fail? Maybe it didn't. This was the crux of my dissertation, or, at least, its current flavor.

I ended my tour in the Meeting House. It was silent. I didn't even turn on the lights. The reflected pallor of the sky and the few remaining dirty banks of snow surrounded me just beyond the wavy windowpane. It felt like I was on another planet.

Ten boys were raised in Ubique. These were the faces I gazed at in the display in the old school room. I visited this photo every time I came, wondering about these boys raised completely in a world of women. Each time, feeling guilty, like this interest was a betrayal to my research. Why them? Why *their* story? Hadn't they been given enough? But I kept returning to the thought of writing about these ten boys.

I'd discovered several of their stories: two had become inventors, one a semi-famous poet, another a respected Congressman. Still another grew up to become an artist of regional renown. A wall-sized enlargement of one of his earliest paintings met visitors entering Ubique's Meeting House. In the foreground, it showed a field in springtime, obviously the farmland that surrounded Ubique. In the distance were two wide oaks and the old well. You could just make out the rooflines of the community's buildings. It was almost as if the painter wanted you to experience looking back at Ubique, a place that was a home before it was abandoned.

From my research, it appeared as if the children raised in Ubique almost universally recalled a magical childhood. Several had written that the education they'd received in Ubique set them on their paths in a particular way. "I was never afraid to try," one wrote. I could never read those words without envy.

My own two children were no longer in flight. I looked at my phone. No messages. It would be even darker soon.

As I walked back to the Coffin House to unpack my things, my phone buzzed. It was my thirteen-year-old. *Miss you Mom. Wish you were here. Iggy does too.* I stood outside, almost in the exact middle of Ubique, and hated everything in that moment, except for them. I would have gotten in my dented car and driven, right then and there, to them. I wanted to type, that for me, everything was just the two of them. That they were my—

Dad says hi and not to worry.

It's going to be okay, I told myself. First world problems—*they were skiing*! Cursing aloud, I typed a few cheerful lines about snow and love and fun, sprinkled with emojis. I became light, so light I almost didn't need to breathe.

And that's when I saw her.

She was across the road, in the cemetery. She was staring at me. I waved. Her right hand moved slightly in my direction. A tiny, bent old woman in a blue coat, her car parked beside her. I hadn't heard a car. Maybe she'd driven up while I was in the Meeting House or the dormitory or freezing in the blacksmith's shop.

"Hello," I called. She looked to be in her nineties. Curly white hair, glasses, thick-soled sneakers, and insulated work gloves. Her pants nearly the same blue as her coat. She leaned on a wheeled walker that she began folding up as I crossed the road.

"May I help you?" I asked.

"No," she answered curtly, stowing the walker in the reclined passenger seat of the car. Then her eyes fell on the keys in my hand. "How did you get those?"

I introduced myself. "I'm doing research," I said. "The director has kindly given me the run of the place. I'm very lucky."

"You think?" Then, her squint grew wide-eyed. "It takes a certain kind of person to want to spend Christmas in Ubique."

I wasn't sure what to say.

She walked carefully over to the driver's seat, got in, and closed the door. She turned the car on as I waved.

"Merry Christmas," I said, still trying.

She barely nodded and then nearly ran me over.

I walked back to the Coffin House, unsure of myself. My phone buzzed again. *Miss you Mom. Love you. Dad said we can call you tomorrow to say HappyCmasEve.* Deer Emoji. Red Heart Emoji. Green Heart Emoji. *Iggy* = Crying Emoji. *But now he's okay. Dad and Trish brought us a bunch of new*

. . .

Iggy says he misses you.

Miss you both too, I typed, *but you are going to have SO MUCH FUN and be back before you know it. Call me ANYTIME.*

Lately, we communicated better on the small screen. In unpunctuated lines and symbols, we were somehow our best essential selves. Our words could be fundamental—joy, sadness, sorrow, humor, boredom, fear, hope, exhaustion, grief. Be it about dinner or a test or what I could pick up on my way home from work, it was a relief to autocorrect parenthood one emoji after another.

Three more text messages, a flotilla of meaning, and then good night.

I took off my coat and consumed all the junk food without tasting a bite. No television in utopia, the WIFI code not working, I crawled under the quilt fully clothed and drank a bottle and a half of hibiscus-colored wine. Everything smelled of mildew, and I was unsure if I would ever be warm or happy again.

The next morning, I woke with a headache and a pimple on the side of my nose. Rudolph without the cocoa, I thought, looking in the cloudy bathroom mirror. I showered and brushed my teeth, nauseous and full of self-loathing. Angry especially that I hadn't noticed that there was no real coffee in the Mary Bedford Coffin House. An anachronistic Keurig sat on the counter of the makeshift kitchen, but I could only find decaf pods in the basket beside it. I grabbed my keys, noting that I had yet to unpack my research.

No messages. There was a time difference, of course—and skiing—and a chocolate fountain.

I drove to the same gas station where I'd stopped the day before. But this time it was early morning, much colder, and Christmas Eve. I felt incapable of gas station banter, but when I saw the elderly woman from the cemetery sitting in a booth with a newspaper, half a donut, and a cup of coffee. I said hello. It's what you do, even if your heart's broken and your head isn't far behind.

"You have kids?" she asked.

I said their names and ages in a tone that sounded as if I was auditioning for a game show instead of suffering under the fluorescent lighting of a gas station. And then I went ahead and told her—about missing my kids, about the dissertation that refused to die or come to life, about everything. She told me to get myself a coffee and sit down. She said her name was Betty Davis. "Y not E," she said, frowning at my smile. Then she leaned towards me with a question. "Ever hear the story of Mary Fisher?"

Mary Fisher came to Ubique with her mother and two sisters when she was a toddler. She ran away from Ubique at the age of fifteen after falling in love with a member of the infamous Simeon gang. Rem Simeon and his brother invented a new form of robbery. On October 6, 1866, the Simeon brothers got on an Ohio & Mississippi passenger train near Seymour, Indiana, and committed the first train robbery in history. That day, wearing masks, the brothers stole an estimated $10,000 in gold coins and $33 in bank notes.

Mary left even the conventions of the unconventional Ubique when she ran off with Rem Simeon. "He was an outlaw through and through," Betty Davis explained. She told the story of how Rem and his brother, John, got their start as bounty jumpers during the Civil War. "Men would get called up, you see. The draft. And they'd pay the Simeon boys to take their place. Rem and John would enlist under someone else's name and, a little while later, desert. Then they'd find another bounty and do it again."

The story didn't end well. The Simeon gang was hung by a "local vigilante mob."

"Pinkertons had something to do with it," Betty said. "Fat cats were sick of losing their money to a bunch of Indiana country boys."

Mary Fisher and her children—there were at least five of them by that time— returned to Ubique. "The ladies took them in, of course, Mary being their own. But she was marked, you know. Never really trusted. Probably no longer really belonged."

"An outcast of the outcasts," I muttered, not remembering the name Fisher from any of my lists.

"The story goes that Mary didn't come back to Ubique completely empty-handed." Betty Davis took a moment and blew her nose, staring at me the entire time. I leaned forward, and I think it was that moment that decided it.

"There's a treasure in Ubique," Betty said. "You gonna help me find it?"

The metal detector in the trunk of Betty's car was too heavy for her to lift on her own. She told me this after we pulled up to the cemetery. Looking into the trunk, I touched the label on the metal detector, which read *The Bounty Hunter*. "Does the director know you're hunting for buried treasure on the grounds?"

Betty ignored the question. "Put the headphones around your neck" she said and turned up the volume.

She opened her purse and threw a quarter, a penny, and what looked to be a man's gold wedding ring onto the cold ground. "Lucky it isn't icy today. Too much snow last Christmas. Okay, now set it to Tone. Discrepancy about 12 o'clock." Betty pointed to each dial. "Sensitivity . . . oh, about two."

I did as I was told.

"There, now go," she said, directing me to wave the metal detector over each item. With both coins, I heard a high-pitched bleet, but as I waved the machine over the gold ring, a low, deep sizzle filled my ears.

"You hear that?" Betty asked, her face barely coming to my shoulder, her dentures appearing when she smiled.

"Where should we begin?" I asked, unable to keep the excitement from my voice.

"You can start by picking those up," she said, nodding towards the ground.

All day we looked. It was bright and cold. Betty sat in her car, driving behind me as I listened to the headphones. I was certain we would find the treasure. The Bounty Hunter led me to discover a belt buckle, a black penny, a bent spoon, and the pop top of a beer can. By 2:00, my elbow ached. The clouds were rolling in, and the wind grew. I pulled my phone from my pocket. No messages.

"Let's stop and eat something," Betty grunted. We were wearing our winter coats inside the old Ubique chicken coop. We'd been through every building and barn, every garden space and orchard, and alongside each of Ubique's three roads.

It was growing dark as I followed Betty in my own car. Her house, about a mile from Ubique, was small and low-slung. It looked as if it had been bricked over in the 1970s. There were two outbuildings and a leaning pole barn. I followed Betty Davis inside her home as she turned on the lights and the heat.

"I don't boil it like most oldies when I'm not here. Waste," she said, making her way to her tiny kitchen. The cupboards looked to be handmade of cedar. At least it didn't smell of mothballs. I noticed pictures of two children on her refrigerator, and I wasn't sure if I should ask. They were school photos—one child smiling, the other not. A boy and a girl. I looked at my phone.

Betty made us soup from a can and buttered two slices of bread. She washed an apple for me and put a banana down for herself. "Get glasses, and I'll get the whiskey." She poured us each a finger or two of golden liquid from a bottle I didn't recognize.

"Merry Christmas," she mumbled, picking up her spoon.

I responded in kind and took a sip. I'm not sure if it was the day or the soup or the whiskey, but I didn't ask enough. Yes, I learned she was a descendant of Mary Fisher and Rem Simeon. Yes, I learned how many years she'd been searching for treasure. But there were so many questions left unsaid. I didn't ask if she had children, if she'd been married, if she'd ever been in love, if she'd ever had her heart broken. I didn't ask what it was like to grow old. I didn't ask how to keep going after failing at something so important that it feels as if you might never succeed at anything else.

We talked mostly about Ubique and the treasure. And while I listened to Betty Davis, I thought about what I would do with the money. It was a revelation. I had spent so much time looking for meaning, for responsibility and poignancy in everything, and all of it was transcended in an instant. *Treasure*! I felt unburdened by this new task. Is there anything more irresistible than to take something valuable? Especially, when it was lost by someone else.

Before I left that night, Betty Davis pulled out two boxes that she let me look through. One box held photos of her father, the last boy born in Ubique. It even held a photograph of an unsmiling Mary Fisher, surrounded by her unsmiling children. There were also letters. Betty read aloud the one that Rem Simeon wrote to Mary just before he died.

I couldn't help myself. "Why aren't these in the collection?" Until that point, we'd successfully avoided any conversation that involved Ubique's modern incarnation as an Historical Site. Betty made a sound of disgust, and I made amends.

"I understand completely." I looked again at Rem Simeon's handwriting. "I've been through that cemetery and the inhabitant lists a million times," I said, "but I've never seen their names."

"Because she changed them," Betty answered, looking tired all of a sudden. "After they killed Rem like that. Wouldn't you?"

I nodded.

The second box was larger than the first. It held everything Betty Davis had ever discovered in Ubique. Several decades' worth of found objects, including a class ring and an 1873 silver dollar. I added our findings from the day to the stash. Betty closed the lid.

"Just like Christmas." She grinned ruefully. I tried to be hopeful, but Betty only shook her head.

"Bunch of refugees paying taxes. Birth in a barn." Betty ran her fingers up and down the edges of the box. "And we celebrate that."

"We're going to find it," I said.

I shouldn't have driven. I'd had too much to drink. I went so slowly into that night, onto the silent road, expecting disaster. But my headlights only captured snow angling down. Everyone else was already home. I left with the plan to meet Betty in the morning. She would bring gas station coffee and donuts, and we would spend Christmas searching for the treasure.

That didn't happen.

In the morning, my phone rang. It was my children. Their voices were sweet and the ache in my heart was something I could almost bear. After hanging up, I waited for Betty, making a list of the best possible locations. In the letter she had read the night before, Rem Simeon wrote to Mary that even though death might separate them, she could always find him in their spot, a place he called the "valley between loss and wishes." I wrote that line on an index card and stared at it.

I imagined what it would be like to dig up treasure. For some reason, I could only picture it in the summer. It would be humid and I would wear work boots, steel toe against shovel, shovel against dirt. Maybe my children would join us. I would write a book about it. I listed possible titles.

Everything would change, I thought, happily, looking at a topographical map of Ubique, searching for any suggestion of a valley.

Around 9:30, I drove to Betty's house and knocked on the door. I rang the bell. Her car wasn't in the driveway. It wasn't at the gas station. It wasn't in Ubique. I returned to the Mary Bedford Coffin House to wait for her, impatient to begin again. My arm was still sore from the day before, but what did that matter when there was treasure somewhere beneath my feet.

Mary Fisher had been a child in Ubique. I read through my notes again, remembering all the places the children had played. "Down the creek and under the Giants," a line from a poem. Pulling on my coat, I walked out past the cemetery to the shriveled creek. Maybe I will live to be as old as Betty Davis, I thought.

I heard a car pull up, the gravel crunching. It was just before noon. I hurried back to the road, expecting to see Betty, but it was the director and her husband. They'd been to a Christmas service and brought me a plate of cookies on their way to their son's house.

"How's your research going?" the director asked from the passenger seat, still buckled in.

"Great," I said and soon waved them goodbye, thrilled with the secret I shared with Betty, kept.

After they left, I turned back to the cemetery, and that's when I saw it. The gravestone of Mary Remington. Mother of T. S. Remington, the landscape painter. The painting! Two oaks, the wishing well, past the cemetery, a valley between loss and wishes.

I rushed to Betty's house and pounded on the door. I walked around to the back. All the windows were curtained; I couldn't see inside. I started to get a bad feeling. Had something happened to Betty?

I called her name and rang the bell, wondering if I should break a window. It was freezing outside. Putting my ear to the door, I thought I heard something. I waited, listening. In front of her door, the snow held the imprint of a footstep. She must have at least gotten the morning paper.

I wrote a quick note and slipped it inside the front door, waiting in my car to see if Betty Davis would come. She didn't. Eventually, I pulled out of her driveway and ordered a bad pizza from the gas station. On the way back, I tried Betty's house again.

The note was gone.

But still, no one came to the door.

At least she's alive, I thought.

The note had contained everything I could fit onto an index card: the fact I had to leave in the morning to get back to my job and my life, and the place where I thought we'd find the treasure.

The next morning, I left Ubique. I went home, where I worked on the dissertation half-heartedly for another year before I put it down, this time for good. My children grew older. My life kept going, filled both with things done and left undone. But every once in a while—more often than I care to admit—I think back on that note. I turn it over and over in my mind; I've worn the edges round. What I want to know is: Why did I write that note in the first place? If I hadn't written it—if I had just gone after the treasure myself—who would I have become?

I don't know the answer. I'll never know that answer.

All I know for certain is this. The next morning, as I prepared to leave Ubique for home, I opened the trunk of my car and found it. The Bounty Hunter, Betty Davis's metal detector, without a note or explanation. Beside it, a single gold coin.

DECEMBER

EXCERPT FROM *ABE MARTIN'S ALMANACK*

Frank McKinney Hubbard

YOU HAVE BEEN IN THE WEST FOR years, and it has been a constant struggle for existence. You are on the road home for Christmas, and you are bringing a young wife with you—Annie. The railroad fare has cost all that you have been able to save, but how happy you are!

Annie wonders if your mother will like her and how your brothers and sisters will look. You gather your bags and parcels together and put on your wraps many miles from your destination, so eager are you. How slow the train runs!

A tired-looking woman, dressed in dingy black, with two small, sticky children, sits just across the aisle from you. They are embedded in empty paper bags and orange peelings, and the mother's hair is coming down. The forlorn-looking trio was put aboard the train way back in Nebraska by a rough, sullen-looking man who did not even kiss the little ones good-bye or utter one single gentle word to the woman. Annie wonders where they are going and if anyone will be glad to see them.

At last you reach your destination, and your father pushes his way through the crowd of curious, felt-booted villagers to greet you. Father has not changed much. A little dash of white here and there in his shaggy whiskers, and the shoulders of his overcoat have turned a yellowish brown, but he is still strong and hearty.

The old surrey is hitched behind the grain elevator where Lizzie can't see the cars. You all climb in and are soon rolling along the rough country road. You notice so many changes in the advertisements on the barns. The tall oaks that stood about Hiram Green's house have been cut away and sold. There are no doors or windows in the old Williams home—the folks are all dead and gone.

A sudden turn in the road and you can see your home nestled among the cedars on the hill. A woman is walking slowly down the hill. As you draw near you notice how white and frail she looks, how thin and unsteady her hand is as she unfastens the gate. It is your mother. She wanted to be the first to embrace you.

Presently your brothers and sisters are about you, and what a welcome! Annie feels easier now. You all walk up the hill to the house—a tall, thin, unpainted house with a summer kitchen, but the curtains are as white as the driven snow.

Brother Jim doesn't look very prosperous, and when he awkwardly bends over you and whispers that "your wife is all right," you catch a faint odor of cloves. Poor Jim has always been Mother's favorite.

You can't quite figure out sister Nell's hair, but she strikes you as being a stunning woman. Nell is a trimmer in the city, and she does the buying at the spring and fall displays. She opens Annie's eyes when she tells of the wonderful profits on flowers and feathers.

Brother Henry has told his house some sort of a story in order to get home from Duluth to reunite. Henry is your father's favorite and travels on the road and gets a salary and a commission, too. He belongs to all the lodges and looks fine and single. He tells your father that he is going to take him down east some time and show him a few things, but Father only laughs.

You take a peep in the parlor, and the old musty smell is still there. Nothing has been changed since the children went away. The glass cane is in its accustomed corner near the column stove, and the curious little box made of varnished peach seeds still sets off the center table. How it caught your eye when you were a child! You open it, and on the underside of the lid, protected by glass, is a lock of chestnut hair—your mother's hair. The odd cabinet contains old, faded daguerreotypes in clumsy cases, held secure by brass hooks.

You gently close the door and join the family. The heat from the sitting-room fireplace has had its effect on Jim, and he sleeps peacefully on the padded settee. You all go in to dinner without him.

The old, two-leaf table can scarcely stand under the weight of dark-colored preserves in heavy glass dishes of primitive design. The same big blue tureen with which your mother went into business is on the board filled with mashed potatoes. The castor and the bone-handled butter knife—every familiar object, everything you used to like, is there. You are eating at home again.

After dinner you all walk out to the barn, Father ahead, to see the new calf—all except Mother. By three o'clock she has the dining room and kitchen "tidied" and slowly climbs upstairs to her room for a little rest—the same low, back bedroom, overlooking the currant bushes and the smokehouse.

BEASLEY'S CHRISTMAS PARTY

Booth Tarkington

I

The maple-bordered street was as still as a country Sunday, so quiet that there seemed an echo to my footsteps. It was four o'clock in the morning; clear October moonlight misted through the thinning foliage to the shadowy sidewalk and lay like a transparent silver fog upon the house of my admiration, as I strode along, returning from my first night's work on the *Wainwright Morning Despatch.*

I had already marked that house as the finest (to my taste) in Wainwright, though hitherto, on my excursions to this metropolis, the state capital, I was not without a certain native jealousy that Spencerville, the country seat where I lived, had nothing so good. Now, however, I approached its purlieus with a pleasure in it quite unalloyed, for I was at last myself a resident (albeit of only one day's standing) of Wainwright, and the house—though I had not even an idea who lived there—part of my possessions as a citizen. Moreover, I might enjoy the warmer pride of a next-door neighbor, for Mrs. Apperthwaite's, where I had taken a room, was just beyond.

This was the quietest part of Wainwright; business stopped short of it, and the "fashionable residence section" had overlapped this "forgotten backwater," leaving it undisturbed and unchanging, with that look about it which is the quality of a few urban quarters, and eventually of none, as a town grows to be a city—the look of still being a neighborhood. This friendliness of appearance was largely the emanation of the homely and beautiful house which so greatly pleased my fancy.

It might be difficult to say why I thought it the "finest" house in Wainwright, for a simpler structure would be hard to imagine; it was merely a big, old-fashioned brick house, painted brown and very plain, set well away from the street among some splendid forest trees, with a fair spread of flat lawn. But it gave back a great deal for your glance, just as some people do. It was a large house, as I say, yet it looked not like a mansion but like a home; and made you wish that you lived in it. Or, driving by, of an evening, you would have liked to hitch your horse and go in; it spoke so surely of hearty, old-fashioned people living there, who would welcome you merrily.

It looked like a house where there were a grandfather and grandmother; where holidays were warmly kept; where there were boisterous family reunions to which uncles and aunts, who had been born there, would return from no matter what distances; a house where big turkeys would be on the table often; where one called "the hired man" (and named either Abner or Ole) would crack walnuts upon a flatiron clutched between his knees on the back porch; it looked like a house where they played charades; where there would be long streamers of evergreen and dozens of wreaths of holly at Christmastime; where there were tearful, happy weddings and great throwings of rice after little brides, from the broad front steps: in a word, it was the sort of a house to make the hearts of spinsters and bachelors very lonely and wistful—and that is about as near as I can come to my reason for thinking it the finest house in Wainwright.

The moon hung kindly above its level roof in the silence of that October morning, as I checked my gait to loiter along the picket fence; but suddenly the house showed a light of its own. The spurt of a match took my eye to one of the upper windows, then a steadier glow of orange told me that a lamp was lighted. The window was opened, and a man looked out and whistled loudly.

I stopped, thinking that he meant to attract my attention; that something might be wrong; that perhaps someone was needed to go for a doctor. My mistake was immediately evident, however; I stood in the shadow of the trees bordering the sidewalk, and the man at the window had not seen me.

"Boy! Boy!" he called, softly. "Where are you, Simpledoria?"

He leaned from the window, looking downward. "Why, *there* you are!" he exclaimed, and turned to address some invisible person within the room. "He's right there, underneath the window. I'll bring him up." He leaned out again. "Wait there, Simpledoria!" he called. "I'll be down in a jiffy and let you in."

Puzzled, I stared at the vacant lawn before me. The clear moonlight revealed it brightly, and it was empty of any living presence; there were no bushes nor shrubberies—nor even shadows—that could have been mistaken for a boy, if "Simpledoria" *was* a boy. There was no dog in sight; there was no cat; there was nothing beneath the window except thick, close-cropped grass.

A light shone in the hallway behind the broad front doors; one of these was opened, and revealed in silhouette the tall, thin figure of a man in a long, old-fashioned dressing-gown.

"Simpledoria," he said, addressing the night air with considerable severity, "I don't know what to make of you. You might have caught your death of cold, roving out at such an hour. But there," he continued, more indulgently; "wipe your feet on the mat and come in. You're safe *now!*"

He closed the door, and I heard him call to someone upstairs, as he rearranged the fastenings:

"Simpledoria is all right—only a little chilled. I'll bring him up to your fire."

I went on my way in a condition of astonishment that engendered, almost, a doubt of my eyes; for if my sight was unimpaired and myself not subject to optical or mental delusion, neither boy nor dog nor bird nor cat, nor any other object of this visible world, had entered that opened door. Was my "finest" house, then, a place of call for wandering ghosts, who came home to roost at four in the morning?

It was only a step to Mrs. Apperthwaite's; I let myself in with the key that good lady had given me, stole up to my room, went to my window, and stared across the yard at the house next door. The front window in the second story, I decided, necessarily belonged to that room in which the lamp had been lighted; but all was dark there now. I went to bed, and dreamed that I was out at sea in a fog, having embarked on a transparent vessel whose preposterous name, inscribed upon glass life-belts, depending here and there from an invisible rail, was *Simpledoria*.

Editor's note: *Let's skip over the next hundred pages, for the sake of space and also to avoid some material that probably wouldn't have been considered racist at the time, but would make a modern reader cringe hard enough to loosen a filling. Here's a quick synopsis of the story: The mysterious neighbor turns out to be David Beasley, candidate for governor. When his nemesis, Simeon Peck, finds out about this strange behavior, he hatches a plot to bring Beasley to ruin. The dastardly Peck invites reporters to Beasley's Christmas party to expose his insanity, but the situation backfires on him when everyone learns that Beasley is playing make-believe for the benefit of his ward, an infirm child. Okay, onto the lovely ending:*

"My soul!" said the *Journal* reporter, gasping. "And he did all THAT—just to please a little sick kid!"

"I can't figure it out," murmured Sim Peck, piteously.

"I can," said the *Journal* reporter. "This story WILL be all over town tomorrow." He glanced at me, and I nodded. "It'll be all over town," he continued, "though not in any of the papers—and I don't believe it's going to hurt Dave Beasley's chances any."

Mr. Peck and his companions turned toward the street; they went silently.

The young man from the *Journal* overtook them. "Thank you for sending for me," he said, cordially. "You've given me a treat. I'm FER Beasley!"

Dowden put his hand on my shoulder. He had not observed the third figure still remaining.

"Well, sir," he remarked, shaking the snow from his coat, "they were right about one thing: it certainly was mighty low down of Dave not to invite *me*—and you, too—to his Christmas party. Let him go to thunder with his old invitation, I'm going in, anyway! Come on. I'm plum froze."

There was a side door just beyond the bay window, and Dowden went to it and rang, loud and long. It was Beasley himself who opened it.

"What in the name—" he began, as the ruddy light fell upon Dowden's face and upon me, standing a little way behind. "What *are* you two—snowbanks? What on earth are you fellows doing out here?"

"We've come to your Christmas party, you old horse-thief!" Thus Mr. Dowden.

"*Hoo*-ray!" said Beasley.

Dowden turned to me. "Aren't you coming?"

"What are you waiting for, old fellow?" said Beasley.

I waited a moment longer, and then it happened.

[Mrs. Apperthwaite] came out of the shadow and went to the foot of the steps, her cloak falling from her shoulders as she passed me. I picked it up.

She lifted her arms pleadingly, though her head was bent with what seemed to me a beautiful sort of shame. She stood there with the snow driving against her and did not speak. Beasley drew his hand slowly across his eyes—to see if they were really there, I think.

"David," she said, at last. "You've got so many lovely people in your house tonight: isn't there room for—for just one fool? It's Christmastime!"

IN GOD WE TRUST: ALL OTHERS PAY CASH

Jean Parker Shepherd Jr.

IT WAS NOW THE SECOND WEEK OF December and all the stores in town stayed open nights, which meant that things were really getting serious. Every evening immediately after supper we would pile into the car and drive downtown for that great annual folk rite, that most ecstatic, golden, tinseled, quivering time of all kidhood: Christmas shopping. Milling crowds of blue-jowled, agate-eyed foundry workers, gray-faced refinery men, and motley hordes of open-hearth, slag-heap, Bessemer-converter, tin-mill, coke-plant, and welding-shop fugitives trudged through the wildly pulsing department stores, through floor after floor of shiny, beautiful, unattainable treasure, trailed by millions of leatherette-jacketed, high-topped, mufflered kids, each with a gnawing hunger to Get It All. Worried-looking, flush-faced mothers wearing grayed cloth coats with ratty fox-fur collars, their hands chapped and raw from years of dishwater therapy, rode herd on the surging mob, ranging far and wide into the aisles and under the counters, cuffing, slapping, dragging whiners of all sizes from department to department.

At the far end of Toyland in Goldblatt's, on a snowy throne framed with red-and-white candy canes under a suspended squadron of plastic angels blowing silver trumpets in a glowing gold grotto, sat the Man, the Connection: Santa Claus himself. In Northern Indiana Santa Claus is a big man, both spiritually and physically, and the Santa Claus at Goldblatt's was officially recognized among the kids as being unquestionably THE Santa Claus. In person. Eight feet tall, shiny high black patent-leather boots, a nimbus cloud of snow-white beard, and a real, thrumming, belt-creaking stomach. No pillows or stuffing. I mean a real stomach!

A long line of nervous, fidgeting, greedy urchins wound in and out of the aisles, shoving, sniffling, and above all waiting, waiting to tell HIM what they wanted. In those days it was not easy to disbelieve fully in Santa Claus, because there wasn't much else to believe in, and there were many theological arguments over the nature of, the existence of, the affirmation and denial of his existence. However, ten days before zero hour, the air pulsing to the strains of "We Three Kings of Orient Are," the store windows garlanded with green-and-red wreaths, and the toy department bristling with shiny Flexible Flyers, there were few who dared to disbelieve. As each day crept on to the next like some arthritic glacier, the atheists among us grew moodier and less and less sure of ourselves, until finally in each scoffing heart was the floating, drifting, nagging suspicion:

"Well, you never can tell."

It did not pay to take chances, and so we waited in line for our turn. Behind me a skinny seven-year-old girl wearing a brown stocking cap and gold-rimmed glasses hit her little brother steadily to keep him in line. She had green teeth. He was wearing an aviator's helmet with the goggles pulled down over his eyes. His galoshes were open and his maroon corduroy knickers were damp. Behind them a fat boy in a huge sheepskin coat stood numbly, his eyes watering in vague fear, his nose red and running. Ahead of my brother and me, a long, uneven procession of stocking caps, mufflers, mittens, and earmuffs inched painfully forward, while in the hazy distance, in his magic glowing cave, Mister Claus sat each in turn on his broad red knee and listened to exultant dream after exultant dream whispered, squeaked, shouted, or sobbed into his shell-like, whisker-encased ear.

Closer and closer we crept. My mother and father had stashed us in line and disappeared. We were alone. Nothing stood between us and our confessor, our benefactor, our patron saint, our dispenser of BB guns, but 297 other beseechers at the throne. I have always felt that later generations of tots, products of less romantic upbringings, cynical nonbelievers in Santa Claus from birth, can never know the nature of the true dream. I was well into my twenties before I finally gave up on the Easter bunny, and I am not convinced that I am the richer for it. Even now there are times when I'm not so sure about the stork.

Over the serpentine line roared a great sea of sound: tinkling bells, recorded carols, the hum and clatter of electric trains, whistles tooting, mechanical cows mooing, cash registers dinging, and from far off in the faint distance the "Ho-ho-ho-ing" of jolly old Saint Nick.

One moment my brother and I were safely back in the Tricycle and Irish Mail department and the next instant we stood at the foot of Mount Olympus itself. Santa's enormous gleaming white snowdrift of a throne soared ten or fifteen feet above our heads on a mountain of red and green tinsel carpeted with flashing Christmas-tree bulbs and gleaming ornaments. Each kid in turn was prodded up a tiny staircase at the side of the mountain on Santa's left, as he passed his last customer on to his right and down a red chute—back into oblivion for another year.

Pretty ladies dressed in Snow White costumes, gauzy gowns glittering with sequins, and tiaras clipped to their golden, artificial hair, presided at the head of the line, directing traffic and keeping order. As we drew nearer, Santa seemed to loom larger and larger. The tension mounted. My brother was now whimpering steadily. I herded him ahead of me while, behind, the girl in the glasses did the same with her kid brother. Suddenly there was no one left ahead of us in the line. Snow White grabbed my brother's shoulder with an iron grip and he was on his way up the slope.

"Quit dragging your feet. Get moving," she barked at the toiling little figure climbing the stairs.

The music from above was deafening:

JINGLE BELLS, JINGLE BELLS, JINGLE ALL THE WAY. . . . sung by ten thousand echo-chambered reverberating chipmunks. . . .

High above me in the sparkling gloom I could see my brother's yellow-and-brown stocking cap as he squatted briefly on Santa's gigantic knee. I heard a booming "Ho-ho-ho," then a high, thin, familiar, trailing wail, one that I had heard billions of times before, as my brother broke into his Primal cry. A claw dug into my elbow and I was launched upward toward the mountaintop.

I had long before decided to level with Santa, to really lay it on the line. No Sandy Andy, no kid stuff. If I was going to ride the range with Red Ryder, Santa Claus was going to have to get the straight poop.

"AND WHAT'S YOUR NAME, LITTLE BOY?"

His booming baritone crashed out over the chipmunks. He reached down and neatly hooked my sheepskin collar, swooping me upward, and there I sat on the biggest knee in creation, looking down and out over the endless expanse of Toyland and down to the tiny figures that wound off into the distance.

"Uhh . . . uhhh . . . uhhh. . . ."

"THAT'S A FINE NAME, LITTLE BOY! HO-HO-HO!"

Santa's warm, moist breath poured down over me as though from some cosmic steam radiator. Santa smoked Camels, like my Uncle Charles.

My mind had gone blank! Frantically I tried to remember what it was I wanted. I was blowing it! There was no one else in the world except me and Santa now. And the chipmunks.

"Uhhh . . . ahhhh. . . ."

"WOULDN'T YOU LIKE A NICE FOOTBALL?"

My mind groped. Football, football. Without conscious will, my voice squeaked out:

"Yeah."

My God, a football! My mind slammed into gear. Already Santa was sliding me off his knee and toward the red chute, and I could see behind me another white-faced kid bobbing upward.

"I want a Red Ryder BB gun with a special Red Ryder sight and a compass in the stock with a sundial!" I shouted.

"HO-HO-HO! YOU'LL SHOOT YOUR EYE OUT, KID. HO-HO-HO! MERRY CHRISTMAS!"

Down the chute I went.

I have never been struck by a bolt of lightning, but I know how it must feel. The back of my head was numb. My feet clanked leadenly beneath me as I returned to earth at the bottom of the chute. Another Snow White shoved the famous tree gift into my mitten—a barely recognizable plastic Kris Kringle stamped with bold red letters: MERRY XMAS. SHOP AT GOLDBLATT'S FREE PARKING—and spun me back out into Toyland. My brother stood sniveling under a counter piled high with Raggedy Ann dolls, from nowhere my mother and father appeared.

"Did you tell Santa what you wanted?" the Old Man asked.

"Yeah. . . ."

"Did he ask you if you had been a good boy?"

"No."

"Ha! Don't worry. He knows anyway. I'll bet he knows about the basement window. Don't worry. He knows."

Maybe that was it! My mind reeled with the realization that maybe Santa did know how rotten I had been and that the football was not only a threat but a punishment. There had been for generations on Cleveland Street a theory that if you were not "a good boy" you would reap your just desserts under the Christmas tree. This idea had been largely discounted by the more confirmed evildoers in the neighborhood, but now I could not escape the distinct possibility that there was something to it. Usually for a full month or so before the big day most kids walked the straight and narrow, but I had made a drastic slip from the paths of righteousness by knocking out a basement window with a sled runner and then compounding the idiocy by denying it when all the evidence was incontrovertible. This caused an uproar which had finally resulted in my getting my mouth washed out with Lux and a drastic curtailment of allowance to pay for the glass. I could see that either my father or Santa, or perhaps both, were not content to let bygones be bygones. Were they in league with each other? Or was Santa actually a mother in disguise?

The next few days groaned by. Now only three more school days remained before Christmas vacation, that greatest time of all the year. As it drew closer, Miss Iona Pearl Bodkin, my homeroom teacher, became more and more manic, whipping the class into a veritable frenzy of Yuletide joy. We belted out carol after carol. We built our own paper Christmas tree with cut-out ornaments. We strung long strips of popcorn chains. Crayon Santas and silver-paper wreaths poured out of our assembly line.

In the corner of the room, atop a desk decorated with crepe-paper rosettes, sat our Christmas grab bag. Every kid in the class had brought a gift for the grab bag, with someone's name—drawn from a hat—attached. I had bought for Helen Weathers a large, amazingly life-like, jet-black rubber tarantula. I cackled fiendishly as I wrapped it, and even now its beady green eyes glared from somewhere in the depths of the Christmas grab bags. I knew she'd like it.

Miss Bodkin, after recess, addressed us:

"I want all of you to write a theme. . . ."

A theme! A rotten theme before Christmas! There must be kids somewhere who love writing themes, but to a normal air-breathing human kid, writing themes is a torture that ranks only with the dreaded medieval chin-breaker of Inquisitional fame. A theme!

". . . entitled 'What I want for Christmas,'" she concluded.

The clouds lifted. I saw a faint gleam of light at the other end of the black cave of gloom which had enveloped me since my visit to Santa. Rarely had the words poured from my penny pencil with such feverish fluidity. Here was a theme on a subject that needed talking about if ever one did! I remember to this day its glorious winged phrases and concise imagery:

What I want for Christmas is a Red Ryder BB gun with a compass
in the stock and this thing that tells time. I think everybody
should have a Red Ryder BB gun. They are very good for Christmas.
I don't think a football is a very good Christmas present.

I wrote it on blue-lined paper from my Indian Chief tablet, being very careful about the margins. Miss Bodkin was very snippy about uneven margins. The themes were handed in, and I felt somehow that when Miss Bodkin read mine she would sympathize with my plight and make an appeal on my behalf to the powers that be and that everything would work out, somehow. She was my last hope.

The final day before vacation dawned dank and misty, with swirling eddies of icy wind that rattled the porch swing. Warren G. Harding School glowed like a jeweled oasis amid the sooty snowbanks of the playground. Lights blazed from all the windows, and in every room the Christmas party spirit had kids writhing in their seats. The morning winged by, and after lunch Miss Bodkin announced that the rest of the afternoon would be party time. She handed out our graded themes, folded, with our names scrawled on the outside. A big red B in Miss Bodkin's direct hand glowed on my literary effort. I opened it, expecting Miss Bodkin's usual penciled corrections, which ran along the lines of "Watch margins" or "Check Sp." But this time a personal note leaped up, flew around the room, and fastened itself leech-like on the back of my neck:

"You'll shoot your eye out. Merry Christmas."

I sat in my seat, shipping water from every seam. Was there no end to this conspiracy of irrational prejudice against Red Ryder and his peacemaker? Nervously I pulled out of my desk the dog-eared back page of Open Road for Boys, which I had carried with me everywhere, waking and sleeping, for the past few weeks. Red Ryder's handsome orange face with the big balloon coming out of his mouth did not look discouraged or defeated. Red must have been a kid once himself, and they must have told him the same thing when he asked for his first Colt .44 for Christmas.

I stuffed my tattered dreams back into my geography book and gloomily watched other, happier, carefree, singing kids who were going to get what they wanted for Christmas as Miss Bodkin distributed little green baskets filled with hard candy. Somewhere off down the hall the sixth-grade glee club was singing "Oh little town of Bethlehem, how still we see thee lie. . . ."

Mechanically my jaws crunched on the concrete-hard rock candy and I stared hopelessly out of the window, past cut-out Santas and garlands of red and green chains. It was already getting dark. Night falls fast in Northern Indiana at that time of year. Snow was beginning to fall, drifting softly through the feeble yellow glow of distant street lamps while around me unbridled merriment raged high and higher.

By supper that night I had begun to resign myself to my fate. After all, I told myself, you can always use another football, and anyway, there will be other Christmases.

The day before, I had gone with my father and mother to the frozen parking lot next to the Esso station where, after long and soul-searching discussion, we had picked out our tree.

"There's a bare spot on the back."

"It'll fluff out, lady, when it gets hot."

"Is this the kind the needles fall out?"

"Nah, that's them balsams."

"Oh."

Now it stood in the living room, fragrantly, towering, teeteringly. Already my mother had begun the trimming operations. The lights were lit, and the living room was transformed into a small, warm paradise.

From the kitchen intoxicating smells were beginning to fill the house. Every year my mother baked two pumpkin pies, spicy and immobilizingly rich. Up through the hot-air registers echoed the boom and bellow of my father fighting The Furnace. I was locked in my bedroom in a fever of excitement. Before me on the bed were sheets of green and yellow paper, balls of colored string, and cellophane envelopes of stickers showing sleighing scenes, wreaths, and angels blowing trumpets. The zeppelin was already lumpily done—it had taken me forty-five minutes—and now I struggled with the big one, the magnificent gleaming gold and pearl perfume atomizer, knowing full well that I was wrapping what would undoubtedly become a treasured family heirloom. I checked the lock on the door, and for double safety hollered:

"DON'T ANYONE OPEN THIS DOOR!"

I turned back to my labors until finally there they were—my masterworks of creative giving piled in a neat pyramid on the quilt. My brother was locked in the bathroom, wrapping the fly swatter he had bought for the Old Man.

Our family always had its Christmas on Christmas Eve. Other less fortunate people, I had heard, opened their presents in the chill clammy light of dawn. Far more civilized, our Santa Claus recognized that barbaric practice for what it was. Around midnight great heaps of tissue, crinkly, sparkly, enigmatic packages appear among the lower branches of the tree and half hidden among the folds of the white bedsheet that looked in the soft light like some magic snowbank.

Earlier, just after the tree had been finished, my father had taken me and my brother out in the Graham-Paige to "pick up a bottle of wine." When we returned, Santa had been there and gone! On the end table and the bookcase were bowls of English walnuts, cashews, and almonds and petrified hard candy. My brother circled around the tree, moaning softly, while I, cooler and more controlled, quickly eyed the mountain of revealingly wrapped largess—and knew the worst.

Out of the kitchen came my mother, flushed and sparkly-eyed, bearing two wineglasses filled with the special Walgreen drugstore vintage that my Old Man especially favored. Christmas had officially begun. As they sipped their wine we plunged into the cornucopia, quivering with desire and the ecstasy of unbridled avarice. In the background, on the radio, Lionel Barrymore's wheezy, friendly old voice spoke kindly of Bob Cratchit and Tiny Tim and the ghost of old Marley.

The first package I grabbed was tagged "To Randy from Santa." I feverishly passed it over to my brother, who always was a slow reader, and returned to work. Aha!

"To Ralphie from Aunt Clara"—on a largish, lumpy, red-wrapped gift that I suspected to be the crummy football. Frantically I tore off the wrappings. Oh no! OH NO! A pair of fuzzy, pink, idiotic, cross-eyed, lop-eared bunny slippers! Aunt Clara had for years labored under the delusion that I was not only perpetually four years old but also a girl. My mother instantly added oil to the flames by saying:

"Oh, aren't they sweet! Aunt Clara always gives you the nicest presents. Put 'em on; see if they fit."

They did. Immediately my feet began to sweat as those two fluffy little bunnies with blue button eyes stared sappily up at me, and I knew that for at least two years I would have to wear them every time Aunt Clara visited us. I just hoped that Flick would never spot them, as the word of this humiliation could easily make life at Warren G. Harding School a veritable hell.

Next to me in harness my kid brother silently, doggedly stripped package after package until he hit the zeppelin. It was the jackpot!

"WOW! A ZEPPELIN! WHOOPEE! WOW!"

Falling over sideways with an ear-splitting yell, he launched it upward into the middle branches of the tree. Two glass angels and a golden bugle crashed to the floor, and a string of lights winked out.

"It's not supposed to fly, you nut," I said.

"AHH, WHAT GOOD IS A ZEPPELIN THAT DON'T FLY!?"

"It rolls. And beeps."

Instantly he was on his knees pushing the Graf Zeppelin, beeping fiendishly, propellers clacking, across the living-room rug. It was a sound that was to become sickeningly familiar in the months ahead. I suspect even at that moment my mother knew that one day the zeppelin would mysteriously disappear, never to beep again.

My father was on his feet with the first blink of the dying tree lights. He loved nothing better than to track down the continual short circuits and burned-out bulbs of Christmas tree light strings. Oblivious, I continued to ravage my gifts, feigning unalloyed joy at each lousy Sandy Andy, dump truck, and Monopoly game. My brother's gift to me was the only bright spot in an otherwise remarkably mediocre haul: a rubber Frankenstein face which I knew would come in handy. I immediately put it on and, peering through the slit eyes, continued to open my booty.

"Oh, how terrible!" my mother said. "Take it off and put it away."

"I think it looked good on him," my father said. I stood up and did my already famous Frankenstein walk, clumping stiff-legged around the living room and back to the tree.

Finally it was all over. There were no more mysterious packages under the tree, only a great pile of crumpled tissue paper, string, and empty boxes. In the excitement I had forgotten Red Ryder and the BB gun, but now it all came back. Skunked! Well, at least I had a Frankenstein face. And there was no denying that I had scored heavily with the Simoniz and the atomizer, as well as the zeppelin. The joy of giving can uplift the saddened heart.

My brother lay dozing amid the rubble, the zeppelin clasped in one hand and his new fire truck in the other. My father bent over from his easy chair, his eighth glass of wine in his hand.

"Say, don't I see something over there stuck behind the drapes? Why, I think there is something over there behind the drapes."

He was right! There was a tiny flash of red under the ecru curtains. Like a shot I was off, and milliseconds later I knew that old Santa had come through! A long, heavy, red-wrapped package marked "To Ralphie from Santa" had been left somehow behind the curtains. In an instant the wrappings were off, and there it was! A Red Ryder carbine-action range-model BB gun lay in its crinkly white packing, blue-steel barrel graceful and taut, its dark, polished stock gleaming like all the treasures of the Western world. And there, burned into the walnut, his level gaze unmistakable, his jaw clean and hard, was Red Ryder himself coolly watching my every move. His face was even more beautiful and malevolent than the pictures in the advertisements showed.

Over the radio thundered a thousand-voiced heavenly choir:

"JOY TO THE WORLD, THE LORD HAS COME. . . ."

My mother sat and smiled a weak, doubtful smile while my Old Man grinned broadly from behind his wineglass.

The magnificent weapon came equipped with two heavy tubes of beautiful Copproteck BBs, gleaming gold and as hard as sin itself. Covered with a thin film of oil they poured with a "ssshhhing" sound into the two-hundred-shot magazine through a BB-size hole in the side of that long blue-steel tube. They added weight and a feeling of danger to the gun. There were also printed targets, twenty-five of them, with a large bull's-eye inside concentric rings marked "One-Two-Three-Four," and the bull's-eye was printed right in the middle of a portrait of Red Ryder himself.

I could hardly wait to try it out, but the instruction booklet said, in Red Ryder's own words:

Kids, never fire a BB gun in the house. They can really shoot.
And don't ever shoot at other kids. I never shoot anybody
but bad guys, and I don't want any of my friends hurt.

It was well past midnight anyway and, excitement or no, I was getting sleepy. Tomorrow was Christmas Day, and the relatives were coming over to visit. That would mean even more loot of one kind or another.

In my warm bed in the cold still air I could hear the falling snow brushing softly against the dark window. Next to me in the blackness lay my oiled blue-steel beauty, the greatest Christmas gift I had ever received. Gradually I drifted off to sleep—pranging ducks on the wing and getting off spectacular hip-shots as I dissolved into nothingness.

Dawn came. As the gray light crept around the shades and over the quilt, I was suddenly and tinglingly awake. Stealthily I dressed in my icy maroon corduroy knickers, my sheepskin coat, and my plaid sweater. I pulled on my high-tops and found my mittens, crept through the dark living room, fragrant with Christmas tree, and out onto the porch. Inside the house the family slept the sleep of the just and the fulfilled.

During the night a great snow had fallen, covering the gritty remains of past snowfalls. The trees hung rich and heavy with fluffy down. The sun, soaring bright and brilliantly sharp over Pulaski's Candy Store, lit up the soft, rolling moonscape of snow with orange and gold splashes of color. Overnight the temperature had dropped thirty degrees or more, and the brittle, crackling air was still and clean, and it hurt the lungs to breathe it. The temperature stood at perhaps fifteen to twenty below zero, cold enough to make the telephone wires creak and groan in agony. From the eaves of the front porch gnarled crystal icicles stretched all the way to the drifts on the buried lawn.

I trudged down the steps, barely discernible in the soft fluff, and now I stood in the clean air, ready to consummate my great, long, painful, ecstatic love affair. Brushing the snow off the third step, I propped up a gleaming Red Ryder target, the black rings and bull's-eye standing out starkly against the snowy whiteness. Above the bull's-eye Red Ryder watched me, his eyes following my every move. I backed off into the snow a good twenty feet, slammed the stock down onto my left kneecap, holding the barrel with my mittened left hand, flipped the mitten off my right and, hooking my fingers in the icy carbine lever, cocked my blue-steel buddy for the first time. I heard the BB click down into the chamber; the spring inside twanged sharply, and with a clunk she rested taut, hard, and loaded in my chapped, rapidly bluing hands.

For the first time I sighted down over that cold barrel, the heart-shaped rear sight almost brushing my nose and the blade of the front sight wavering back and forth, up and down, and finally coming to rest sharply, cutting the heart and laying dead on the innermost ring. Red Ryder didn't move a muscle, his Stetson flaring out above the target as he waited.

Slowly I squeezed the frosty trigger. Back . . . back . . . back. For one instant I thought wildly: It doesn't work! We'll have to send it back! And then:

CRRAAACK!

The gun jerked upward and for a brief instant everything stood still. The target twitched a tiny tick—and then a massive wallop, a gigantic, slashing impact crashed across the left side of my face. My horn-rimmed glasses spun from my head into the snowbank. For several seconds I stood, not knowing what had happened, warm blood trailing down over my cheek and onto the walnut stock of my Red Ryder two-hundred-shot range-model BB gun.

I lowered the barrel convulsively. The target still stood; Red Ryder was unscratched. A ragged, uncontrolled tidal wave of pain, throbbing and singing, rocked my head. The ricocheting BB had missed my eye by perhaps a half inch, and a long, angry, bloody welt extended from my cheekbone almost to my ear. It was divine retribution! Red Ryder had struck again! Another bad guy had been gunned down!

Frantically I scrambled for my glasses. And then the most catastrophic blow of all—they were pulverized! Few things brought such swift and terrible retribution on a kid during the Depression as a pair of busted glasses. The left lens was out as clean as a whistle, and for a moment I thought: I'll fake it! They'll never know the lens is gone! But then, gingerly fingering my rapidly swelling black eye, I realized that here was a shiner on the way that would top even the one I got the time I fought Grover Dill.

As I put the cold horn-rims back on my nose, the front door creaked open just a crack and I could make out the blur of my mother's Chinese-red chenille bathrobe.

"Be careful. Don't shoot out your eye! Just be careful now."

She hadn't seen! Rapidly my mind evolved a spectacular fantasy involving a falling icicle and how it had hit the gun barrel which caused the stock to bounce up and cut my cheek and break my glasses and I tried to get out of the way but the icicle fell off the roof and hit the gun and it bounced up and hit me and. . . . I began to cry uproariously, faking it at first, but then the shock and fear took over and it was the real thing—heaving, sobbing, retching.

I was now in the bathroom, my mother bending over me, telling me:

"There now, see, it's just a little bump. You're lucky you didn't cut your eye. Those icicles sometimes even kill people. You're really lucky. Here, hold this rag on it, and don't wake your brother."

I HAD PULLED IT OFF!

I sipped the bitter dregs of coffee that remained in my cup, suddenly catapulted by a falling tray back into the cheerful, impersonal, brightly lit clatter of Horn & Hardart. I wondered whether Red Ryder was still dispensing retribution and frontier justice as of old. Considering the number of kids I see with broken glasses, I suspect he is.

WHILE MORTALS SLEEP

Kurt Vonnegut

IF FRED HACKLEMAN AND CHRISTMAS COULD HAVE avoided each other, they would have. He was a bachelor, a city editor, and a newspaper genius, and I worked for him as a reporter for three insufferable years. As nearly as I could tell, he and the Spirit of Christmas had as little in common as a farm cat and the Audubon Society.

And he was like a farm cat in a lot of ways. He was solitary, deceptively complacent and lazy, and quick with the sharp claws of his authority and wit.

He was in his middle forties when I worked for him, and he had seemingly lost respect not just for Christmas but for government, matrimony, business, patriotism, and just about any other important institution you could name. The only ideals I ever heard him mention were terse leads, good spelling, accuracy, and speed in reporting the stupidity of mankind.

I can remember only one Christmas during which he radiated, faintly, anything like joy and goodwill. But that was a coincidence. A jailbreak happened to take place on December twenty-fifth.

I can remember another Christmas when he badgered a rewrite girl until she cried, because she'd said in a story that a man had passed on after having been hit by a freight train.

"Did he get up, dust himself off, giggle, and pass on to wherever he was headed before his little misunderstanding with the locomotive?" Hackleman wanted to know.

"No." She bit her lip. "He died, and—"

"Why didn't you say so in the first place? He died. After the locomotive, the tender, fifty-eight loaded freight cars, and the caboose rolled over him, he died. That we can tell our readers without fear of contradiction. First-rate reporting—he died. Did he go to Heaven? Is that where he passed on to?"

"I—I don't know."

"Well, your story says we do know. Did the reporter say he had definite information that the dead man is now in Heaven—or en route? Did you check with the man's minister to see if he had a ghost of a chance of getting in?"

She burst into tears. "I hope he did!" she said furiously. "I tried to say I hoped he did, and I'm not sorry!" She walked away, blowing her nose, and paused by the door to glare at Hackleman. "Because it's Christmas!" she cried, and she left the newspaper world forever.

"Christmas?" said Hackleman. He seemed baffled, and looked around the room as though hoping someone would translate the strange word for him. "Christmas." He walked over to the calendar on the wall, and ran his finger along the dates until he came to the twenty-fifth. "Oh—that's the one with the red numbers. Huh."

But the Christmas season I remember best is the last one I spent with Hackleman—the season in which the great crime was committed, the robbery proclaimed by Hackleman, gleefully, as the most infamous crime in the history of the city.

It must have been on about the first of December that I heard him say, as he went over his morning mail, "Goddamn it, how much glory can come to a man in one short lifetime?"

He called me over to his desk. "It isn't right that all of the honors that pour into these offices every day should be shared only by management," he said. "It's to you, the working stiffs, that the honors really belong."

"That's very kind of you," I said uneasily.

"So, in lieu of the raise which you richly deserve, I am going to make you my assistant."

"Assistant city editor?"

"Bigger than that. My boy, you are now assistant publicity director of the Annual Christmas Outdoor Lighting Contest. Bet you thought I wasn't even aware of the brilliant, selfless job you've been doing for the paper, eh?" He shook my hand. "Well, here's your answer. Congratulations."

"Thanks. What do I do?"

"The reason executives die young is that they don't know how to delegate authority," said Hackleman. "This should add twenty years to my life, because I hereby delegate to you my full authority as publicity director, just tendered me by the Chamber of Commerce. The door of opportunity is wide open. If your publicity makes this year's Annual Christmas Outdoor Lighting Contest the biggest, brightest one yet, there'll be no ceiling on how high you can rise in the world of journalism. Who's to say you won't be the next publicity director of National Raisin Week?"

"I'm afraid I'm not very familiar with this particular art form," I said.

"Nothing to it," said Hackleman. "The contestants dangle colored electric lights all over the fronts of their houses, and the man whose meter goes around fastest wins. That's Christmas for you."

As a dutiful assistant publicity director, I boned up on the history of the event, and learned that the contest had been held every year, except for the war years, since 1938. The first winner won with a two-story Santa Claus, outlined in lights on the front of his house. The next winner had a great pair of plywood bells, outlined in lights and hung from the eaves, which swung back and forth while a loudspeaker concealed in the shrubbery went ding-dong.

And so it went: each winner bettered the winner of the year before, until no entrant had a prayer of winning without the help of an electrical engineer, and the Power and Light Company had every bit of its equipment dangerously overloaded on the night of the judging, Christmas Eve.

As I said, Hackleman wanted nothing to do with it. But, unfortunately for Hackleman, the publisher of the paper had just been elected president of the Chamber of Commerce, and he was annoyed to learn that one of his employees was squirming out of a civic duty.

The publisher rarely appeared in the city room, but his visits were always memorable—particularly the visit he made two weeks before Christmas to educate Hackleman on his twofold role in the community.

"Hackleman," he said, "every man on this staff is not only a newspaper man, he's an active citizen."

"I vote," said Hackleman. "I pay taxes."

"And there it stops," said the publisher reproachfully. "For ten years you've been city editor, and for ten years you've been ducking the civic duties that come to a man in such a position—foisting them off on the nearest reporter." He pointed at me. "It's a slap in the face of the community, sending out kids like this to do work that most citizens would consider a great honor."

"I haven't got time," said Hackleman sullenly.

"Make the time. Nobody asks you to spend eighteen hours a day in the office. That's your idea. It isn't necessary. Get out with your fellow men once in a while, Hackleman, especially now. It's the Christmas season, man. Get behind this contest and—"

"What's Christmas to me?" said Hackleman. "I'm not a religious man and I'm not a family man, and eggnog gives me gastritis, so the hell with Christmas."

The publisher was stunned. "The hell with Christmas?" he said, hollowly, hoarsely.

"Certainly," said Hackleman.

"Hackleman," said the publisher evenly, "I order you to take part in running the contest—to get into the swing of Christmas. It'll do you good."

"I quit," said Hackleman, "and I don't think that will do you much good."

And Hackleman was right. His quitting did the paper no good. It was a disaster, for in many ways he was the paper. However, there was no wailing or gnashing of teeth in the paper's executive offices—only a calm, patient wistfulness. Hackleman had quit before, but had never managed to stay away from the paper for more than twenty-four hours. His whole life was the paper, and his talking of quitting it was like a trout's talking of quitting a mountain stream to get a job clerking in a five-and-ten.

Setting a new record for an absence from the paper, Hackleman returned to his desk twenty-seven hours after quitting.

He was slightly drunk and surly, and looked no one in the eye.

As I passed his desk, quietly and respectfully, he mumbled something to me.

"Beg your pardon?" I said.

"I said Merry Christmas," said Hackleman.

"And a Merry Christmas to you."

"Well, sir," he said, "it won't be long now, will it, until old soup-for-brains with the long white beard will come a-jingling over our housetops with goodies for us all."

"No—guess not."

"A man who whips little reindeer is capable of anything," said Hackleman.

"Yes—I suppose."

"Bring me up to date, will you, kid? What's this goddamn contest all about?"

The committee that was supposed to be running the contest was top-heavy with local celebrities who were too busy and important to do a lick of work on the contest—the mayor, the president of a big manufacturing company, and the chairman of the Real Estate Board. Hackleman kept me on as his assistant, and it was up to us and some small fry from the Chamber of Commerce to do the spadework.

Every night we went out to look at entries, and there were thousands of them. We were trying to make a list of the twenty best displays from which the committee would choose a winner on Christmas Eve. The Chamber of Commerce underlings scouted the south side of town, while Hackleman and I scouted the north.

It should have been pleasant. The weather was crisp, not bitter; the stars were out every night, bright, hard, and cold against a black velvet sky. Snow, while cleared from the streets, lay on yards and rooftops, making all the world seem soft and clean; and our car radio sang Christmas carols.

But it wasn't pleasant, because Hackleman talked most of the time, making a bitter indictment against Christmas.

One time, I was listening to a broadcast of a children's choir singing "Silent Night," and was as close to heaven as I could get without being pure and dead. Hackleman suddenly changed stations to fill the car with the clangor of a jazz band.

"Wha'd you do that for?" I said.

"They're running it into the ground," said Hackleman peevishly. "We've heard it eight times already tonight. They sell Christmas the way they sell cigarettes—just keep hammering away at the same old line over and over again. I've got Christmas coming out of my ears."

"They're not selling it," I said. "They're just happy about it."

"Just another form of department store advertising."

I twisted the dial back to the station carrying the children's choir. "If you don't mind, I'd enjoy hearing this to the end," I said. "Then you can change it again."

"Sleee-eeep in heav-en-ly peace," piped the small, sweet voices. And then the announcer broke in. "This fifteenminute interlude of Christmas favorites," he said, "has been brought to you by Bullard Brothers Department Store, which is open until ten o'clock every evening except Sunday. Don't wait until the last minute to do your Christmas shopping. Avoid the rush."

"There!" said Hackleman triumphantly.

"That's a side issue," I said. "The main thing is that the Savior was born on Christmas."

"Wrong again," said Hackleman. "Nobody knows when he was born. There's nothing in the Bible to tell you. Not a word."

"You're the last man I'd come to for an expert opinion on the Bible," I said heatedly.

"I memorized it when I was a kid," said Hackleman. "Every night I had to learn a new verse. If I missed a word, by God, the old man knocked my block off."

"Oh?" This was an unexpected turn of events—unexpected because part of Hackleman's impressiveness lay in his keeping to himself, in his never talking about his past or about what he did or thought when he wasn't at work. Now he was talking about his childhood, and showing me for the first time an emotion more profound than impatience and cynicism.

"I didn't miss a single Sunday School session for ten years," said Hackleman. "Rain or shine, sick or well, I was there."

"Devout, eh?"

"Scared stiff of my old man's belt."

"Is he still alive—your father?"

"I don't know," said Hackleman without interest. "I ran away when I was fifteen, and never went back."

"And your mother?"

"Died when I was a year old."

"Sorry."

"Who the hell asked you to be sorry?"

We were pulling up before the last house we planned to look at that night. It was a salmon-pink mansion with a spike fence, iron flamingos, and five television aerials combining in one monster the worst features of Spanish architecture, electronics, and sudden wealth. There was no Christmas lighting display that we could see—only ordinary lights inside the house.

We knocked on the door, to make sure we'd found the right place, and were told by a butler that there was indeed a lighting display, on the other side of the house, and that he would have to ask the master for permission to turn it on.

A moment later, the master appeared, fat and hairy, and with two prominent upper front teeth—looking like a groundhog in a crimson dressing gown.

"Mr. Fleetwood, sir," said the butler to his master, "these gentlemen here—"

The master waved his man to silence. "How have you been, Hackleman?" he said. "It's rather late to be calling, but my door is always open to old friends."

"Gribbon," said Hackleman incredulously, "Leu Gribbon. How long have you been living here?"

"The name is Fleetwood now, Hackleman—J. Sprague Fleetwood, and I'm strictly legitimate. There was a story the last time we met, but there isn't one tonight. I've been out for a year, living quietly and decently."

"Mad Dog Gribbon has been out for a year, and I didn't know it?" said Hackleman.

"Don't look at me," I said. "I cover the School Board and the Fire Department."

"I've paid my debt to society," said Gribbon.

Hackleman toyed with the visor of a suit of armor guarding the entrance into the baronial living room. "Looks to me like you paid your debt to society two cents on the dollar," he said.

"Investments," said Gribbon, "legitimate investments in the stock market."

"How'd your broker get the bloodstains out of your money to find out what the denominations were?" said Hackleman.

"If you're going to abuse my hospitality with rudeness, Hackleman, I'll have you thrown out," said Gribbon. "Now, what do you want?"

"They wish to see the lighting display, sir," said the butler.

Hackleman looked very sheepish when this mission was announced. "Yeah," he mumbled, "we're on a damn fool committee."

"I thought the judging was to take place Christmas Eve," said Gribbon. "I didn't plan to turn it on until then—as a pleasant surprise for the community."

"A mustard gas generator?" said Hackleman.

"All right, wise guy," said Gribbon haughtily, "tonight you're going to see what kind of a citizen J. Sprague Fleetwood is."

It was a world of vague forms and shades of blue in the snowy yard of J. Sprague Fleetwood, alias Mad Dog Gribbon. It was midnight and Hackleman and I stamped our feet and blew on our hands to keep warm, while Gribbon and three servants hurried about the yard, tightening electrical connections and working over what seemed to be statues with screwdrivers and oil cans.

Gribbon insisted that we stand far away from the display in order to get the impact of the whole, whenever it was ready to be turned on. We couldn't tell what it was we were about to see, and were particularly tantalized by what the butler was doing—filling an enormous weather balloon from a tank of gas. The balloon arose majestically, captive at the end of a cable, as the butler turned the crank of a winch.

"What's that for?" I whispered to Hackleman.

"Sending for final instructions from God," said Hackleman.

"What'd he get sent to prison for?"

"Ran the numbers in town for a while, and had about twenty people killed so he could keep his franchise. So they put him away for five years for not paying his income taxes."

"Lights ready?" bawled Gribbon, standing on a porch, his arms upraised, commanding a miracle.

"Lights ready," said a voice in the shrubbery.

"Sound ready?"

"Sound ready, sir."

"Balloon ready?"

"Balloon aloft, sir."

"Let 'er go!" cried Gribbon.

Demons shrieked from the treetops.

Suns exploded.

Hackleman and I cowered, instinctively threw our arms across our faces.

We uncovered our eyes slowly, fearfully, and saw stretching before us, in blinding, garish light, a life-sized nativity scene. Loudspeakers on every side blared earsplitting carols. Plaster cattle and sheep were everywhere, wagging their heads, while shepherds raised and lowered their right arms like railroad-crossing gates, jerkily pointing into the sky.

The Virgin Mary and Joseph looked down sweetly on the child in the manger, while mechanical angels flapped their wings and mechanical wise men bobbed up and down like pistons.

"Look!" cried Hackleman above the din, pointing where the shepherds pointed, where the balloon had disappeared into the sky.

There, over the salmon-pink palace of Mad Dog Gribbon, hung in the Christmas heavens from a bag of gas, shone an imitation of the star of Bethlehem.

Suddenly, all was black and still again. My mind was numb. Hackleman stared blankly at the place where the star had been, speechless.

Gribbon trotted toward us. "Anything else in town that can touch it?" he panted proudly.

"Nope," said Hackleman bleakly.

"Think it'll win?"

"Yup," murmured Hackleman. "Unless somebody's got an atomic explosion in the form of Rudolph the Red-nosed Reindeer."

"People will come from miles around to see it," said Gribbon. "Just tell 'em in the newspaper story to follow the star."

"Listen, Gribbon," said Hackleman, "you know there isn't any money that goes with the first prize, don't you? Nothing but a lousy little scroll worth maybe a buck."

Gribbon looked offended. "Of course," he said. "This is a public service, Hackleman."

Hackleman grunted. "Come on, kid, let's call it a night, eh?"

It was a real break, our finding the certain winner of the contest a week before the judging was to take place. It meant that the judges and assistants like myself could spend most of Christmas Eve with our families, instead of riding around town for hours, trying to decide which was the best of twenty or so equally good entries. All we had to do now was to drive to Gribbon's mansion, be blinded and deafened, shake his hand and give him his scroll, and return home in time to trim the tree, fill the stocking, and put away several rounds of eggnog.

As thoughts of Christmas made Hackleman's neurotic staff gentle and sentimental, and the preposterous rumor that he had a heart of gold gained wide circulation, Hackleman behaved in typical holiday fashion, declaring that heads were going to roll because Mad Dog Gribbon had been out of prison and back in town for a year without a single reporter's finding out about it.

"By God," he said, "I'm going to have to go out on the street again, or the paper'll fold up for want of news." And, during the next two days, the paper would have done just that, if it hadn't been for news from the wire services, because Hackleman sent out almost everybody to find out what Gribbon was up to.

Desperate as Hackleman made us, we couldn't find a hint of skullduggery in Gribbon's life since he'd left prison. The only conclusion to draw was that crime paid so well that Gribbon could retire in his early forties, and live luxuriously and lawfully for the rest of his days.

"His money really does come from stocks and bonds," I told Hackleman wearily at the end of the second day. "And he pays his taxes like a good boy, and never sees his old friends anymore."

"All right, all right, all right," said Hackleman irritably. "Forget it. Never mind." He was more nervous than I'd ever seen him be before. He drummed on his desk with his fingers, and jumped at unexpected sounds.

"You have something special against him?" I asked. It wasn't like Hackleman to go after anyone with such zeal. Ordinarily, he never seemed to care whether justice or crime won out. What interested him were the good news stories that came out of the conflict. "After all, the guy really is going straight."

"Forget it," said Hackleman. Suddenly, he broke his pencil in two, stood up, and strode out, hours before his usual departure time.

The next day was my day off. I would have slept till noon, but a paperboy was selling extras under my bedroom window. The headline was huge and black, and spelled one terrible word: KIDNAPPED! The story below said that plaster images of Jesus, Mary, and Joseph had been stolen from Mr. J. Sprague Fleetwood, and that he had offered a reward of one thousand dollars for information leading to their return before the judging of the Annual Christmas Outdoor Lighting Contest on Christmas Eve.

Hackleman called a few minutes later. I was to come to the office at once to help trace down the clues that were pouring in.

The police complained that, if there were any clues, hordes of amateur detectives had spoiled them. But there was no pressure at all on the police to solve the robbery. By evening the search had become a joyful craze that no one escaped—that no one wanted to escape. And the search was for the people to make, not for the police.

Throngs went from door to door, asking if anyone had seen the infant Jesus.

Movie theaters played to empty houses, and a local radio giveaway program said mournfully that nobody seemed to be home in the evenings to answer the telephone.

Thousands insisted on searching the only stable in the city, and the owner made a small fortune selling them hot chocolate and doughnuts. An enterprising hotel bought a full-page ad, declaring that if anyone found Jesus and Mary and Joseph, here was an inn that would make room for them.

The lead story in every edition of the paper dealt with the search and every edition was a sellout.

Hackleman remained as sarcastic and cynical and efficient as ever.

"It's a miracle," I told him. "By taking this little story and blowing it up big, you've made Christmas live."

Hackleman shrugged apathetically. "Just happened to come along when news was slow. If something better comes along, and I hope it will, I'll drop this one right out of sight. It's about time somebody was running berserk with an automatic shotgun in a kindergarten isn't it?"

"Sorry I opened my mouth."

"Have I remembered to wish you a merry Saturnalia?"

"Saturnalia?"

"Yeah—a nasty old pagan holiday near the end of December. The Romans used to close the schools, eat and drink themselves silly, say they loved everybody, and give each other gifts." He answered the phone. "No, ma'am, we haven't found Him yet. Yes, ma'am, there'll be an extra if He turns up. Yes, ma'am, the stable's already been checked pretty carefully. Thank you. Goodbye."

The search was more a spontaneous, playful pageant than an earnest hunt for the missing figures. Realistically, the searchers didn't have much of a chance. They made a lot of noise, and went only where they thought it would be pleasant or interesting to go. The thief, who was apparently a nut, would have had little trouble keeping his peculiar loot out of sight.

But the searchers were so caught up in the allegory of what they were doing that a powerful expectation grew of its own accord, with no help from the paper. Everyone was convinced that the holy family would be found on Christmas Eve.

But on that eve, no new star shone over the city save the five-hundred-watt lamp hung from a balloon over the mansion of J. Sprague Fleetwood, alias Mad Dog Gribbon, the victim of the theft.

The mayor, the president of a big manufacturing company, and the chairman of the Real Estate Board rode in the back seat of the mayor's limousine, while Hackleman and I sat on the jump seats in front of them. We were on our way to award the first-prize scroll to Gribbon, who had replaced the missing figures with new ones.

"Turn down this street here?" said the chauffeur.

"Just follow the star," I said.

"It's a light, a goddamn electric light that anybody can hang over his house if he's got the money," said Hackleman.

"Follow the goddamn electric light," I said.

Gribbon was waiting for us, wearing a tuxedo, and he opened the car door himself. "Gentlemen—Merry Christmas." His eyes down, his hands folded piously across his round belly, he led us down a path, bounded by ropes, that led around the display and back to the street again. He passed by the corner of the mansion, just short of the point where we would be able to see the display. "I like to think of it as a shrine," he said, "with people coming from miles around, following the stars." He stepped aside, motioning us to go ahead.

And the dumbfounding panorama dazzled us again, looking like an outdoor class in calisthenics, with expressionless figures bobbing, waving their arms, flapping their wings.

"Gangster heaven," whispered Hackleman.

"Oh, my," said the mayor.

The chairman of the Real Estate Board looked appalled, but cleared his throat and recovered gamely. "Now, there's a display," he said, clinging doggedly to his integrity.

"Where'd you get the new figures?" said Hackleman.

"Wholesale from a department-store supply house," said Gribbon.

"What an engineering feat," said the manufacturer.

"Took four engineers to do it," said Gribbon proudly. "Whoever swiped the figures left the neon halos behind, thank God. They're rigged so I can make 'em blink, if you think that'd look better."

"No, no," said the mayor. "Mustn't gild the lily."

"Uh . . . do I win?" said Gribbon politely.

"Hmmm?" said the mayor. "Oh—do you win? Well, we have to deliberate, of course. We'll let you know this evening."

No one seemed able to think of anything more to say, and we shuffled back to the limousine.

"Thirty-two electric motors, two miles of wire, nine hundred and seventy-six lightbulbs, not counting neon," said Gribbon as we pulled away.

"I thought we were going to just hand him the scroll right then and there," said the real estate man. "That was the plan, wasn't it?"

"I just couldn't bring myself to do it then," sighed the mayor. "Suppose we could stop somewhere for a stirrup cup."

"He obviously won," said the manufacturer. "We wouldn't dare give the prize to anyone else. He won by brute force—brute dollars, brute kilowatts, no matter how terrible his taste is."

"There's one more stop," said Hackleman.

"I thought this was a one-stop expedition," said the manufacturer. "I thought we'd agreed on that."

Hackleman held up a card. "Well, it's a technicality. The official deadline for entries was noon today. This thing came in by special delivery about two seconds ahead of the deadline, and we haven't had a chance to check it."

"It certainly can't match this Fleetwood thing," said the mayor. "What could? What's the address?"

Hackleman told him.

"Shabby neighborhood out on the edge of town," said the real estate man. "No competition for our friend Fleetwood."

"Let's forget it," said the manufacturer. "I've got guests coming in, and . . ."

"Bad public relations," said Hackleman gravely. It was startling to hear the words coming from him, enunciated with respect. He'd once said that the three most repellent forms of life were rats, leeches, and public relations men . . . in descending order.

To the three important men in the back seat, though, the words were impressive and troubling. They mumbled and fidgeted, but didn't have the courage to fight.

"Let's make it quick," said the mayor, and Hackleman gave the driver the card.

Stopped by a traffic signal, we came abreast of a group of cheerful searchers, who called to us, asking if we knew where the holy family was hidden.

Impulsively, the mayor leaned out of the window. "You won't find them under that," he said, waggling his finger at the light over Gribbon's house.

Another group crossed the street before us, singing:

For Christ is born of Mary,
And gathered all above,
While mortals sleep, the angels keep
Their watch of wondering love.

The light changed, and we drove on, saying little as we left the fine homes behind, as the electric lamp over Gribbon's mansion was lost behind black factory chimneys.

"You sure the address is right?" said the chauffeur uncertainly.

"I guess the guy knows his own address," said Hackleman.

"This was a bad idea," said the manufacturer, looking at his watch. "Let's call up Gribbon or Fleetwood or whatever his name is, and tell him he's the big winner. The hell with this."

"I agree," said the mayor. "But, as long as we're this far along, let's see it through."

The limousine turned down a dark street, banged over a chuckhole, and stopped. "This is it, gentlemen," said the chauffeur.

We were parked before an empty, leaning, roofless house, whose soundest part was its splintered siding, a sign declaring it to be unfit for human habitation.

"Are rats and termites eligible for the contest?" said the mayor.

"The address checks," said the chauffeur defensively.

"Turn around and go home," said the mayor.

"Hold it," said the real estate man. "There's a light in the barn in back. My God, I came all this way to judge and I'm going to judge."

"Go see who's in the barn," said the mayor to the chauffeur.

The chauffeur shrugged, got out, and walked through the snow-covered rubbish to the barn. He knocked. The door swung open under the impact of his fist. Silhouetted by a frail, wavering light from within, he sank to his knees.

"Drunk?" said Hackleman.

"I don't think so," murmured the mayor. He licked his lips. "I think he's praying—for the first time in his life." He got out of the car, and we followed him silently to the barn. When we reached the chauffeur, we went to our knees beside him.

Before us were the three missing figures. Joseph and Mary sheltered against a thousand drafts the sleeping infant Jesus in his bed of straw. The only illumination came from a single oil lantern, and its wavering light made them live, alive with awe and adoration.

On Christmas morning, the paper told the people where the holy family could be found.

All Christmas Day the people streamed to the cold, lonely barn to worship.

A small story inside announced that Mr. Sprague Fleetwood had won the Annual Christmas Outdoor Lighting Contest with thirty-two electric motors, two miles of wire, and nine hundred and seventy-six lightbulbs, not counting neon, and an Army surplus weather balloon.

Hackleman was on the job at his desk, critical and disillusioned as ever.

"It's a great, great story," I said.

"I'm good and sick of it," said Hackleman. He rubbed his hands. "What I'm looking forward to is January when the Christmas bills come in. A great month for homicides."

"Well, there's still got to be a follow-up on the Christmas story. We still don't know who did it."

"How you going to find out who did it? The name on the entry blank was a phony, and the guy who owns the barn hasn't been in town for ten years."

"Fingerprints," I said. "We could go over the figures for fingerprints."

"One more suggestion like that, and you're fired."

"Fired?" I said. "What for?"

"Sacrilege!" said Hackleman grandly, and the subject was closed. His mind, as he said, was on stories in the future. He never looked back.

Hackleman's last act with respect to the theft, the search, and Christmas was to send me out to the barn with a photographer on Christmas night. The mission was routine and trite, and it bored him.

"Get a crowd shot from the back, with the figures facing the camera," said Hackleman. "They must be pretty damn dusty by now, with all the sinners tramping through. Better go over 'em with a damp cloth before you make the shot."

CONTRIBUTORS

GEORGE ADE (1866–1944) was a writer, newspaper columnist, and playwright. Born in Kentland, Indiana, Ade went on to study at Purdue University, where he roomed with George Barr McCutcheon, who is also featured in this anthology. One of the luminaries of the "Golden Age of Indiana Literature," Ade is best remembered for his humorous "fables in slang," which earned him the nickname "Aesop of Indiana."

AMBROSE BIERCE (1842–1914) wrote short stories, poems, and journalism. He grew up in Kosciusko County and went to high school in Warsaw. Later he served in the Civil War, and his experience informed his famous story "An Occurrence at Owl Creek Bridge." Though his realistic war stories are read to this day, Bierce is best known for his biting satire. His master-work is *The Devil's Dictionary*, which consists of satirical definitions, one of which is included in this anthology as a palate cleanser for the sweetness around it.

MATTHEW BRENNAN recently retired from Indiana State University in Terre Haute, where he taught courses in Romanticism and poetry writing for thirty-two years. He has authored five books of poetry, including *The House with the Mansard Roof*, a finalist for the 2010 Best Books of Indiana. He has received two Indiana Arts Commission grants as well as the Theodore Dreiser Distinguished Research and Creativity Award. His latest book is *One Life* (Lamar University Literary Press, 2016).

CURTIS L. CRISLER was born and raised in Gary, Indiana. Crisler has written four full-length poetry books, two young adult books, and four poetry chapbooks. He's been published in a variety of magazines, journals, and anthologies. He's been a contributing poetry editor, and he also created the Indiana Chitlin Circuit. Crisler is Associate Professor of English at Purdue University Fort Wayne. He can be contacted at www.poetcrisler.com.

KAREN JOY FOWLER is the author of six novels, including *The Jane Austen Book Club*, and three short story collections. She grew up in Bloomington, Indiana. Her most recent novel, *We Are All Completely Beside Ourselves*, was published in May 2013 and won the PEN/Faulkner Award that year. In 2016, she was named Indiana Writer of the Year. She currently lives in Santa Cruz, California, and is working on a historical novel.

MELISSA FRATERRIGO is the author of the novel *Glory Days*, which was named one of "The Best Fiction Books of 2017" by the *Chicago Review of Books*, as well as the short story collection *The Longest Pregnancy*. Her fiction and nonfiction has appeared in more than forty literary journals and anthologies from *storySouth* and *Shenandoah* to *Notre Dame Review*, *Sou'wester*, and *The Millions*. She was born in Hammond, Indiana, and is the founder and executive director of the Lafayette Writers' Studio in Lafayette, Indiana, and teaches in Indianapolis at Indiana University–Purdue University Indianapolis.

BRYAN FURUNESS is the author of a couple of novels, *The Lost Episodes of Revie Bryson* and *Do Not Go On*. In addition to this anthology, he is the editor of *My Name Was Never Frankenstein: And Other Classic Adventure Tales Remixed* and co-editor (with Michael Martone) of *Winesburg, Indiana: A Fork River Anthology*. He grew up in the Region (Schererville), went to college in Bloomington, and currently lives in Indianapolis, where he teaches at Butler University.

FRANK McKINNEY HUBBARD (1868–1930) was a cartoonist, humorist, and journalist better known as Kin Hubbard. Born in Ohio, Hubbard moved to Indianapolis, where he began publishing the cartoon strip *Abe Martin* in 1904 in the *Indianapolis News* and other papers. He was renowned for quips such as "Next to a circus, there ain't nothing that packs up and tears out any quicker than the Christmas spirit."

GEORGE KALAMARAS served as Poet Laureate of Indiana (2014–2016) and is the author of ten books of poetry and seven chapbooks, including *Kingdom of Throat-Stuck Luck*, winner of the Elixir Press Poetry Prize (2011), and *The Theory and Function of Mangoes*, winner of the Four Way Books Intro Series (2000). He is

Professor of English at Purdue University Fort Wayne, where he has taught since 1990. He lives in Fort Wayne with his wife and colleague, the writer Mary Ann Cain, and their beagle, Bootsie.

KAREN KOVACIK is a native of Lake County, Indiana, and for over twenty years has been Professor of English at Indiana University–Purdue University Indianapolis. She's the author of the poetry collections *Metropolis Burning* and *Beyond the Velvet Curtain*; the translator, most recently, of Jacek Dehnel's *Aperture*, a finalist for the 2019 PEN Award for Poetry in Translation; and the editor of *Scattering the Dark*, an anthology of Polish women poets. From 2012 to 2014, she was Indiana's Poet Laureate.

NORBERT KRAPF, former Indiana Poet Laureate, is a native of Jasper, Indiana. His thirteen poetry collections include *Somewhere in Southern Indiana*, *The Country I Come From*, *Looking for God's Country*, *Bloodroot: Indiana Poems*, and *Indiana Hill Country Poems*. He is the winner of a Glick Indiana Author Award, the Lucille Medwick Memorial Award from the Poetry Society of America, and a Creative Renewal Grant from the Arts Council of Indianapolis. His poems have been read on *The Writer's Almanac* and his poem "Back in Indiana" is included in stained glass at the Indianapolis International Airport and was also part of the Indiana Bicentennial play *Finding Home: Indiana at 200* at the Indiana Repertory Theatre. His play *Catholic Boy Blues* was produced in the Indy Eleven Theatre of IndyFringe.

JAYNE MAREK has published in *The Lake*, *One*, *Grub Street*, *Cortland Review*, *Women's Studies Quarterly*, *Spillway*, and Indiana-based publications such as *And Know This Place: Poetry of Indiana* (2011), *Notre Dame Review*, *The Bend*, *Flying Island*, and *Tipton Poetry Journal*. She received her MFA in creative writing from Notre Dame, and her poetry books include *In and Out of Rough Water*, *The Tree Surgeon Dreams of Bowling*, and the co-authored *Company of Women*, with Indianapolis's Chatter House Press. She has received two Pushcart Prize nominations and a Best of the Net nomination, and she won the Bill Holm Witness poetry contest. She lived in Franklin and Greenwood, Indiana, for twenty years and was an Indiana Master Naturalist.

GEORGE BARR McCUTCHEON (1866–1928) was a novelist and playwright. Born in Tippecanoe County, he went on to attend Purdue University, where he roomed with George Ade, who is also included in this anthology. A major contributor to the "Golden Age of Indiana Literature," McCutcheon is best remembered for his novel *Brewster's Millions*, later adapted into a movie with the same title. The excerpt included in this collection is from his novel *Mr. Bingle*, which reads like a love letter to Dickens's *A Christmas Carol*.

SUSAN NEVILLE was born in Indianapolis and teaches English at Butler University in Indianapolis. Her parents and grandparents and brother and aunts and uncles and children were also born in Indianapolis. She is the author of eight books of fiction and nonfiction, including *The Town of Whispering Dolls*.

MEREDITH NICHOLSON (1866–1947) was an author and a diplomat, serving as an envoy to Paraguay, Venezuela, and Nicaragua in addition to writing best-selling novels, including *The House of a Thousand Candles* and *A Hoosier Chronicle*. Born in Crawfordsville, Nicholson grew up in Indianapolis. Along with Booth Tarkington, James Whitcomb Riley, George Ade, and others, Nicholson was a major contributor to the "Golden Age of Indiana Literature." When he passed in 1947, the *New York Times* proclaimed him to be the "last leaf on a famous literary tree that grew in Indiana."

As a traveling actor barnstorming across Indiana, EDWARD PORTER stayed in Don Hall's Guesthouse in Fort Wayne several times. It made a strong impression on him, and he's tried to put what he learned there to good use. His short fiction has been published in *Glimmer Train*, *The Hudson Review*, *The Gettysburg Review*, *Colorado Review*, *Barrelhouse*, *Booth*, *Catamaran*, *Best New American Voices*, and elsewhere. His work has been supported by Stegner and Madison fellowships, the Bread Loaf and Sewanee writers' conferences, and residencies at MacDowell, Yaddo, VCCA, and Millay. Currently he's a Jones Lecturer in Creative Writing at Stanford University.

ERNEST "ERNIE" PYLE (1900–1945) was a journalist and war correspondent. Born in Dana, Indiana, Pyle went on to attend Indiana University, which has since erected a bronze sculpture of the journalist. Today, Pyle is best known for his reports from the European theater and the Pacific theater during World War II. Of his writing, President Truman said that "no man in this war has so well told the story of the American fighting man as American fighting men wanted it told. He deserves the gratitude of all his countrymen." Pyle was killed in action on the island of Ie Shima, near Okinawa, in April 1945, just months before the end of the war.

LORI RADER-DAY is a native of central Indiana and a proud alumna of Ball State University. Now a resident of Chicago, Lori is the author of *The Lucky One*, *Under a Dark Sky*, *The Day I Died*, *Little Pretty Things*, and *The Black Hour*. She is an Edgar Award nominee and the recipient of the Mary Higgins Clark Award, the Anthony Award, and the Indiana Author Award.

JAMES WHITCOMB RILEY (1849–1916) was born in Greenfield, Indiana, in an age when newspapers published poems, and famous poets could make a fine living on the lecture circuit by performing for large crowds. One of the most popular poets of the era, Riley was known as the "Hoosier Poet" for his verses about midwestern life and also the "Children's Poet" for his poems for young readers. His poem "Little Orphant Annie" inspired the popular comic strip character. Upon his death, children began donating coins to build his memorial, and to this day, his grave site in Indianapolis's Crown Hill Cemetery glitters with coins.

SCOTT RUSSELL SANDERS is the author of more than twenty books of fiction and personal narrative, including *A Conservationist Manifesto*, *Hunting for Hope*, and *A Private History of Awe*. His recent books include *Earth Works: Selected Essays* and *Stone Country: Then and Now*. Among his honors are the Lannan Literary Award, the John Burroughs Essay Award, and the Eugene and Marilyn Glick Indiana Authors Award. He is Distinguished Professor Emeritus of English at Indiana University and a fellow of the American Academy of Arts and Sciences. He and his wife, Ruth, a biochemist, have reared two children in their hometown of Bloomington, in the hardwood hill country of southern Indiana.

JEAN PARKER SHEPHERD JR. (1921–1999) was a writer, actor, radio and television personality, and general raconteur. He grew up in Hammond, Indiana, and turned his experiences into a book of loosely autobiographical stories—*In God We Trust: All Others Pay Cash*—that was adapted into the movie *A Christmas Story* (which he narrated).

BARBARA SHOUP is the author of eight novels for adults and young adults, most recently *An American Tune* and *Looking for Jack Kerouac*, and two books about writing, *A Commotion in Your Heart: Notes on Writing and Life* and *Novel Ideas: Contemporary Authors Share the Creative Process*. A high school creative writing teacher for twenty-five years, she served as executive director of the Indiana Writers Center for ten years and is currently the organization's writer in residence.

Shoup was born and raised in Hammond, Indiana, attended Indiana University, and has lived in Indianapolis since 1968.

GENE STRATTON-PORTER (1863–1924) was a writer, photographer, and naturalist. She was born in Wabash County, in the town of Lagro. She had eleven siblings, including a brother she called Laddie (which I mention because her chapter in this anthology is from a novel titled *Laddie: A True Blue Story*). Today, Stratton-Porter is best known for *A Girl of the Limberlost*, a novel set in the Limberlost swamp that she loved to explore. Though much of the Limberlost was drained and destroyed for commercial purposes during her lifetime, her stories, articles, and photographs of the swamp endure. Additionally, two of her nearby residences have been preserved as historic sites, and nearly a hundred acres of wetlands around the Cabin at Wildflower Woods are undergoing restoration.

BOOTH TARKINGTON (1869–1946) was born in Indianapolis and attended Shortridge High School (a veritable cradle of authors, Shortridge is also the alma mater of Kurt Vonnegut and Dan Wakefield). Tarkington is best known for two novels, *The Magnificent Ambersons* and *Alice Adams*, both of which won the Pulitzer Prize. While he spent many of his later years in Maine, he maintained a home on North Meridian in Indianapolis and is buried in Crown Hill Cemetery.

KELSEY TIMMERMAN is the *New York Times* best-selling author of *Where Am I Wearing? A Global Tour to the Countries, Factories, and People That Make Our Clothes*; *Where Am I Eating? An Adventure through the Global Food Economy*; and *Where Am I Giving? A Global Adventure Exploring How to Use Your Gifts and Talents to Make a Difference*. He lives with his family in Muncie, Indiana.

ELIZA TUDOR grew up in Indiana and holds an MA in English and an MFA in writing from Butler University. Her stories have appeared in *PANK*, *TLR*, *Hobart*, *Annalemma*, *Paper Darts*, and *The Conium Review*, among others, as well as in the anthologies *Mythic Indy* and Dark Ink Press's *Fall*. Her novella, *Wish You Were Here*, won the 2017 Minerva Rising Press Novella Prize. After spending the last few years living in places as varied as Silicon Valley; the south coast of England; and Austin, Texas, she currently resides on an island near Seattle. You can find more at www.elizatudor.com.

KURT VONNEGUT (1922–2007) was born in Indianapolis. He attended Shortridge High School—cradle of authors!—and Cornell University before serving in the army during World War II. Vonnegut was in Dresden when it was firebombed by the Allies, and he only survived by taking refuge in a meat locker—an incident that gave rise to his masterpiece, *Slaughterhouse-Five*. (*Editor's note*: I once saw Vonnegut speak at a theater in Louisville, and it was clear to me that I was in the presence of a living saint. In my opinion, Vonnegut is the finest writer to ever come from Indiana, and this anthology would not be complete without his presence.)

SHARI WAGNER, a former Indiana Poet Laureate, is the author of three books of poems: *The Farm Wife's Almanac*, *The Harmonist at Nightfall*, and *Evening Chore*. She has an MFA in creative writing from Indiana University and teaches for the Indiana Writers Center, Bethany Seminary, and Indiana University–Purdue University Indianapolis's Religion, Spirituality and the Arts Initiative. She was born in Goshen, Indiana; grew up in rural Wells County; and currently lives in Westfield.

JESSAMYN WEST (1902–1984) was born in North Vernon, Indiana. When she was six, her family moved to California, where West later attended Whittier College. While studying for a PhD at the University of California, West was diagnosed with tuberculosis. After spending two years in a sanatorium, she came home to die, but under her mother's care, she began to improve. While she recovered, her mother told her stories about her own childhood and their Quaker heritage, and eventually West began writing her own stories inspired by her mother's tales. "I thought my life was over," said West. "Instead, for me, it was the beginning of my life." Her story in this anthology is from *The Friendly Persuasion*, her best-known book.

LIZ WHITEACRE is Assistant Professor of English at the University of Indianapolis. She teaches creative writing and is the author of *Hit the Ground*. Her poetry has appeared in *Disability Studies Quarterly*, *Wordgathering*, *Kaleidoscope*, and other literary magazines.